Nell Grant

Exitum: A Classic Disappearance

This paperback edition published in 2024

Cover design by Dave Sneddon, Firehouse Design

ISBN: 9798875782473

The author would like to express her sincere thanks to Rod Grant, Stewart Anderson, Roddy Irvine and Maggie McQueen for all their help and expertise.

Chapter 1

Kira's desk in Ivan Cole's Estate Agency was partially facing the window. During a lull in her day, she found herself staring out at the passers-by, creating an intriguing back story for their lives. In truth, Kira had more than enough complications in her own life without fascinating over other people's.

The estate agency was situated within the area of Bruntsfield, a highly desirable village within a city. The heart of Edinburgh was a short walk away, and yet Bruntsfield held all the charm of a small community. The housing around the area was a blend of high-quality tenements interspersed with large, elegant villas. Unique, independent shops lined both sides of the street with pavement cafes on almost every street corner. Amidst the small businesses a wide variety of restaurants covering all culinary tastes could be found. The town had been built around a tree-lined park, which was enjoyed by Students, the elderly and everyone in between. While selling houses in this sought after district was typically effortless, Kira possessed a knack for achieving sale prices beyond expectations. Her approach, characterised by sweetness, feminine charm, and an honest, pretty face, set her apart in a world where pushy tactics were the norm. Ivan Cole left Kira to her own selling technique, but it was not a method that he endorsed for the rest of the sales team.

Balancing the phone under her chin, Kira opened the large three year diary which sat on her desk. In the 2.30pm section, she recorded all the details supplied to her by the potential viewer on the other end of the line. The caller requested a viewing of a three bedroomed property which had recently arrived on their books. Although Ivan Cole's agency had an excellent I.T. infrastructure, he still insisted that all data be entered into an appointments diary as a back-up. In his experience, modern technology could not be relied on. 'If the computers go down, we'll be stuffed!' he told the staff. Larger estate agencies would have found this system antiquated, but Kira Carmichael's preference would have been the desk diary over the computer any day.

Kira's attention was elsewhere as she continued to ask for the caller's details. It was standard procedure to inquire if he had a mortgage set in place and whether or not his existing property was on the market. Estate agents had zero patience for timewasters who were simply spending an afternoon coveting the lives of others. She found herself growing increasingly agitated with his lengthy narrative about his impending house move. The patient, sympathetic Kira of yesteryear was fading fast and a more direct version of herself was beginning to take over.

Interrupting the caller, she announced, 'So, I will be doing the viewing myself. I will see you there at two-thirty pm. Goodbye.'

The rather stunned caller allowed his sentence to dwindle before stuttering, 'Oh, eh, yes, well that will be fine. See you then.' The line was dead before he could return her goodbye.

A strong urge to escape from the office overwhelmed her. Throwing a glance in the direction of the diary, she could see that her first appointment was not until mid-morning.

In an impromptu gesture, she shouted to her colleagues, 'I'm going to Costa, would anyone like coffee?'

All the hands in the office were raised by the team, as they spoke on the phones. After several years of working with the

same people, she had become all too familiar with their preferred coffee options.
Reaching for her pink mohair cardigan from the back of the chair, she slipped it on as she left the agency. Navigating the traffic was easy, as Wednesdays were usually quiet; she had no idea why. Looking both ways, she ran to the middle island in the road and stopped. Two cars drove past, a third slowed to a crawl when it drew near to her. The driver tooted the horn as he passed. Thinking it might be someone she knew, she ducked slightly to look in the driver's window. It was just two young men admiring a pretty blonde in a short dress.
Dresses always seem to draw attention from males, Kira thought. *Perhaps it's because women so often dress in jeans and tracksuits these days*. Crossing to the other side of the road, she walked down the hill to the coffee shop.
Once inside Costa Coffee, she waited to be served by either of the two baristas. The tall, young man with the long, tied back hair, raced over to serve her first.
'Hi, what can I get for you?' he asked, in an overly attentive manner.
Using her fingers, she listed the varying selection of five coffees, one by one.
'Absolutely no problem,' he replied. 'Do you work around here?' he asked.
'Yes, I work in Ivan Cole's Estate Agents at the top of the hill,' she told him, smiling.
'I thought so. I see you in here often. Have you noticed that I push past everyone to serve you?' He gave a nervous laugh.
Kira's cheeks flushed; this made her feel a little awkward. 'No, I hadn't noticed.'

He made a face that she couldn't quite read before walking over to the machine to make the hot drinks. Kira turned to look out of the window at the passers-by as she waited.
'Okay, Kira, that's you all set up,' he said, placing the cardboard carrier of drinks on the counter.
'Thank you,' she said, lifting her purchases.
'Maybe see you tomorrow,' he asked, smoothing his hair flat with his hand.
'Maybe,' she replied.
As she walked back up the hill towards the office, she thought, *Why did I tell him where I worked?* A fear of offending him had forced her into answering his questions. Seeing a gap in the traffic, she ran straight across without stopping at the island.
The bell above the estate agency door dinged as she entered.
'Oh, finally! What kept you?' her colleague Derek joked, reaching for his Americano.
Everyone gathered round to collect their drink from the cardboard carrier.
'You can't beat a strong coffee in the morning,' Ivan announced, sipping on the hot liquid. 'It just gets your wheels in motion.'
Kira lifted the latte to her lips, but suddenly stopped. 'Wait a minute,' she said, verbalising her thoughts. 'How did he know my name? Did any of you tell that guy who works in Costa, my name?'
They all shook their heads, mumbling no.
'I mean the one with the long hair, tied back in a strange bun,' she clarified.
Again, her colleagues shook their heads, muttering, 'No, not me.'

'Why?' the boss asked her.
'He called me by my name when he served me. Oh, and he asked me where I worked, and I stupidly told him.'
'Oh, that's a bit odd,' Connie piped up. 'Anyway, before I forget, Mr Swanson asked if he could change the time of the viewing at Morningside Mews, from two-thirty to three p.m. Could you call him back to confirm?'
Replying with a nod, she sat down at her desk to make the call.
Kira looked in her diary to check her appointments for the day. There was one at eleven thirty, now one at three, another at five. Normally, she didn't take appointments after four, but she had made an exception for the gentleman that phoned, as he needed a place to live urgently. His full-time working hours made it impossible to attend a viewing before 5pm. The tone of desperation in his voice had made Kira feel sorry for him. The idea of a quick sale was also a factor as she was on a commission-based salary.
I wonder what is going on in his life, she thought. *Probably a broken relationship. Perhaps his wife walked out, leaving him for someone else; his childhood sweetheart.* She tried to imagine how painful that experience would be.
Reality dragged her out of her thoughts when Connie shouted across the room, 'Kira, your mum is on line one. Do you want to speak to her, or will I tell her you're out of the office?'
'Just put her through.'
Kira braced herself as she pressed line one. 'Hi mum.'
'Hello darling. Are you remembering that we have an appointment at the Prestonfield Hotel today at half past five?'

'Yes, of course,' she said, suddenly remembering. 'I may be running a little late, but I'll get there as soon as I can.'
'Oh, and Kira, make sure you look presentable.'
'Mum, I always look presentable. See you later.' Kira replaced the phone back on to the receiver. Her mother had a real talent for making her feel worthless, hence the reason she avoided her calls. *'Make yourself look presentable'* she quoted in her head. *What a charmer she is.* The sparkle from her engagement ring distracted her. It was undoubtedly the most valuable thing she had ever owned. Its three large diamonds shone under the overhead spotlights, bouncing a spectrum of light in every direction. Moving her hand backwards and forwards, she maximised the glimmer from the multifaceted stones. Wasn't she lucky to have such a beautiful possession?
Mrs. Carmichael had favoured the Prestonfield Hotel for Kira's wedding. Most dignitaries and heads of state booked to stay there when visiting Scotland. It was understandable that a mother would want everything to be perfect for her only daughter. This occasion would be talked about in the influential circles in which both families were very much a part of. Contacting 'Hello' magazine to take some 'who's who' photographs at the event had been on her extensive to-do list. The planning of Kira and Jeremy's wedding took up all of Mrs. Carmichael's time and energy; in fact, it baffled her to think of what she ever did before. It was highly convenient for her that Kira did not interfere in the planning procedure, she obviously realised that mothers knew best.
Kira logged off her computer, grabbed her handbag and slipped her pink cardigan over her shoulders. 'I'm going to show the property at Morningside Mews. I have another

appointment at five so tell the boss that I won't be back in the office until tomorrow,' she relayed to Connie. Slinging her bag over her shoulder, she headed for the door.
'No problem. See you tomorrow,' Connie shouted after her. It had occurred to Connie that Kira had not been herself lately, nothing she could put her finger on, just a little off. There had been no point in asking her about it, as Kira was an exceptionally private person. Kira never attended any of the nights out with her colleagues; Connie suspected that this was because she only had room in her life for Jeremy. It had crossed her mind often how wonderful it must feel to meet someone of whom you can't get enough.
The first two appointments of Kira's day had gone well. The viewers had certainly asked all the right questions. She felt quietly confident that there would be an offer on the house in Morningside before the end of the week. Both houses had been immaculate, so there was no real selling involved; the properties spoke for themselves.
Ivan preferred the occupants of the house to leave the selling to his sales team. The statistics showed that the success rate was higher when a neutral party carried out the viewings. However, when Kira was involved, the data made for even more positive reading. Ivan's sales team were all skilled professionals, but Kira was the golden girl, employee of the day, week, year, decade, as far as he was concerned.
The last appointment of the day for Kira was within walking distance of the Estate Agency. The early evening sun illuminated only half of Bruntsfield Place, the hub of the town, so Kira crossed to the sunny side of the street. It was not the area she had originated from, but she had grown to love the bustling vibrancy of it. Passing the pavement cafes,

she looked at the young student-types drinking cappuccinos as they worked on their laptops. Memories of her own university days flooded back to her. *What a bittersweet time that had been,* she thought, shuddering. In the distance, she could hear the laughter of children from the grassy expanse on Bruntsfield Links. Seeing the families laughing and playing together in the park, prompted her to ask herself the ever recurring question, *Will I ever have my own family?*

Nearing the property for sale, Kira glanced at her watch; she was half an hour early. It was commonplace for estate agents to arrive at the establishment in plenty of time to prepare it for viewing. Switching on lights, plumping cushions and lowering toilet seats could do wonders for first impressions. However, she had read the home report, deducing from it that this property was way beyond cushion plumping. It was badly in need of a full up-grade, kitchen, bathroom, central heating, electrics, the works. Enjoying the last rays of the sun, she decided instead to order a latte in the cafe on the corner of the street.

There were only two seats left that were not shaded from the sun by the building across the road. The seat Kira chose was an excellent viewpoint for the arrival of her client. The property was on a quiet side street with no through road, so there would be every chance that the next gentleman to walk down it would be the client.

Oh no! I've forgotten the name of the man I'm meeting, she panicked, reaching for her phone from her handbag. *I know there is something unusual about it, but I just can't think what it is.*

Connie's name was top of her contacts. With the surname Abbot, she was always going to come first on any alphabetical list.
'Hi Connie, I can't remember the name of the client I'm about to meet at five o'clock. Can you look it up for me.'
'Kira, this is not like you. You're normally so organised. I don't need to look it up. Don't you remember, we made a joke of it, it's David Cameron.'
'Oh, so it is, how did I forget that. Thanks Con.'
'No problem. I hope you don't mind me asking but are you alright, Kira? 'You haven't been yourself lately.'
Kira laughed, 'Of course I'm alright. It's all this ridiculous wedding business that's occupying my mind. Thanks for asking. See you tomorrow.'
'David Cameron,' Kira whispered under her breath, shaking her head. How could she have forgotten that? Her father knew the actual David Cameron well, they weren't close friends, but they had worked together when he had been Prime Minister. There were only a handful of politicians that her father didn't know and less than a handful that he liked. In fact, had she ever heard him speaking highly of any politician? She racked her brains; no, there was no one that he had a high opinion of. Mind you, she thought, the feeling was probably mutual. This led her to wonder why so many of these gentleman that her father thought so little of were on the guest list for her wedding.
A bearded man wearing a suit walked past the cafe, heading in the direction of the flat for sale. Kira glanced at the clock on her phone, 4:55. *That could be him,* she thought, slinging her bag over her shoulder.

The latte had already been paid for, so she was free to leave and go after the would-be viewer. A fast walk followed by a semi-run, kept her close behind the man. Sure enough he strode down the pathway leading to the block of tenements which held the flat for sale. Kira watched as he pushed the heavy communal door, disappearing inside. She followed. Hot on his trail, almost bumping into him on the first landing. To her surprise, he took a key from his trouser pocket, letting himself into his flat. Whoever the man with the beard was, he wasn't David Cameron. Kira walked on by, heading upward to the top floor. *I could have sworn he was my guy, but alas no. Never presume anything,* she thought.
The front door of the flat for sale was difficult to push open, this was due to the fact that a year's worth of junk mail had been dropped through the letterbox.
This is quite a place! she thought, entering the hallway.
Décor-wise, the place had not been touched since the seventies. Bold swirls of brown and orange adorned the walls, clashing with the busy pattern on the carpets. It was difficult to describe the smell that hung in the air, Kira could only liken it to the musty odour in her parent's garden shed. Looking around, she saw a standard lamp in the corner of the room behind the settee. The room improved slightly in the warm glow when she switched it on. She held no great desire to touch anything in the room, but she saw that the sagging cushions could do with a plump. The dust caught the back of her throat when she punched the offending item vigorously. *Oh, I hate this place. Please hurry up,* she willed the viewer in her head.
The toilet bowl was awash with brown staining; Kira gagged. Using one finger, she flicked down the seat before

running back through to the lounge. Her preferred option for sitting on was the battered, leather pouffe in the centre of the room. She perched on the edge, body rigid. All she wanted to do was leave; now.

It was half past five and looking like a 'no show'. *I'll stay five more minutes,* she told herself for the fourth time. *My mother is going to be furious that I haven't turned up at the Prestonfield. I know how important it is to her, so I'll just leave it in her capable hands. She'll seal the deal without me. Why would she need my approval now when she's done everything else on her own?*

Her thoughts were far, far from the neglected hovel that time had forgotten. The sound of a distant siren snapped her back to reality. To her absolute horror, she saw that she had waited for over forty minutes. Why had she done that? She knew why.

Kira drove across the city in rush hour traffic, arriving at 'The Prestonfield Hotel' just as her mother was walking to her car in the carpark.

'I'm so sorry I'm late. I waited and waited for a client, but he didn't show up. Did you make another appointment?' she babbled nervously to her stony-faced mother.

'No. I just went ahead and booked it. Trust me, you'll love it. Must fly, see you soon,' she announced, swinging her legs into her Maserati.

Kira climbed back into her still-warm car, driving off in the direction of home. The traffic was typically heavy in the town centre, all Kira could do was sit it out. *I need to stop making my mother angry. It's happening more and more these days. I will try harder.*

Indicating left, she swerved into one of the permit holders' parking spaces close to her house in Palmerston Place. Home had been a six bedroomed townhouse with Jeremy for the past three years. The house was in the centre of Edinburgh with St. Mary's Cathedral and The Sir Arthur Conan Doyle Spiritualist Centre a short walk along the road. When they purchased the house, it had been way out of their price range, but both sets of parents pulled together to supply the money for the deposit. At the time, Jeremy's father had said, 'A house says a lot about the man. It is not just a lifestyle but a symbol of stature and success.' Kira's father gifted her share of the money. For Jeremy, it had been a loan from his father, to be paid back within ten years.

Kira's heartbeat quickened frantically, as it always did when she turned the key in her front door. As usual, Jeremy was there to greet her, eyeing her short, floral dress approvingly. Without a word being exchanged, she felt him slide his warm hands up her legs, under her skirt. She knew the routine; her lacy knickers were ripped and discarded. Once naked below, she was roughly spun round to face the wall near the front door. She heard the zip of his trousers go down, before he entered her from behind. Slowly, rhythmically, she felt him rock her back and forth. The pace quickened, faster and faster, harder and harder. She screamed loudly, 'Jeremy, Jeremy!'

When it was over, they sat together at the dinner table. They chatted about their day as they drank fine Argentinian Malbec.

Chapter 2

The following morning, Kira arose with the song of lark. Wearing what she referred to as her Julia Roberts 'Pretty Woman' dress, she looked in the mirror and smiled. The dress was spotty with a full skirt; it made Kira feel extremely feminine. Jeremy walked her to the front door, she kissed him goodbye, then gave him a wave before she entered her little pink car. The early morning sun was shining; there wasn't a cloud in the April sky. As she pushed the button for the radio, the car was instantly filled with music that she couldn't help singing along to. Turning up the volume, she sang a duet at the top of her voice with Jason Derulo.

There was nothing Kira liked more than starting the day early, partly because she could almost guarantee securing a parking place outside her work. Feeling truly happy, she drove through the city, alongside the castle. *I never tire of that view of Edinburgh Castle,* she thought, looking out the window on her left. Her journey then took her straight up the hill into Bruntsfield until she came to the row of shops where the Ivan Cole Estate Agency stood. *Will there be a parking place? Please, please!* she begged, avoiding looking until the last moment. *Yes, yes, I knew it. Today is going to be a great day.*

Kira's boss, Ivan, was already in the office when she breezed through the door.

'Hi Ivan, it's a beautiful day and I got parked outside the door. What more could a girl ask for?'

'Big sales for a start!' he told her, in a mock angry voice. 'How's your day looking?'

Reading aloud her list of appointments from the large diary, she waited for her computer to load. For some reason, the

internet had been slow over the past week. *Ivan was right about the diary,* she thought, *Sometimes the old ways were the best.*
'Four viewings throughout the day but I'm going to contact a few potential buyers to alert them to the properties that are due to come on the market soon. So, I'll be busy, busy, busy!'
Her four o'clock appointment caught her eye. Mr Darcy - viewing the property in Regent Terrace.
*Mr Darcy…*she laughed to herself, as she visualised Colin Firth walking out of the lake, his shirt soaked through. *How exciting. Mr Darcy viewing a property in the city.* Using her red ballpoint pen, she circled the appointment several times.
When her computer was fully loaded, she clicked on the database of current clients, the list was extensive. She began working her way down the names, leaving a message for those who were not available. The bell above the office door made its familiar ding as the staff arrived to start the day. Kira spoke sweetly to the would-be viewers on the line, waving to her colleagues as they passed her desk.
Connie rushed in, hurling herself onto her swivel chair. She took a small mirror from her bag and began applying her make-up.
Derek sauntered in late, wearing a smart grey suit. As he walked past the phone, it rang. He answered it in a relaxed, professional manner, as though he had been in the office for hours.
Eric was the next to arrive. His entrance was made in the usual quiet, apologetic manner. There was no selling involved in his job description, he simply erected the Ivan Cole 'for sale' signs outside the new properties. It was also up to him to travel around slapping on 'Under Offer' or

'Sold, Subject to Completed Missives' stickers to the sign when the appropriate time arose. Eric was awkward in his manner, eye contact and conversation were not his best assets. It would also be fair to say that he was not plagued with initiative; he had to be instructed, every inch of the way. Kira quite liked him, although, subconsciously, she avoided ever being alone with him.

It was Connie's turn to get the morning coffees. She always struggled to remember what her colleagues liked, even after all this time. Taking a pen from her desk, she wrote down the list on a piece of scrap paper. The town was busy on a Thursday and just as she suspected, there was a lengthy queue in Costa Coffee. Although attractive in her own pleasing way, Connie was no traffic stopper, nor did the baristas rush forward to serve her.

Kira made the last of her phone calls, jotting down the names of her clients in her notebook. If Connie got back sharply, she would have time to drink her latte in the office rather than take it on the road. Her next appointment was about fifteen minutes away, but it was on a new housing estate that she was not familiar with; she would allow herself an extra half hour.

'Hey, you guys,' she said to her colleagues, 'Did any of you take a call from a David Cameron who was viewing the flat in Bruntsfield? I sat for ages in that dreary joint. He didn't turn up and he hasn't returned any of my calls.'

Everyone answered with a shake of the head, or a 'No, not me.'

'Strange,' she thought. 'Maybe he'll call today.'

The overhead bell chimed when Connie walked in with the cardboard carrier of hot drinks.

'Sorry I took so long,' she apologised. 'The traffic is horrendous out there.'
Everyone walked over to collect their drinks.
'Hey Con, where the hell is my Americano?' Derek shouted.
Connie made a face and began removing the lids from the cups to check. She then turned to Kira, 'By the way, that tall guy with the bun was asking about you.'
'Oh no, what did he say?' Kira asked, feeling uncomfortable.
'He wanted to know if you were single. He then asked what time the office shut. I told him you were getting married and that the office shuts when we are finished for the night. If you ask me, I'd say he is really smitten by you.'
'Does anyone actually say smitten anymore?' Derek asked her.
'Yes, me!' Connie said, slapping him on the arm.
'Don't you dare *smite* me. Help, I've been smitten!' Derek shouted, impersonating Connie's upper-class accent.
'Oh Derek, I'm sorry, I got you an Expresso instead of an Americano,'
Derek made a childlike face, folding his arms, pretending to be in the huff.
'I'm sorry, I just got mixed up. I couldn't read my own writing on the list. Anyway, it serves you right for making fun of me.'
Draining the last drop of her latte, Kira announced, 'I'm off now but I will be back into the office about lunchtime. If you need me, just phone. Enjoy your day, guys.'
Walking out the door, she smiled, looking at her little pink car, parked so conveniently outside the office. *It really pays to be an early bird*, she thought smugly.

Her first appointment was in a street called Orchard Way. Her sat nav took her in the direction of the new development, just outside of town. On arrival, she saw that there were beautiful five-bedroomed houses standing elegantly on a generous plot at the entrance to the estate, but as she ventured further in, she saw that the houses at the back were less impressive, lacking a little in character.

Indicating left, she found herself on a street that she had already driven down, it was a maze. The houses were all so similar, the street names were not clearly visible. The clock in her car showed her that she had five minutes to find the house. *I hate being late,* she thought. *Where the hell am I?* Pressing the Sat Nav button on her phone, she spelled out the address and post code. The map began to calculate the fastest route. *Come on, come on.*

'You have reached your destination,' the Sat Nav voice announced.

Distrusting technology, she lowered her window, preparing to ask a gentleman approaching with his dog on a leash.

'Excuse me, can you tell me the name of this street?' she asked him.

'Orchard Way,' he told her, pointing up at a sign a few yards away.

'Thank you,' she shouted. He nodded his reply. 'What is wrong with me? My mind's all over the place. Come on, Kira, hold it together,' she warned herself.

Kira completed her morning appointments, feeling confident that at least one couple she had shown were seriously interested in buying. In her experience, the people who say nothing on a tour around a house, are usually the interested parties. It's not until they ask questions about entry and closing dates, that she presumes that the sale is in the bag. Likewise, the viewers who gush overenthusiastically around every room, in Kira's thinking, are feeling guilty that they have wasted her time.

Back in the car, Kira took her sunglasses from the glove compartment; it was such a beautiful morning. Lowering the visor above her head, she started the engine and drove back towards the office. Ivan insisted that they all regroup for a short meeting on a Monday and Thursday at lunchtime. It was a chance to get an update on the progress of the properties on their books. Each member of the sales team gave a brief rundown of what was happening. They discussed closing dates, early offers and houses that would benefit from lowering the selling price to arouse interest. Once in a while, a fixed price was even applied to a property to move things along. It was a typical trend to have an excess of houses for sale in springtime. Statistically, people tended to buy and sell more often at this time of year.

Of course, her parking place had been taken by the time she returned. A brisk walk up to the office would do her good, as the majority of her time was spent sitting at a desk. Passing the window of Costa, she heard knocking on the glass from inside the shop. Glancing furtively, she saw that it was the assistant with the tied back hair. He was waving frantically at her. She flicked her hand up, in an embarrassed semi-wave without stopping.

He's becoming a pest! she thought.

Much to the delight of Kira and the rest of the team, Ivan wrapped the lunchtime meeting up early. This gave Kira an opportunity to take a look at her appointments, some of which she had organised herself, others that had been entered into the system for her. It was important to work out the logistics and time frame of getting from house A to house B. The selling business had come naturally to Kira and although she had grown to enjoy it, it had never even been on her radar as a profession; she had Jeremy to thank or blame for that. When she left university, she met Jeremy soon after. A close relationship between the two of them developed fairly early on. It was an all-consuming love affair with barely any room for anyone else in their lives. After running into Ivan Cole one day in the city, Jeremy decided to ask him for a job for her. The men had attended boarding school together, which, he informed her later, made him feel comfortable enough to ask for a favour. Kira had been embarrassed walking into the office on that first day but by the time Ivan had shown her the ropes, they all agreed that she was a good fit.

Her three-thirty appointment had left her with the feeling that she had wasted her precious time. The client informed her that she was unsure whether she wanted to move house or not. 'I was merely curious to see what was out there,' she told her. This kind of thing happened from time to time; it was exasperating. However, Kira never showed her true feelings. To her mind, this week's browser could be next week's buyer.

Before leaving for her final appointment of the day, she sat in her car with the engine off. She wanted to take a moment to reflect on everything that was going on in her life; things seemed so up in the air for her. The mirror on the back of the sun visor reflected her face; too many sleepless nights had taken their toll. Reaching over for her handbag on the passenger seat, she retrieved her lipstick and the small bottle

of perfume. A quick spray on the neck then wrists, followed by the pursing of her fuchsia coloured lips. 'There,' she said aloud as she checked her reflection once more, 'That is what my mother would call presentable.'
Flipping the sun visor back up, she straightened her 'Pretty Woman' dress over her knees and started up her beloved little pink car. It was now time to drive across town to Regent Terrace where Mr Darcy would be waiting.

Chapter 3

Jeremy paced the floor in front of the bay window of their Victorian property. He couldn't understand why Kira was so late. She would never go socialising after work nor would she ever book appointments after five. It was now half past seven and Jeremy was beside himself with worry. He picked up his phone and pressed the 'Kira' button. The phone rang a few times before going to answering machine. 'Kira, it's Jeremy. Call me when you get this message.' He then phoned Kira's mother by hitting the 'Celia' button.

'Celia, are you with Kira? She hasn't come home from work yet. I can't get in touch with her.'

Celia paused to think of where Kira could be, but answered, 'No, she's not with me, Jeremy. We went to the Prestonfield Hotel last night, but we didn't have any appointments today. By the way, I went ahead and booked the Prestonfield, it's an excellent hotel; absolutely everything that we're looking for. I think you'll love it. Anyway, let me know when she turns up.'

'Yes, yes, the Prestonfield is an excellent choice. You did the right thing booking it. I trust your judgement. I'll give you a call when she eventually walks through the door. Bye Celia.'

Once he had cut off Celia's call, he smashed his finger down on the Kira button again. Waiting impatiently for rings to pass, he left another message after the long beep.

'Kira, where the fuck are you?'

Feeling distraught, but equally furious, he threw himself down on the leather Chesterfield in the front room, listening intently for the sound of a key in the front door. It didn't come.

His mobile phone sat on the small occasional table, and staring at it, he thought, *Who the fuck can I phone now*?' Snatching it up, he began flicking through his contacts until he came to 'Ivan Cole'.

'Ivan, my friend! How are you? It's been too long. Listen, I'm looking at my watch and noticing that Kira hasn't returned home yet. Any idea of her plans this evening? Her phone's just ringing out.' This information was relayed casually, Ivan would never have suspected the inner turmoil going on within him.

'Jeremy, good to hear from. Yes, you're right, it's been too long. It's our turn to have you two over for dinner. We must organise something. Let's check our diaries for a date around the week of the 28th. Does that work for you?' Ivan asked.

'Yes, that sounds like a plan to me. Er, about Kira, any ideas?' Subconsciously, he found himself crossing his fingers as he waited for a reply.

'Oh, well, I know that her last appointment was at four o'clock. She didn't come back into the office after that, but then, I wouldn't have expected her to. I know that she has been looking at wedding venues with her mother after work, so she could be with her. If my memory serves me correctly, her mother, Celia, is a real talker, so she's probably just been held up.'

'Yeah, that'll be it. Thanks Ivan. Get onto Sarah about that dinner date. I'll keep my diary free.'

Hysteria began to set in, altering Jeremy's breathing pattern. Strange squeals escaped his lips. This had never happened before. *Where is she*? he wondered. *Why is she not answering her fucking phone*?

By ten o'clock, Jeremy had been physically sick down the toilet. Something was wrong, he knew it. From the crystal decanter on the sideboard, he poured himself a large Grouse. With his hands shaking, he threw it down his throat before replenishing the glass. 'What the Hell should I do?' he found himself asking out loud, wandering from room to room. He was drunk and demented with worry. A nervous rumbling came from his insides, forcing him to run to the toilet. It felt like his innards had just given way. His knees bobbed up and down in an involuntary action while sitting on the toilet seat. Loud sobs blurted from his lips.

The best option, he decided, would be to give it until the morning, then he would call the police. Calling the cops would be a last resort as they were a high profile, yet private, family. Still, what else could he do if she had not returned by the morning?

Arranging two of the cushions on the Chesterfield, he settled down for the night. The several whiskies he had consumed took the edge off his panic. A calm, hopeful feeling washed over him, as he drifted off into a deep sleep; tomorrow would bring his Kira back home.

His phone blasted the ringtone of 'William Tell Overture'. In his disorientated state, he sat bolt upright as he reached to answer the call.

'Yes?' he answered, experiencing a raging thirst in his throat.

'Hello, Mr Ward, your nine o'clock appointment is in the waiting room. Will you be long?' Jeremy's secretary asked.

'No, no, I'm on my way. Just stuck in a bit of traffic. Make him a coffee and butter him up.' Wincing from the pain, he clambered from the Chesterfield. Hammers pounded upon his skull from every direction. He attempted to straighten his

back, which had stiffened into the arched position he had slept in.
Suddenly, he remembered why he felt so bad. Swaying unsteadily at the foot of the stairs, he shouted 'Kira, Kira are you home?' There was no reply. Something deep within him knew that there wouldn't be. There was only a graveyard silence from the two floors above him.
Stumbling his way to the front window, he harboured a flicker of hope that he may see her little pink car, but there was no sign of it parked in either direction.
'Where is she?' he wailed, as he picked up his phone and pressed the 'Kira' button once again. As before, it rang out before switching to her answering machine:
'Hi, I'm busy at the moment, but I'll call you back when I can.' Beep, beep, beep.
Jeremy broke down crying when he heard Kira's cheerful voice. 'Where are you?' he shouted. 'Where the bloody hell can you be?'
He donned his pinstripe suit, before setting off to the office for his nine o'clock appointment. It was closer to ten when he walked through the glass doors of his business. Apologising profusely, he led the client into his impressive corner office, which boasted views of Edinburgh Castle, Arthur's Seat and a glimpse of the Parliament Building.
Jeremy conducted the meeting with absolute decorum, managing to hold himself together for the duration. By the end of discussion, his client shook his hand, thanked him and left.
When the door to his office clicked shut, Jeremy laid his head in his hands.
Where is she, where the fuck is she?

He pounded on his aching skull with his fists. He was, quite literally, in pieces.
Picking up the phone on his desk, he dialled 999.
'Hello, what service do you require?' the voice asked on the other end.
'I would like the police, please.'
'Police, what's your emergency?' the voice asked officially.
'It's about my fiancé. She didn't come home last night. She is not answering her phone, it's just ringing out and her car is gone. Before you ask, we haven't had a fight, she has never done anything like this before. I have a terrible feeling that something has happened to her.' He began to cry.
'Right, sir, try to stay calm. Give me the full name of your fiancé and a description of her. It would be very helpful if you could tell me what she was wearing when you last saw her. I will also need the make, model and the registration number of her car,' the police handler asked softly.
Jeremy came off the phone with a sense of relief knowing that the police would be looking for Kira. Feeling completely emotionally drained, he walked out to the reception area where his secretary, Lucy, was sitting typing up a formal letter to a rival company.
'Lucy, cancel the rest of my appointments for today. I'm not feeling at all well. I'm going home.' Without waiting for an answer, he walked robotically out of the building.
Functioning purely on autopilot, he weaved his way through the city traffic. The driver from the side road on his left tooted, as Jeremy drove out in front of him, through a red traffic light. He had no recollection of reaching his house or parking his car badly, with the front wheels on the pavement. He staggered his way to the Oxford blue front

door where he opened it with his key. Without shutting the outer storm door behind him, he stumbled to the lounge where he threw himself down on the leather wing chair. *I'll wait here until the police decide to arrive,* he thought. *I won't even move a muscle.*

Jeremy had no idea how much time had passed when his thoughts were interrupted by the loud shrillness of his front doorbell ringing. He rose up out of the chair, walking unsteadily to answer it.

'Come in,' he said rather thinly to the two cops on the doorstep. They followed as he led them through to the front lounge, pointing at the Chesterfield, motioning for them to sit down. There was no offer of refreshments.

'So, Mr Ward, to the best of your knowledge could you give us an idea of your fiancé's last movements,' the female police officer asked.

'She works in the Ivan Cole Estate Agency. All I know is that her last appointment was at four o'clock yesterday afternoon. No one saw her after that. She's never done this before.'

'Can you tell us the last time you spoke to her? What I mean by that is, does she call you throughout the day?' the male police officer enquired.

'The last time I spoke to her was in the morning when she left for work,' Jeremy replied, thinking back.

'How did that conversation go?'

'She was wearing what she referred to as her 'Pretty Woman' dress and I told her she looked great. I kissed her and said, 'See you tonight'. We never have a cross word.'

'Thanks for your help, Mr Ward. We don't need anything further at this stage. What happens now is that we'll write out a missing person's report. That will go out to all police personnel, right across the capital. In the next hour or so, we'll take a trip over to the estate agency where she works to check out where her last appointment took place. Keep your phone handy and we'll call with any developments. I know it's easy for me to say but try not to worry. There could be a perfectly logical explanation for all of this.'

Jeremy looked at them both with narrowed eyes. 'Such as?'

'Well, she could have met a group of friends, lost track of the time or something. The important thing is that if you think of anything that we should know, just dial 101 and ask to be put through to the on-duty supervisor at St Leonard's Police Station.'

Jeremy was only too aware of how crucial the first few days were when it came to searching for a missing person. He also knew that he would be the number one suspect until they were able to rule him out. Walking the cops to the door, he reminded them that he wanted to know any piece of information they uncovered, good or bad.

'One last thing before we go, Mr Ward,' the female officer asked. 'Could we take a quick look upstairs please? It's just routine procedure.'

They explained that the first attending officers always had to complete a basic search of the home before leaving. Sometimes people would inform the police of a missing person when that person was actually upstairs in bed asleep, dead from a heart attack or murdered. This would cause great embarrassment for the police if they went ahead and put out an alert for a missing person.

'You want to search my home?' Jeremy questioned in disbelief. 'If she were just missing in the house, I think I'd be

able to find her, don't you? The reason I called you is because she is *not* in the house!'
'Like I said Mr Ward, it's just routine procedure.'
Jeremy shook his head in despair as the police officers climbed the stairs to carry out a search.
The officers were back downstairs within fifteen minutes. They had found nothing.
'We'll be in touch,' one of them shouted, as they saw themselves out.
Within the hour, the police had made their way over to the Ivan Cole Estate Agent office.
Derek, Connie, Eric and Ivan all stared as the imposing looking uniformed officers walked through the door. Ivan walked forward to address them.
'How can I help you?' he asked, his heartbeat quickening. A fleeting thought crossed his mind that the police had found out about a favour he had pulled off for a good friend, which was not exactly legal. His friend's submitted offer on a house had not been the highest at the closing date, but he felt that his friend needed it the most, so he had sent him a quick text advising him to up his offer by several thousand pounds. He justified his dishonesty by telling himself that the sellers got a better price and his friend got what he needed. All the other people involved would soon find another house, perhaps even a better one; it could be seen as fate.
'We're here to ask you a few questions about Kira Carmichael. Is there somewhere we can talk in private?' the female officer asked.
'Yes, come through to my office at the back.' Ivan felt a huge wave of relief wash over him as he led the two cops through a door at the back, into a very small, untidy space. There

were only two chairs in his office, so he brought a chair through from the front office.
'Now, what's this all about?' Ivan asked.
'Kira Carmichael, who I believe is an employee of yours…' The policeman paused for confirmation of this suggestion while Ivan obliged with a nod, '…did not arrive home last night and has not been seen since. We are hoping that you can shed some light on where she was going and who she was meeting.'
'That's unbelievable,' he said, quite obviously shocked. 'Although, Jeremy, her partner, did call me last night because she hadn't come home. He didn't seem overly concerned. In fact, we talked about making plans for the four of us to have dinner at my house.'
'How would you describe their relationship, Mr Cole?'
Ivan thought for a moment. 'It's good, I think. I mean, they're getting married next year, so it must be good.' This was the most honest answer he could give the police. There had been a few signs of Jeremy's controlling behaviour, but that was just Jeremy. He liked things done his way.
'Could you tell us about the last appointment Miss Carmichael had in her diary for yesterday?
Ivan thought for a moment. 'I'll have to go and get her diary, just to be certain.'
He left the room to fetch Kira's desk diary. As he walked into the main office, Derek mouthed, 'What the fuck?'
Ivan shook his head, whispering, 'I'll tell you later.'
He took the large appointments' diary from Kira's desk at the window and headed back through to the police officers. The staff all watched closely. They stared at each other wide-eyed, looking for answers.

The policewoman flicked through the pages until she came to the correct day. She scanned down the page until she came to the last appointment.
'The last appointment appears to be at four o'clock with a Mr Darcy at a house in Regent Terrace. I can see that the appointment has been circled several times. Have you any idea why she would do that, Mr Cole?'
Ivan shook his head, 'No, I haven't a clue; although that property is worth over a million pounds, so it could be that she circled it because it's important to the company financially. She is on a commission based salary so selling this house would be worth a lot of money to Kira.'
'Do you know who lives in this property?'
'I can't remember the name off the top of my head, but I think he's an Asian gentleman working in Dubai at the moment,' Cole told them.
'Did you hear from her after she had visited the property?'
'No, she didn't check in after that, but then she wouldn't normally do that anyway,' he told them.
'Do you have any information on this Mr Darcy?' they asked.
'No, I haven't heard that name until now. She didn't mention it, but his details will have been taken at the time the appointment was booked. I will look on the system and contact you with anything I can find on him.'
'That would be helpful,' the male cop answered. 'Now, could you describe Miss Carmichael's mood or state of mind when she left the office yesterday?' the woman asked.
'Happy, laughing, her usual chipper self, I would say.'
The police officers stood up at the same time, as if they knew instinctively that they had asked the last question.

'If you think of anything significant, no matter how small, get in touch. Just call 101 and ask to be put through to the duty supervisor.' She handed Ivan a card with a reference number written on it. He put it in the top drawer of his desk. 'Thank you for your time, Mr Cole. We may be back at some point to speak to your staff.'
They headed out the door, through the front office, out onto the street.
Ivan didn't think that it was relevant to mention the fact that Kira had taken money from the petty cash box on several occasions. A camera had been installed in his office in the back when he discovered that there were small amounts of money going missing regularly. Kira was the last person he had expected to see when he played back the footage. He had been waiting for the right moment to ask her about it. There was no shortage of money in Kira's household, if there had been, Ivan knew that her parents would have helped her out. It made no sense to him that someone like her would steal from her employer.

Chapter 4

Jeremy had never felt so helpless in his entire life. He was the kind of person who liked to be in control of a situation. If there was a problem, he fixed it. If he didn't like something, he changed it. It was as simple as that. Now, he found himself in a position where he was utterly at a loss as to what to do next. His instincts told him to go out and search for Kira, but he was afraid that she would return home and he wouldn't be there; besides, he would have no idea where to start looking.

Work and home were the only two facets to Kira's life. She did not have friends nor was she a member of any gyms or clubs. Jeremy was all she had. In fact, she raced home each day to be with him. There was nowhere to look, no one to call. He knew that she had to be in trouble because this behaviour was completely alien to Kira's nature. It could be said that, over the years, he had come to know her every thought, mood, desire and movement. Now, how many men could say that about their partners? Not many, he guessed.

With the last of his depleted strength, he dragged the solid wing chair over to the bay window to enable him to watch for Kira. People out on the street, chatting and laughing, filled him with unbearable anger. The normalcy of life outside the house was becoming an irritant to him. *How can these fools behave like nothing is happening?* he thought irrationally. *Do they not realise that my world is crumbling around me*? Yanking the cork out of the whisky bottle with his teeth, he poured himself a large measure to settle his nerves. He rested his head on the back of the chair, sipping on the smooth, golden elixir.

In an instant, a lightbulb moment came to his mind. It dawned upon him that he had a phone app for Kira's phone. She had given him no reason to use it of late, but in the beginning of their relationship he needed to check that she was where she said she would be. It was important that he could trust her before he proposed. After checking her whereabouts each day, he then questioned her when she got home. This was done to make sure that her story tied in with the evidence he had gleaned from her phone. His findings revealed that she was absolutely by the book dependable. Everywhere she said that she had been, was everywhere the app had told him. This was a very good indication of her character.

Phone in hand, he nervously tapped on the app. His heart began to bang painfully in his chest, his fingers trembled. Why hadn't he thought of this before?

A map appeared on the screen with an arrow showing Kira's phone. It showed him clearly that her phone was situated somewhere off the M9 motorway. It seemed to be pointing somewhere past Linlithgow, on the way to Falkirk. Thrusting the phone into his pocket, he grabbed his car keys and ran out of the front door. Knowing that he shouldn't be driving, as he had consumed a generous measure of whisky, he eased his conscience by telling himself that this was an emergency. This could be a 'life or death' situation. Was it possible that Kira was being held somewhere against her will? He couldn't thole the thought of her crying for him, willing him to burst through the door to save her. Rage began to swell within him at the thought of some thug laying his filthy hands on his precious girl.

An afterthought occurred to him as he drove through the busy streets, *I should have brought a weapon from the house.* But he had no time to turn back, he was on the way to finding Kira, nothing was going to slow him down. There would be time to formulate a plan when he got there. Once he'd had a chance to case the joint, he'd find out how many perpetrators were involved, then act on his intuition.

The speedometer on Jeremy's car had reached ninety miles per hour as he raced out of the city of Edinburgh towards Stirling. The phone resting on the dashboard showed him that he was getting closer and closer to Kira.

'I'm coming for you baby,' he muttered, over and over again, under his breath. 'I'm coming for you. Everything is going to be all right. I will save you.' His foot flattened on the accelerator, his fingers closed tightly around the steering wheel. He kept to the outside lane of the motorway, moving in close behind any car that got in his way. Tooting erratically on his car horn, he warned the other drivers that he was not in the mood to be messed with. The other drivers gave him the space that he was looking for, presuming that he was either a cop in an unmarked vehicle or a madman.

The pressure he was applying on the gas eased as he drew close to the area in which the arrow pointed. Frantically, he scanned the scene around him from every window in his car but saw only countryside. There were no people, houses or ruined shacks. All that was visible were hills, surrounded by sparse wooded areas and large patches of marshy ground. There was only one explanation for it all, he surmised, *She is being held underground.* There had been an article he read some time ago about a kidnap victim who had been incarcerated for weeks underground, in a coffin. The girl in question had been supplied air by a copper tube leading up out of the earth. *Yes, that must be it. They've laid her in a coffin then buried her,* he thought, scouring the ground for a protruding object which could be construed as a breathing tube.

The phone indicated that he was now in the actual vicinity of where Kira was being held. Pulling the car over onto the hard shoulder, he climbed out, phone in hand. Staring at his screen, he walked over to the grass verge until he was standing on the arrow. He reached down to feel through the long reedy grass. There was nothing there. Dropping to his knees, he crawled around, patting the damp marshland on either side of him.

An idea suddenly came to him. *Idiot; I'll just call her.*

With his peaty hands, he took out his phone, pressing the 'Kira' button. An object lit up in the grass, followed by the ringtone 'We Found Love (in a Hopeless Place)', by Rihanna. It was her phone, he snatched it up. It was cracked but was otherwise perfectly intact. He looked all around, wondering how on earth Kira's phone had ended up on the M9 motorway. Scrambling back up to his feet, he put the phone in his pocket. Disappointed by the find, he realised that rather than solving anything, it had only made matters a whole lot worse.

Jeremy drove back towards Edinburgh. Driving through the city centre, tears rolled down his face. Aloud, he asked himself questions that he was unable to answer. He was utterly distraught. Arriving at Palmerston Place, he parked the car down the street from his house. A fleeting thought entered his head when he pulled Kira's phone from his pocket. Imagine if she were in the house right now, sitting in the lounge waiting for him, telling him that someone had stolen her phone. The thought dissipated in seconds, as he knew that too much time had elapsed. *Anyway,* he reasoned, *if someone steals your phone, you can still call from the office, you can still make your way home, you still have your car. Someone stealing your phone is inconvenient, but it doesn't make you disappear without a trace.* His head began to hurt. He had followed every possible idea in his mind, only to be met with a dead end. Just like a children's puzzle of a maze, there was a starting point, with only one true road leading you to the end conclusion. All the other routes on the maze were put there to confuse you, they were no more than red herrings. This now meant that he was back, no further than the original starting point, once again.

Just as he turned the key in the front door, his own phone rang. An unfamiliar number rather than a name appeared on his screen, for a second he hoped it could be Kira.

'Mr Jeremy Ward?' the voice on the other end of the line asked.

'Yes,' Jeremy answered nervously.

'This is the police. Would it be possible for you to come down to the station as soon as possible? We are situated on St. Leonard's Street.'

'Of course, I'll head over there now. Have you found Kira?' he asked, desperately.

'No, I'd rather not discuss the matter over the phone. I'll explain everything when you come in.'

She's dead, Jeremy thought, as his mind raced. Why did they want to see him? Why were they so brief?

It must be bad news, or they would have given me a hint as to what they know. His hands began to tremble, as did his knees. *They don't want me breaking down hysterically when I'm about to drive my car to the police station.*

Jeremy ran at full speed back down the hill and into his car, screeching his way out of the neat parking place. The BMW parked in front of him unfortunately lost a wing mirror as Jeremy clipped it, speeding off toward the police station. With no consideration for the other drivers on the road, he weaved in and out of cars, switching from lane to lane. Horns were tooting, drivers were throwing their hands in the air, shaking their heads. A lorry driver rolled down his window to shout, 'Maniac!' in the hope that Jeremy would hear. But all Jeremy could hear was the policeman's voice in his ears saying, 'I'll explain everything when you get here.'

When he arrived, he was led through to an interview room through the back of the police station. Two officers from CID introduced themselves to him. Further events had accelerated their investigation into a crime in action.

'What's this about?' Jeremy asked. 'Have you found her?'

'Mr Ward, we visited the house in Regent Terrace where your fiancé was heading to her last appointment of the day. We did an informal search of the area, and we found this dress pushed down into a wheelie bin at the back of the property.' One of the men held a paper bag with a polythene window. The bag contained a spotted dress, which had been torn in several places.

'We would like you to take a close look at it.' The short dress was laid flat on the table. 'It is important for us to know if this dress belongs to Kira. Do you think you can identify it for us?' the detective asked him gently, as he noticed Jeremy's quivering hands.

Jeremy nodded, gripping on to the table in front of him. His knees, once again, began to bob up and down involuntary, he slipped one hand down, leaning heavily on them to suppress the nervous reaction.

The polka dot dress in the bag was laid on the table in the middle of the room. It was kept within the transparent wrapping to preserve potential traces of DNA that may be present and to stop any further contamination.

Jeremy leaned forward studying the dress through the polythene window. An image of Kira wearing it that morning, entered his head. He had admired the way the hem of her dress flicked up as she walked, showing a little of her smooth, brown thighs. He had watched her walking out onto the front doorstep before shouting, 'See you tonight.' She had turned around and given one of those sweet smiles that made her look so innocent; childlike almost. The memory cut through him like a dagger.

Tears filled his eyes as he looked at the detectives, whispering, 'Yes, this is Kira's dress.'

'Are you certain?' one of them asked.

Jeremy nodded.

'We're going to send a forensic team out to the house on Regent Terrace. The area will be cordoned off. The dress will be sent to the lab and tested for DNA. We'll check all CCTV footage in the area around that time. You did supply a description of Miss Carmichael's car when you originally reported her missing, but can you confirm the make, model and registration once again please, Jeremy?'

'Yes, it's a pink Mini Cooper with the registration, K174 CAR.'

'Thank you, we just needed to double check. Miss Carmichael's car has been found parked outside the house in Regent Terrace. Her handbag was found on the passenger seat of the vehicle. The bag contained her money, bankcards and other personal items. However, there was no sign of a mobile phone. This is a good thing because she may still be able to make a call if she is in trouble. There is also a strong possibility that we will be able to trace her from her phone.'

Jeremy dropped his head in defeat as he reached into his pocket. He pulled out Kira's phone, placing it gently on the table.

'I tracked her phone this morning using an app that I set up a year ago. I found the phone at the side of the road, on the M9 near Falkirk.'

Jeremy laid his head down on the table in front of him. There was no logical explanation for all of this. His mind could not cope with the harsh reality that she may have been kidnapped or murdered. Remaining silent, he waited for the CID officers to inform him of the next steps in the procedure of finding his beloved Kira.

The elder of the two officers awkwardly shuffled some notes on the table. Seeing this young man before him in such a distraught state had affected him adversely. After over forty years on the force, he suspected that it was time to retire, his toughened shell was beginning to show cracks. He cleared his throat before speaking, 'Mr Ward, we need you to assist us in this investigation, so if you could stay strong, that would be really helpful for all of us.'

The young detective took over at this point to explain the procedure. 'As we believe that this has become a criminal investigation, the area is now being cordoned off and a general trawl for information is taking place at the scene where Miss Carmichael's belongings have been found. We will appeal for witnesses and carry out house-to-house enquiries. A thorough search of the whole area will be carried out by forensic experts. You can rest assured that no stone will be left unturned. Our team will do everything in their power to find out what has happened to Miss Carmichael.'

The senior of the two continued, 'We usually get a positive response from a media appeal, so we will set that up as soon as possible. All CCTV footage from that area will be combed through thoroughly. Someone out there will know something, so we just have to hope that the public will do their civic duty by coming forward with information.'

Jeremy thanked the detectives as he left. Deep down in his core he held out no hope of them solving the case and finding Kira, dead or alive. At this point, he truly believed that the disappearance of Kira Carmichael would forever be an unsolved mystery which would then become a story that would resurface every ten years or so. Perhaps retired detectives in the future would open the cold case file and attempt to unravel the facts for a television documentary. Kira was gone, she was never coming back, of this he was almost certain.

Chapter 5

Ramsay Carmichael comforted his overwrought wife as they waited for the police to arrive. He pledged to her that he, personally, would find out who had done this to Kira. Once the culprit was caught, he vowed to rip out his throat. Celia was comforted by his confident, fighting talk. Her faith in him was steadfast. As he held her crying face in his hands, he promised her, 'No one messes with the Carmichael family. Not if they want to see another day.'

'Do you promise; do you promise you'll find her?' Celia sobbed.

A heavy banging from the doorknocker resounded through the stillness of the house. With their arms around each other for support, the Carmichaels walked through the hall to the front door. A detective and a young, fair-skinned woman whose black hair looked too dark for her pale complexion, stood on the doorstep. Ramsay Carmichael invited them in and led them through to the more informal lounge at the back of the house.

'I am DCI Bryce, and this is Shirley Reid, your liaison officer. We want to give you an update on the investigation and get some background information from you about Kira. So, can I start with you Mrs Carmichael? Just tell me all about your daughter. What kind of girl is she?'

Celia took the handkerchief from up her sleeve to gently dab her tear-filled eyes.

'She's a wonderful human being, so kind and caring. She is naïve, a little, er…' she searched for the right word, '… green. She has needed a lot of guidance in her life as she hasn't always made the right decisions.'

DCI Bryce interrupted at this point, asking Celia to clarify this statement.
Celia continued, 'Well, over the years, we haven't approved of many of her friends. Would you say that was fair, Ramsay?'
'Yes, yes, I would say that was a fair comment, Celia.'
Shirley, the liaison officer, asked what it was about these friends that deemed them unsuitable for their daughter.
'I can't really put my finger on it,' Celia said. 'They were a different class from Kira. They were working class people from working class backgrounds. I, I mean *we*, didn't really approve of Kira moving in such circles, if you know what I mean. We have always brought her up to believe that you have to set your sights high when it comes to success, marriage and friendships.'
No, DCI Bryce did not know what she meant, and he was developing an uncomfortable dislike for this woman. He wondered if she ever factored happiness into her formula for a good life.
Celia continued, 'When she was at university she got in tow with a boy; Ramsay, what was the name of that boy?'
'Oh, what was it again?' he said, searching the recesses of his memory. 'I've got it!' he announced, suddenly remembering. 'It was Fraser, I think, Fraser Jackson.'
'Yes, that was it, Fraser Jackson. Well, this Fraser Jackson character was highly unsuitable. For her own good, we had to put a stop to the whole thing. We then found out that she was sneaking out of the house at night to meet him. It was a terrible time for us all. He obviously had some kind of hold over her because she behaved completely out of character. Anyway, he disappeared off the scene, thankfully.'

'Did you say she was at university at this time?' DCI Bryce asked.
'Yes.'
'Wouldn't she have been around eighteen years of age?' DCI Bryce asked, knowing that it was none of his business to judge these people. However, he had an eighteen-year-old daughter at home who had brought home some real 'beauties' for him to meet. He would never have dreamt of interfering in her life. As far as he was concerned, making mistakes was all part of the growing up process.
Celia could see what the detective was getting at; this irritated her. 'DCI Bryce, I am trying to explain the situation to you. She is a naïve, vulnerable girl who has needed guidance in her life's decisions. I didn't want to put my foot down about her relationships, but it was necessary because of the way she is. Don't you see?'
'Tell us about her relationships now. Does she seem happy with Jeremy? Does she have any close friends that she sees regularly?' DCI Bryce asked.
Ramsay took over answering the questions as he could see that Celia was becoming distressed.
'Kira and Jeremy are joined at the hip. They are always together. They have a few friends that are couples, such as Ivan Cole, Kira's boss and his wife, but Kira doesn't go out on girls' nights, if that's what you mean. She would prefer to be home with Jeremy.'
'How did she meet Jeremy?'
'He is the son of a very good friend of mine. We can take full credit for the relationship. Jeremy's father and I set it up,' Ramsay announced, suddenly feeling rather proud.

Celia contributed to this statement. 'Hey, I was in on the mix too, you know!'
'What else can you tell us about your daughter?'
'She's hardworking and very good at her job,' Ramsay explained. 'Look, she's a good girl who never does anything to hurt anyone. She is decent, certainly not promiscuous, if that's what you're thinking. She's excited about getting married. I don't know what else we can tell you. Now, could you start telling us some information about what you've found out?'
'As you know, a torn dress was found in the bin at the rear of property where Kira had visited. Jeremy has positively identified the dress as being Kira's. The discovery of the dress and the fact that her car and personal belongings were also found at the scene means that Kira's disappearance has now become a criminal investigation. Her dress has been sent to the lab for DNA testing and the forensics team are now on site. We are in the process of tracking down the owner of the property who resides in the middle east. He may be able to tell us if he had allowed anyone to stay there while he was away.' The detective could see Kira's mother becoming fraught with the lack of positive news. The irritation that he had previously felt for her had now melted away, only compassion remained. 'The door to door enquiries will hopefully bring forward some new information and all local CCTV footage is being checked thoroughly.'
Celia reached for her handkerchief once again. 'Do you think that you'll find her?' she asked mid sob.

'I hope so. We will do everything we can. Now, would you be prepared to take part in a media appeal at a press conference?'
'I would normally prefer to keep things out of the media but if you think this might bring Kira back, then yes, of course we will,' Ramsay answered. 'I would also be prepared to offer a reward of fifty thousand pounds to anyone who can help bring her back to us.'
Celia remained in the lounge as Ramsay saw the detective and liaison officer to the door.
Shirley turned to Ramsay before leaving. 'I will come and see you both at the end of the week, but if you need anything before that, just call. I am here to support you both.'
Ramsay nodded. Tea and sympathy were the last things he needed right now. The only thing on his mind was finding Kira, his own investigation would begin as soon as these useless cops left.

Chapter 6

Jeremy didn't leave his house. Many days had passed since he had shaved, showered or dressed. The encrusted food stains on the front of his dressing gown were multiplying daily and the tartan wool fabric reeked of spilt whisky. Wearing his slippers all day, he shuffled from room to room, muttering to himself. Every so often, his pent up frustration would manifest itself with an object being thrown at the wall. All he wanted was privacy and to be left alone, but the press had set up camp outside his home in Palmerston Place. They had no intentions of leaving until they had a statement from him about his missing fiancé. If he were seen to be distraught, it would really get the sympathy of the readers and viewers. On the other hand, if he presented himself in a calm, composed manner, then he could look intriguingly suspicious. Either way, it was a winner for making news headlines. Well-wishers posted cards and letters to him. He received messages of hope, encouragement, lucky charms, theories of alien abduction and vindictive messages telling him that he was a rich bastard that deserved everything he got. There had even been several messages accusing him of murdering Kira. Amidst all of this overwhelming attention, there was the perpetual dull ache of loss. He missed Kira terribly and dreamt about her every night. In some of his dreams, she was back in bed beside him. When he awoke, drenched in sweat, he reached across the pillow for her but found only the empty space. This made him cry. On other occasions, he dreamt that a gang of kidnappers had snatched her with the intention of selling her into sex slavery. He awoke sobbing. As each new day arrived, he hoped that there would be comforting news to soothe his tortured soul. At best, he yearned for her to be found alive. At worst, he wanted her body to be found, with information as to how she died and who had killed her. But for now, he was in the waiting room of purgatory, unable to think, concentrate or move forward in any kind of new life.

Chapter 7

The police trawled through Kira's bank statements, but no money had been taken from her account since the day she had disappeared. They scrutinised her phone records but there were no unexplained calls or unrecognised numbers. At one point, the police asked if the mobile phone was only used as a business line as there were no photos, very few texts and only work-related calls. Jeremy explained that it was her own personal phone, but Kira had no need for friends; he was her best friend, and she was his. Why waste valuable time with people that don't mean anything to you? Life was too short for that.

All the staff members of Ivan Cole's Estate Agency were interviewed individually about Kira. There was a recurring thread running through each of the statements. She never joined them for nights out in the pub, instead she rushed home to her fiancé, Jeremy, every night. Her relationship seemed all consuming and her wedding plans were her top priority. However, during the interview process a red flag was raised when three separate workmates mentioned a barista in Costa Coffee that seemed to be harbouring an obsession for Kira. This had apparently caused her some concern. Both police officers wrote down descriptions of the young gentleman along with directions to the coffee shop.

After leaving the Estate Agency, the two policeman walked across the road, then down the hill to Costa. Once they had ascertained which of the two assistants was the one in question, they then asked him to come into the station at the earliest opportunity to assist them with their enquiries.

In the car, on the way back to the station, the police officer who was driving asked his partner, 'What did you think of Eric?'
'Who's Eric?' the officer in the passenger seat asked, retrieving his notebook from his pocket.
'He is the shilpit one in Ivan Cole's Estate Agency. The one that couldn't look us in the eye.'
'Yeah, he was a bit strange. Do you think he deserves a closer look?'
'It certainly wouldn't do any harm.'
The young gentleman from Costa appeared at the station the following morning. He was questioned and released without further investigation. On the day Kira had disappeared, he had been working all day. After arriving at the coffee shop around 7am in the morning, he had not left the premises until the establishment had been cleaned and set up for the following day, which was after 7pm. His lunch had been consumed on the premises. His colleague had confirmed his movements.
As time rolled by, the trail began to turn lukewarm. Jeremy commissioned posters to be made with Kira's smiling face on them. In the evenings, he walked the streets distributing the flyers to every restaurant and bar that he passed. Most people were happy to display Kira's picture in the window of their business or in the vestibule of the church. Seeing Jeremy's grief-stricken face made people want to help in any way that they could. After all, if it had been their loved one, wouldn't they have wanted everyone to care and unite in the search.
Every day for a week, Jeremy left the house armed with a bag filled with posters and a staple gun. In the beginning, he

secured Kira's picture to every lamp post in the street, starting with Regent Terrace where she had disappeared. It soon became apparent that his mission would be too time consuming, he then changed his tactic to every second lamp post. Towards the end of the week his desired outcome was simply to have at least one poster in every street in the area. When his stash of posters was finished, he returned home for the final time. Once inside the house, he headed straight upstairs to the bathroom where he tended his blistered feet with a soothing aloe vera gel. His legs and hips ached but his spirits had lifted somewhat. Someone, somewhere, will pass one of the posters, see Kira's face and they will be reminded of the time they saw her being taken away in a car by a stranger.

Celia and Ramsay Carmichael decided to make a public appeal via a press conference for any information on the disappearance of their daughter. Ramsay had contacted Jeremy asking him to join them in this process, but he declined. The Carmichaels were disappointed in him but accepted that he had his own reasons for not appearing before the wider public. Ramsay also had reservations about carrying out such an arduous task, but it had been explained to him that in all missing persons cases, it was essential to get the message out to as many people as possible to uncover any information. Displaying a grieving family on television could help a story to stay in the headlines. In short, the more publicity, the better. Ramsay was also told that in around 10% of missing person cases, public pleas yielded tips that would be helpful in locating their loved one. He reckoned that 10% was high enough odds for him to put himself out there.

During the public appeal, Celia Carmichael broke down sobbing.
Ramsay took over. 'Somebody out there must know what has happened to our daughter, Kira. There may even be people watching this who know something helpful but may not realise it. Kira is a sweet and beautiful girl; we miss her terribly.' At this point, Ramsay's voice began to waiver. Celia detected her husband's emotion and pulled herself together.
Patting Ramsay's hand, Celia took over. 'On the day Kira went missing, she was wearing a spotty dress just like the one Julia Roberts wore in 'Pretty Woman'. In fact, she called it her 'Pretty Woman' dress,' she told the camera with a brave attempt at a smile. She then picked up a photograph that she had brought with her to the press conference. 'Take a good look at Kira's pretty face. Have you seen her? Please, please think back, do you remember anything, no matter how small a detail? Help us bring back our wonderful daughter, Kira, please.'
Ramsay composed himself in time to add some factual information about the last known movements of his daughter. The closing statement was made into the camera by DCI Bryce.
The detectives were pleased with the way the appeal had gone. Both parents had used Kira's name several times just as they had been advised to do. Celia's appeal had been powerful in the way she talked so lovingly about her daughter.
The public appeal did not yield the harvest of information that the Carmichaels had hoped for. It had turned up reports of possible sightings of Kira in Greece and Turkey, but as Kira's passport was still in a drawer in her home in

Palmerston Place, these leads were not followed up. During the investigation, it became clear that Kira had not bought a property, rented a house, earned a wage, paid any tax or claimed benefits. She had quite literally disappeared without a trace.

The police arranged for Ramsay and Celia to help with a reconstruction of Kira's last known movements. Celia begged Jeremy for his input in this latest appeal, and he reluctantly agreed. The fact that it would be an advisory role for him, rather than in the public eye, helped to sway his decision.

The actress they chose for the re-enactment had long blonde hair and was of similar height and build to Kira. Jeremy showed the lookalike how to style her hair by giving her a diamante clasp belonging to Kira. The clasp had come from a pack which had originally contained three. Jeremy had brought the pack of the remaining two clasps along to the reconstruction, as he knew that she had worn one on the day she had disappeared. The police managed to source a spotty 'Pretty Woman' dress, which was very similar to the one Kira had worn. Kira's car with the cherished number plate was also used.

The film started with the actress leaving her desk in Ivan Cole's Estate Agency. She walked down the hill, past Costa Coffee, round the corner to her parked car. The actress then drove, via the most direct route, to the house in Regent Terrace. The cameraman was in the passenger seat of a vehicle which travelled closely behind.

When the filming was complete, the actress changed into her own clothes in the office of Ivan Cole's Estate Agency before leaving to meet friends. Jeremy ran after her to ask for the diamanté clasp back which belonged to Kira. The lookalike apologised, telling Jeremy that she had forgotten that she was wearing it. Jeremy took the clasp back, saying nothing before he walked away.

Forgot you were wearing it? he thought. *Yeah, sure thing. Everyone wants a memento these days. A souvenir to show your friends when you tell them that you have just played the starring role in a film about the disappearance of Kira Carmichael. Bitch!*

The reconstruction was aired on prime-time television on the BBC programme, 'Crimes Unsolved'. The presenter, Bob Foster, stared into the camera at the end of the show and appealed to the public in a closing monologue:

'These are the last known movements of Kira Carmichael. Someone out there may know something that would help in this investigation. Think back to that Thursday in April. Try to remember if you saw this woman. We would also like to appeal to Mr Darcy, who viewed the property in Regent Terrace in Edinburgh, to come forward, so that he may be eliminated from the police enquiries. Thank you for watching. Goodnight.'

The phone numbers to call ran along the foot of the television screen. The familiar theme tune then played as the credits rolled.

There had been a few phone calls that night, following the programme, but nothing concrete. Several people phoned to say that they did remember seeing her, but they had nothing to add to what the police already knew. The calls soon dried up and 'Crimes Unsolved' focused on a different investigation the following week. Mr Darcy did not come forward to the police and a dead end had been reached in their attempts to trace him. He was the main person of interest in the investigation, but the police were now convinced that he had used a false name.

Chapter 8

Days turned into weeks, then months, the posters in the shop windows came down, the letters from the public slowed to a trickle. The world carried on as normal and Kira's disappearance became just another unsolved mystery that was rarely spoken of.

Jeremy did not throw himself into his work; quite the contrary, he stayed away. Within the confines of his house was the only place he wanted to be. The comforting scent of Kira had remained in several of the rooms but with each day that passed the smell grew fainter. There were still occasions when he could sense her presence around. In the darkness of his bedroom at night, he was convinced that he could see her standing over his bed. However, illumination from the bedside lamp soon told him that he was imagining things. After these occurrences, he would reaffirm to himself that Kira was gone, and he would probably never know what had happened to her.

Usually, in the afternoons, he sat in the wing chair at the window in the front lounge, thinking over the different scenarios that could have happened to her. When he had exhausted all the possible theories, he would look at his watch, realising that four or five hours had passed; and that he had not moved a muscle. The worst times for him were when he came under attack in the night from the punishing torment of regrets. Asking himself if he had treated her as well as he could have. Did he put her feelings first? Was he a bit controlling at times? Did everything have to be his way or no way? Worst of all, was he a little heavy handed with her? These torturous thoughts were unbearable, so he made sure that he justified his every action to himself. It was a survival mechanism to keep his sanity intact.

Chapter 9

Celia was awakened early on the Sunday morning by a resounding knock at the front door. Leaving Ramsay sleeping, she reached for her dressing gown and slid her feet into her slippers. Holding tightly to the banister, she ran down the curving staircase. Her dressing gown flapped behind her; the belt hung loose. After undoing the bolts on the glass door, she then moved onto the locks on the heavy storm door.

DCI Bryce and a police officer that she did not recognise stood on the doorstep, stern faced.

'Yes?' she said, half-hiding behind the door.

'Mrs Carmichael, would it be possible for us to come inside. We would like to have a word with you and your husband, if he's home.'

Celia invited them into the formal lounge, telling them to take a seat. Feeling a little embarrassed, she apologised for her attire, then told them that she would be back shortly. At full speed, she ran upstairs and shook Ramsay awake. He opened his eyes saying, irately, 'What are you playing at, woman?'

'The police are here, and they want to have a word with us both. Oh, Ramsay, maybe someone knows where she is. Perhaps they've found her. Hurry up, will you!' Celia screeched, as she pulled on her jeans and jumper, which were lying on the chaise longue from the night before.

They held hands as they walked downstairs to hear the news of their precious daughter.

DCI Bryce and the police officer rose to their feet as Celia and Ramsay entered the room. Bryce cleared his throat before announcing, 'I am sorry to inform you, but the body of a young woman, fitting the description of your daughter, has been retrieved from The River Almond. Could you accompany us to the Edinburgh Royal Infirmary to help us in the identification of the body?'

Ramsay made a call to Jeremy on the way to the mortuary to tell him that there was a possibility that Kira had been found, dead. Jeremy became vaguely detached saying, 'Okay, let me know how it goes.' It sounded as though he didn't care, but Ramsay and Celia knew that the opposite was true. They could see that Jeremy was not coping with the loss of Kira; he was withdrawing more and more into his own dark world.

The Carmichaels were led into a small, clinical room in the lowest level of the hospital building. Everything around them became detached from reality as they walked mechanically towards the stretcher on wheels that stood in the centre of the room. Ramsay placed his arm around his wife to support her as they stood in front of the covered body. Both parents stared at the dead woman's height and form, desperately trying to determine if it could be Kira, before the sheet was finally pulled back.

Beforehand, the medical examiner had presented the couple with a photograph of the body, but it had been impossible to tell if it was her. It was explained to them that the body had been in cold water for some time, which had slowed down the decomposition process; however, when the body was taken from the water, putrefaction was accelerated. The examiner also warned them that obstacles and structures in the water had interacted with the remains. In short, they needed to brace themselves for a very upsetting sight.

The medical examiner held the sheet and looked at Ramsay. Ramsay nodded to let him know that they were as ready as they would ever be.
The Carmichaels stared at the hideously bloated, bruised corpse. It was extremely distressing but neither of them had to think twice. They both spoke simultaneously, 'That's not our daughter.'
'Are you one hundred percent sure?' the medical examiner asked.
'One hundred percent,' they both replied.
With a quickened pace, the Carmichaels left the hospital, clearly relieved. Ramsay retrieved his phone from his pocket as soon as they were outside in the fresh air. He knew that Jeremy would be waiting for news from them, he had to put him out of his misery.
'Jeremy, it's not her.'
All he could hear on the other end of the line was a sound that resembled the yelping of an injured animal.
'I just thought you'd like to know,' Ramsay said, ending the call.

Chapter 10

Jeremy slowly climbed the stairs to the bathroom. Looking at himself in the mirror, he did not recognise the man he saw staring back at him. After splashing his face with cold water, he ran Kira's brush through his hair. He looked at the brush before he sat it down. It was filled with strands of her fine blonde hair. In an attempt to extract her scent, he inhaled deeply over the bristles. Then pulling all the hair from the brush, he separated out every strand. The fine hairs were laid out straight, on the side of the sink. It was a time-consuming task, but to him, it was important. By the time he had finished, he had a pretty lock of Kira's hair. Reaching into the bathroom cabinet, he took one of the diamante clasps from the pack of two. Carefully, he slid the clasp onto the lock of hair to keep it nicely together. 'There now,' he thought, 'that was a good job, well done.'

Slowly, he trundled downstairs, grabbed his lightweight jacket from the coat hook in the vestibule before walking out the front door. He had no idea where he was going, all he knew was that he needed to get out of the house for a while. He walked to the end of Palmerston Place, stopping at St. Mary's Cathedral, which was situated at the end of the road. The heavy wooden doors of the church were open wide; he saw that as an invitation to enter.

The cathedral was restfully quiet as he wandered in. Strolling down the aisle, he looked along the pews until he saw a seat that he fancied to sit in. The cathedral was almost empty so he could have had his pick of seats, but it was important for him to get the right seat. For a moment he felt at peace, which was a feeling he had not experienced for many months. His shoulders drooped as he bowed his head, enjoying the comfort that he felt around him. Gentle organ music played, 'Breathe on me, Breath of God'. Glancing up at the large wooden cross behind the altar, he whispered, 'Where is Kira? Please God, help me find Kira.' He waited for an answer to be whispered in his ear or for a sign to appear before him.

A feeling of anger began to manifest within him. The rage he was experiencing was directed towards God for not answering him immediately. With his full force, he banged his fist on the hymnbook shelf before storming out of the pew and back down the aisle towards the door. He needed to get out of there quickly, it was impossible for him to settle anywhere. There was no respite from the torture that was constantly being inflicted upon his soul.

Jeremy walked back along Palmerston Place in the direction of his home. Lifting his eyes from the pavement for a moment, he caught sight of 'The Sir Arthur Conan Doyle Spiritualist Centre', which stood a few doors along from his house. Feeling a little intrigued, he stopped to read the information board attached to the wrought iron railings around the Victorian Townhouse.

Sir Arthur Conan Doyle Centre

Home of the Edinburgh Association of Spiritualists.

Upcoming events:

Mysticism, Spirituality and Everyday Life.

Death, Near-Death, DMT & Discarnate Entities.

Heart-Centred Meditation.

Astrology: The ancient art.

An Evening with Psychic and Spiritualist: Florence Fields.

Private Readings with Claire Voyant.

Jeremy read the list through. The last two events caught his interest; he jotted down the dates and times. It was quite astonishing that he had walked past this building so many times but had never really looked at it. Who would have guessed that all of these spiritualist events took place in this establishment. In fact, he had always presumed that it was a museum, set up in honour of the late Sir Arthur Conan Doyle to celebrate his literary works of Sherlock Holmes.

What if he went to a psychic meeting and received a message from Kira? What if she were able to contact him to tell him what had happened to her? He held out little hope that she could still be alive after all this time, but the not knowing what had happened to her was like a plague eating away at him from the inside. Being completely honest, he would have to admit that he had no belief in anything of a supernatural nature, but he was desperately willing to try anything. All he wanted in the world was to bring this nightmare to a conclusion.

Tucking the piece of paper that he had written the details on into his jacket pocket, he walked along the road to his house. It had been a spiritually uplifting morning. A cathedral and a psychic centre right there on his doorstep. Firstly, he had sent out a prayer to God, now he was going to be present while the dead were contacted. *I think I've covered all bases, hedged all bets,* he thought to himself.

A call came to the police station from an elderly lady by the name of Alma Glass-Waters. She reported that she had seen the missing girl, Kira Carmichael. She confessed that she had managed to take a photo of the young woman without

alerting her. The officer in charge asked her to email the photo through to the police station.
The girl in the photo was dark haired, her frame was extremely thin. Kira was curvaceous, her hair was blonde. However, it was obvious that there was a resemblance in some of her facial features, despite that fact that the photo had been taken side on.
Mrs Glass-Waters told the police that she had seen the girl resembling Kira, walking a dog near the harbour area of the village that she resided in. The girl in the picture was wearing a grey, loose-fitting tracksuit with white trainers. Her dog was similar to a collie but with short hair. The dog was wearing a red collar with matching lead. In great detail, she explained to the police that she had followed the woman up the hill, then along the cliff road where there were six recently built houses standing in a row. The girl had entered the last house by simply walking in the front door; she did not knock. This led Mrs Glass-Waters to believe that the girl in the tracksuit resided there. The police officer who took the phone call had a feeling that nothing much happened in this small town up north. He sensed by the official way she relayed the information that Mrs Glass-Waters was thoroughly enjoying 'helping the police with their enquiries'. Excitement like this didn't happen every day in Portmahomack.
The police showed the photograph to Celia and Ramsay Carmichael. They also showed it separately to Jeremy Ward. All agreed that the woman in the photo did have some facial similarities to Kira, but they also recognised that the hair colour was completely wrong, as was the very slight build of the girl. Jeremy also confirmed that Kira would never have

worn an ill-fitting tracksuit like the one in the photo. He was able to confirm confidently to the policeman that the idea of Kira owning a dog was simply not plausible. 'This could not possibly be Kira,' he explained to the officer, 'because if she were walking freely along the road on her own, why would she not try to escape or phone for help?' The possibility of her being there of her own free will was simply not an option.

All things were considered, the lead was not followed up. There had been many reports of sightings the length and breadth of Great Britain, as well as several countries in Europe.

The previous month, the police force in Edinburgh had alerted the police in Cornwall to investigate a young woman who had been reported to them as a possible sighting of Kira. The young woman was Scottish. It seemed that she had moved to Cornwall in the same month that Kira had disappeared. The woman had blonde hair and similar elfin features to Kira's. From what the witness said in her statement, the girl seemed to be under the control of a raven haired, foreign man who held her tightly by the hand. He appeared to be pulling at her. Police had paid the young woman a visit, interviewing her at length. The woman turned out to be exactly who she said she was. She had laughed when the police reported that a member of the public had seen her being dragged along the road against her will. The girl then produced a card with the time and date of her dental appointment on it. Even although she had been experiencing severe toothache, she had refused treatment due to her fear of dentists. Her husband had told her that if she didn't go to the appointment which he had booked for her, he would drag her there himself. The police had smiled at this explanation, deciding that no further investigation was necessary. They were satisfied that this was not Kira Carmichael.

Chapter 11

Ramsay Carmichael was confident that the cash reward he was offering for the safe return of his daughter would bring forth information in abundance. It didn't happen. DCI Bryce told him that for anyone who had information on a crime, the reward could be a tipping point or trigger for them to make contact, but he said that, in truth, very few people ever came forward to claim a reward. Ramsay realised that all the money in the world couldn't make this problem go away. His beautiful daughter was out there somewhere, dead or alive, and there was damn all he could do to help her.

Celia stopped attending her golf club at Archerfield. No longer could she tolerate the sympathetic comments from her fellow golfers. The 'Any news, Celia?' questions had long since stopped, and it had now become, 'How are you bearing up, Celia?' These questions were always asked with a soft voice and a tilted head. She hated it. Golf no longer interested her, she preferred to stay at home.

Some of her friends from the past had contacted her to invite her out for afternoon tea, but if it wasn't going to bring Kira back, she had no desire to do it. Going out with friends for drinks or dinner were simply time fillers that she could do without. Kira dominated her every thought. On good days, she relived happy memories of Kira as a child, laughing and playing. The bad days brought darker memories of regret. On those days she had to keep herself busy to shut out her thoughts.

Whilst walking through the hallway to the kitchen, Celia heard the click of the letterbox, with the sound of mail dropping through her front door. She was intrigued as it was late afternoon and they had never received an afternoon post. Opening up the inner, glass door, she saw a card with no envelope sitting on the doormat. It had been hand delivered. With the absence of her glasses, she had to hold the card inches from her eyes to be able to see it clearly. On one side was a painted scene of a cottage overlooking the sea. It was very pleasing. Celia looked at every detail in the picture. *I think that's a painting of Mull,* she decided.

The mountainous scenery brought back a wonderful memory of a holiday they had taken in Mull when Kira was young. They had gone for a week to the newly refurbished five-star country house hotel which was situated in the small village of Pennyghael. The weather had been so hot and balmy, it felt almost like being abroad. Ramsay had relaxed for the first time in years, becoming more like the man Celia used to know and love. The memory of the deserted beaches returned to her as she visualised Kira wearing her blue polka dot bathing suit, splashing in and out of the waves. It had been a very happy time with so much laughter. Laughter had been missing from the Carmichael household for many years, Celia realised with sadness. *We must bring the happy times back,* she thought. *We will return to Mull to stay in the same hotel, as soon as Kira is found*. Turning the card over, she saw that there was a handwritten message.

Dear Mrs Carmichael,

I just wanted to invite you to our meeting on Friday. It is held in a hall at the back of St. Mary's Cathedral in Palmerston Place. We all have a missing person in our family, so we understand what you are going through. Sometimes it just helps to talk to people who are in a similar

situation. If you don't feel like talking, that's fine too, you could come simply to listen.
The meeting starts at 7pm and we would love to see you there.
Best wishes
Lynette Cochrane
Celia folded the card in half before taking it through to the kitchen. Pressing the pedal with her foot, the lid of the bin sprung open allowing her to drop the card inside before releasing the pedal to close. No sooner had she walked away, but second thoughts came to her mind. Stopping in her tracks, she returned to the bin to retrieve the card. She straightened out the fold that cut through the landscape, then wiped off a speck of spaghetti sauce with her handkerchief. The picture of Mull had reminded her of happier times, so it was worth displaying on the shelf, next to her collection of pottery jugs. There was no harm in keeping the card, it wasn't like she had to respond to it.

Chapter 12

Jeremy showered before putting on his pale blue shirt and chinos. Running the comb through his now shoulder length hair, he could see that he badly needed to visit the barbers. But that was far too much effort to even think about it. He skilfully manoeuvred a pair of tan loafers from the stack of shoeboxes in his wardrobe. A quick glance at the leather soles showed him that they had never been worn. The tower of boxes almost reached the ceiling in the cupboard. *I wonder how many pairs of shoes I have that have never seen the light of day?* he pondered, looking up at the collection. *Buying shoes used to please me greatly.* He always took great pride in keeping his half of the wardrobe impeccable. The suits were hung shoulder to shoulder in a perfect row; a separate rack was designed for ties, all of which were colour coded. With an ironic smirk, he marvelled at the things that used to be of importance to him. How his priorities had changed since the disappearance.

Kira's side of the wardrobe was also immaculate. The sight of it brought back memories of how untidy she had been when they first moved in together. Her sloppy, disorganised ways had irked him greatly. Something had to be done, so he took charge. It had taken a long time to train her into the neat and tidy girl she became. Admittedly, he had been strict, perhaps even a little too harsh at times. But looking now at her neatly folded clothes in front of him, he could see that it had paid off. *If she were here now,* he thought, *she would graciously thank me. After all, love was about helping people to become the very best version of themselves.*

It had been a long, long time since he had gone out of an evening, in fact he could not recall when he last did. The heavy front door of his house needed quite a tug to pull it closed behind him. When he was sure that it was secure, he wandered along the road to the meeting at the Sir Arthur Conan Doyle Spiritualist Centre. There was a certain feeling of vulnerability about going to a meeting that he knew nothing about, but he had decided that if he sat at the back, near the door, he could slip away if it wasn't for him.

On entering the Victorian townhouse, he was greeted with a warm welcome from two ladies, perhaps in their late sixties, one wearing a full length fur. Making conversation, they asked him if this was his first visit to the centre. He told them that it was.

The next question that was about to be asked of him was what enticed him along to their meeting, but he pre-empted it and swiftly walked on past before the sentence was fully out. The purpose of coming along to the Sir Arthur Conan Doyle Spiritualist Centre was not to make small talk with newfound friends. There was one reason, and one reason only for his visit: finding out what had happened to Kira.

Following the crowd, he was led into an impressively fitted out conference style hall with a stage at the front. There were rows of bleacher seating, which made things a little difficult for an early departure. Most of the rows were full, but Jeremy spied an aisle seat halfway up. There was a lot of chatter coming from all directions; presumably, most people knew each other. It appeared that they were all regulars of this establishment. There was nothing he could do but listen as the gentleman in the row behind asked someone across the aisle if they had been at last week's meeting. When the person had answered no, the gentleman gave a blow-by-blow account of everything that had happened. 'It was a wonderful experience,' the gentleman had added, clasping his hands together.

Yeah, I'm sure it was, now shut the fuck up, Jeremy thought.

The guest speaker was given a lengthy introduction, outlining her achievements. Everyone was told to put their hands together for Miss Florence Fields. There was uproarious applause accompanied by a few ear-splitting whistles. Jeremy surmised from this that the crowd had heard this woman before and liked her.

Florence Fields, a woman fast approaching seventy, walked onto the stage smiling at everyone in the auditorium. Standing before her audience, she soaked up the applause before raising her hands, gesturing for everyone to be still.

'It's an honour and a privilege to be here with you tonight. Hopefully, the spirits will feel comfortable in this environment. We would like to welcome them in to speak to us.'

Shutting her eyes, she murmured as though she were talking to someone. Nodding her head, she said, 'I have a beautiful young woman who would like to speak to her loved one who is sitting here tonight.'

Jeremy's heart began thudding. Sweating profusely, he reached his hands down between his knees to stop them shaking.

'She wants to give her loved one a message. She says, 'Please don't worry about me. I am happy and in a good place.'

Jeremy found himself crying softly. In his mind, he could hear her saying the words in her gentle voice; her face smiling radiantly. 'I am so glad that I came here tonight,' he thought, as the burden began to ease from his heavy-laden back.

'The message is from a woman by the name of Violet. Does the name Violet mean anything to anyone? Violet is giving this message to her loved one, Frank. Is there anyone here called Frank?'

Jeremy's burden returned tenfold when he realised it wasn't Kira.

'Yes, is that you Frank? Raise your hand right up high so that we can all see you. Do you know someone called Violet, Frank?'

Frank managed to say, 'Yes, that's my daughter. She was taken from us three years ago in a car accident.'

Florence continued, 'Well Frank, she wants you to stop worrying about her because she is happy. She wants you to know that she loves you and her mother very much.'

It was Frank's turn to sob. He thanked Florence for the desperately yearned for words.

'Frank, she is telling me about honeysuckle in your garden. She wants you to know that when you are in the garden where the honeysuckle grows, she sees you crying.'

Frank was uncontrollable at this point.

'Do you cry beside the honeysuckle for your daughter, Frank?' Florence asked.

'Every day.'

The audience gasped, simultaneously bursting into applause. Frank sat back down in his seat. He had now heard the words that he had come for.

Florence closed her eyes again. Her head began to nod, which was followed by a frown. 'Yes, yes, I'll tell her,' Florence assured the spirit. 'Cathy, are you with us tonight?

Donald knows that you have lost the ring that he gave to you on your wedding day. Does this make sense to anyone here?' she asked, scanning the crowd for a recipient.

Cathy stood up. 'Yes, I'm Cathy, Donald is my husband. He passed away five years ago from cancer. I lost my wedding ring three weeks ago,' she told Florence tearfully.

'Well, Cathy, when you go home tonight, look behind the cistern at the back of the toilet because that's where your ring is. You sat it on top of the toilet when you washed your hands, and it slipped down the back.'

Cathy stood crying, 'I can't believe it! I'll look tonight when I go home.'

Florence then added, 'Cathy? Donald said that you've to be more careful in future.'

Everyone laughed and again, applauded loudly. Cathy sat down. Another satisfied customer.

Florence contacted a mother, two grandmothers and a young child, before she wrapped up the evening. Jeremy sat in his seat feeling disappointed, but he was hooked!

Everyone left the auditorium. Jeremy followed the crowd as they filed through to the plush-carpeted foyer. A few of the members had gathered near the front door, discussing the evening's events. Jeremy asked them politely if they could move to enable him to pass; they did so. Delivering a cordial nod of thanks, he left the building and carried on his way back home. The night air smelt good to him as he strode purposefully along, swinging his arms, feeling charged with excitement. The next meeting would yield something for him, he felt sure of that. Meanwhile, he had the private reading to attend on Thursday. He had booked himself in for an evening appointment with a highly renowned psychic called, 'Claire Voyant'. It was a corny name, but it certainly drew attention to who she was and what she did. It wasn't a name that anyone would forget in a hurry. If she were genuine in helping his cause, then he didn't care what she called herself.

For the first time since Kira's disappearance, Jeremy slept until morning without stirring. Feeling totally refreshed when he awoke, he found that his outlook on life had become a little more positive than it had been of late. Finding Kira was his only priority, he would try to achieve that by whatever method it took. At this moment in time, he felt that he was on the right track. This mystery was going to be unravelled soon, he could sense it.

Chapter 13

Ramsay Carmichael had set up his own office in one of the many spare bedrooms within the house. It was where he spent most of his time since he retired. The idea of isolating himself for several hours every day, undisturbed, was highly appealing to him. Before he retired, he hardly saw his wife, now he was expected to spend every waking moment of the day with her. In order for them to live out their lives together harmoniously, the hideout was essential.

Since Kira disappeared, he was even more absent from the rest of the house, his office had become his headquarters. For hours on end, he stared at his computer screen, trawling through all the information that he could find on missing girls in Scotland and England. The previous night an idea had crept into his thoughts, preventing him from sleeping. When dawn had broken the following morning, he was still lying there next to Celia, staring at the ceiling, crafting his plan. What if whoever took Kira had done this before? What if it were a serial killer who had been getting away with it for years? His search had revealed several girls who had gone missing without a trace in the past ten years. There had even been an estate agent of the same age who had never been found.

Leaving all the information up on the screen, he took a notebook from the filing cabinet and began writing down everything he could glean. As he jotted down names, ages, descriptions, locations and dates, he was convinced that a pattern was emerging. Combing through the details of each case, he noted all the similarities in each disappearance, cross referencing them with Kira's details. What if these girls were alive, being held against their will somewhere? It was important to dig deeper, widen his search. *I will create a highly detailed document,* he thought. *When I have completed my investigation, I will hand it over to the police.* He made a solemn promise to Celia that he would get Kira back and by God, he was going to do it. 'The devil is in the detail,' he said aloud; 'the devil is definitely in the detail.' Finding connections whilst following clues was going to take time, but he had all the time in the world. *I will take a fine tooth comb through every detail of every missing person,* he told himself.

Celia wandered through to Ramsay's study, 'What are you up to darling?' she asked him, peeking over his shoulder.

'It's nothing for you to concern yourself with. I'm building up a dossier, if you must know.'

'A dossier, Ramsay? What kind of a dossier?' she asked him, feeling curiously hopeful that this might be something that was going to bring results. There were so many unanswered questions that needed explaining. Ramsay had climbed every rung on the ladder of success until he reached the top because he was a highly intelligent problem solver who never gave up. Celia rubbed the back of his neck fondly. Without a shadow of a doubt, she knew that he would put things right for the Carmichael family, like he always did. *How comforting,* she thought.

'You know, Celia, I'm actually doing the work that the police should be doing. I'm going to catch whoever took Kira. But I need peace and quiet, so shut the door behind you.'

'Would you like a coffee and perhaps one of those spicy cinnamon buns with the little raisins in it?' she offered him as she was leaving.

'Yes, but bring it, then leave. This is not Mickey Mouse stuff that I'm involved in here. This is proper investigative research. Now go.'
Celia left, shutting the door behind her. She did not appreciate being spoken to like that but if it brought Kira back then it was a price worth paying. As soon as she entered the kitchen, the postcard of the Island of Mull caught her eye. It made her happy, yet so sad, when she fleetingly relived a scene with the three of them on the beach, laughing. *Don't torture yourself,* she thought, switching on the kettle. Spooning the coffee into the cups, she once again stole a furtive glance at the beauty of Mull. She poured the hot water, added the milk and stirred. Stopping suddenly in her tracks, she threw down the teaspoon and snatched the postcard down from the shelf, reading the message on the back. *Tomorrow night, 7pm at St. Mary's, hmm. I'm not doing anything important at that time, maybe I'll go along for a while. I'll sit near the back so that I can slip away without anyone seeing me.*
'Where the hell's the coffee and spiced bun you promised?' a harsh voice bellowed from the office.
'It's coming, it's coming,' she said, rushing through, ensuring she didn't spill a drop.
'Oh, you're still here?' he said sarcastically. 'I thought you'd gone to Brazil for the coffee and The Spice Islands for the flaming bun.'
Celia laughed. 'You're a big torment, Ramsay, do you know that?'
'Get out and shut the ruddy door behind you!'

Chapter 14

The Ivan Cole Estate Agency was busier than ever. The name of the business had appeared several times in the newspaper as well as the news channels in connection with Kira's disappearance. Ivan couldn't help thinking selfishly that he could never have afforded to pay for that kind of publicity. The name 'Ivan Cole' now seemed to resonate in the minds of people when it came to buying or selling a house. There were also the clients who were morbidly curious about the last place Kira Carmichael disappeared from. As far as Ivan was concerned, business was business whatever the reason. In the beginning, people would enquire, 'Is there any news on Kira Carmichael?' but latterly they simply asked, 'Did they ever find that missing girl?'

Ivan had hired a new girl to do Kira's job, but the shoes were too big to fill. She turned out to be frustratingly hopeless. There were so many missed opportunities when it came to sealing a deal. In short, she lacked the flair that came naturally to Kira.

The first meeting Ivan ever had with Kira had followed a phone call from Jeremy Ward almost pleading with him for a favour. Jeremy wanted his girlfriend to start working in the Estate Agency. Kira's quietly confident manner had impressed Ivan; in fact, he found himself feeling rather attracted to her. She was intelligent, funny and when she laughed Ivan was knocked sideways. Of course, he never shared this information with anyone, and Kira would never have suspected. Ivan had known Jeremy from Fettes College, where they had boarded together as boys. Back then, Ivan had zero time for Jeremy because he was a highly unlikeable individual. He cried constantly, telling teachers that he was being bullied. The truth of the matter was that he rubbed the older boys up the wrong way by being an annoyance. In the beginning, he had felt sorry for Jeremy because he had no friends. He had also noticed that when the holidays came around, all the boarders were taken home, but Jeremy would still be at school. Later, he found out that Jeremy's parents booked Christmas and summer holidays without him. Ivan could remember feeling a sharp pang of guilt leaving Jeremy alone in the common room when he left to go home with his parents.

The phone call from Jeremy had taken him by surprise, he had not heard from him or of him, in years. Based on past experience, he wanted nothing to do with Jeremy, or his girlfriend for that matter. If he were being honest, he was surprised that he even had a girlfriend. Despite his many reservations, his softer side had kicked in and he found himself inviting them into the office for an informal chat. Jeremy had waited in the car whilst Kira came into the office to be interviewed. Although she had no sales experience, he was convinced that she was perfect for the business. When she left the office that evening, he found himself thinking, *What on earth does a girl like that see in someone like Jeremy Ward?*

Connie really missed Kira. Most days she would imagine that she saw her walking down the street or browsing in a busy shop. It seemed that when someone was always on your mind, their face became superimposed onto the people around you. As far as she was concerned the heavy burden of suspicion lay with the bun wearing barista in Costa Coffee. It couldn't have been a coincidence that he knew everything about her on the very day she disappeared. Connie found herself visiting the coffee shop regularly in a hope that her suspect would serve her. Whenever he did, and without fail, she would bring up the subject of Kira, in an attempt to make him slip up. Perhaps even to divulge a piece of incriminating information.

On one occasion, he said, 'She'll turn up one day when you least expect it.' Another time he said, 'Sometimes people just vanish into thin air. Poof!' He emphasised the statement with a magician's hand gesture. He made it sound like he had made her disappear. Or perhaps that was her imagination. She decided to write down all the comments that he made, in order to build up a picture. Her trips into the shop became ever more frequent in order to add as many statements as she could to her list. Eventually, the Costa worker stopped serving her. He began to suspect that she may be involved in the girl's disappearance. The final time she stood in the queue for coffee, she heard him say to his colleague, 'Geordie, could you serve that nutcase with the raincoat, she creeps me out.'

Chapter 15

Jeremy had been looking forward to this night all week. It was the evening of his private reading with 'Claire Voyant'. A half hour slot at 8pm had been available, so he went ahead and booked. He felt that the private reading was more personal and would hopefully furnish him with some long awaited answers. On the centre's website, he saw that there was an event at seven o'clock that he was also interested in. It only lasted an hour, so it was possible to dash from that meeting to his reading. The event was hosted by a Medium and Clairvoyant from Leeds who went by the name of Duncan R.C. Davidson, who was only going to be in Scotland for one night. His reputation was excellent, and after checking out a few of his YouTube videos, Jeremy was thoroughly impressed with the psychic ability of the man. It was a great opportunity, and one not to be missed. *Why settle for one event when I can have both?* he thought. 'Covering all bases' was one of Jeremy's regularly used mottos.

It soon became apparent to Jeremy that he had to prioritise what was important in life and what was not. The final reminders, in connection with his business, were coming through the door at a steady rate. His secretary had forwarded the bills to the house because he had not made an appearance in the office for months. Her calls were never answered nor returned. Debtors visited the office several times to chase up the money they were owed, and, at times, they were anything but pleasant. Jeremy's long suffering secretary, Lucy, was on the verge of leaving the company, even though she had been there since its infancy. There was no one to turn to for advice, she was left making all the big

decisions that her boss should have been handling. Jeremy's situation was undeniably tragic, but this was not what she had signed up for. The pressure was becoming intolerable and she lived in constant fear of a backlash from making a wrong decision. She was neither qualified nor balsy enough for the managerial role in which she had found herself.
White envelopes with red 'Final Notice' lettering on them, lurked menacingly beneath the letterbox of the house in Palmerston Place. Jeremy stood staring at them for a time before lifting them, pincer grasp by their corners, and dropping them into the bin. Rinsing his fingers under the hot tap after touching them, he subconsciously washed his hands of them. They were not important to him, all that mattered was getting in touch with Kira to find out what had happened to her. All the business problems could wait. By his own sheer hard work and commitment, he had built his empire from the bottom up, but now his focus was on more pressing issues. Surely there was someone out there who was equipped with enough intelligence to hold the reigns at work until he cracked the Kira case. Was that really too much to ask?
Tonight may be the night, he thought, walking down the road to the Sir Arthur Conan Doyle Centre. The centre had been the best thing that had happened to him in months. He wished that it had been the church that had given him the comforting strength, but it wasn't. An amusing thought entered his head as he strolled along. *I have become Sherlock Holmes since I began attending the Sir Arthur Conan Doyle Centre. Let's hope I'm as successful as he was at solving a mystery.* The amazing coincidence of it all made him chuckle to

himself. It was almost like fate had played him an unexpected hand.
Strutting through the door of the Victorian Townhouse, he smiled at the gathering of people in the foyer. There was a small exchange of pleasantries with a few regulars, who appeared to find him utterly charming. Once inside, he felt at home, part of something special that revealed the mysteries of life. It was a place that could give him the answers that were way beyond the understanding of the incompetent police force.
Being a creature of habit, he chose the same seat that he had sat on during his previous visit. As the auditorium began to fill up, he recognised many of the faces around him. Nodding a greeting to a young couple on his left, he then gave a small wave to a woman who was walking up the aisle. Checking his watch, he began to fret. *I hope it starts on time because I only have seconds to get to my reading with Claire Voyant.*
The guest Medium was introduced. This incited the crowd to cheer and clap. Duncan R. C. Davidson walked onto the stage with a man-of-importance attitude. His grey locks were unruly, matching his cliffhanger eyebrows perfectly. The gold chain of his pocket watch glinted as he slipped his hand into the pocket of his suit trousers. Although he was tall and slim in stature, the buttons on his waistcoat strained slightly against his middle aged waistline. Leaning on the podium, he nodded, smiling, as he drank up the adoration that was being bestowed upon him.
'Good evening, ladies and gentlemen.'
The crowd replied.

There was no preamble. He did not want to waste a second of spirit contacting time.
'Ishbel? Is there an Ishbel in here tonight? Make yourself known Ishbel, if you are here.' He looked up to the top row of seating, searching for a sign of recognition.
A small, elderly lady on the front row raised her hand. 'I'm Ishbel,' she croakily announced.
'Ishbel, your father fought in two World Wars, he suffered from pancreatic cancer, but he had a long and full life. The only thing that he needs now in order to be at peace is your forgiveness. He is asking me tonight to beg you for forgiveness. Ishbel, do you forgive your father, so that he may truly rest in peace?'
The elderly lady gripped the back of the seat in front of her, to aid her stance. Her spine was curved, her hands gnarled with arthritis. Wide eyed, she looked directly at Duncan R.C. Davidson, tears in her eyes.
'Do you forgive your father, Ishbel, so that he may be at rest?' the medium coaxed softly.
'I will never, ever, forgive that abomination of a father!' she croaked. 'May he scorch in Hell!'
The crowd gasped; Duncan R. C. Davidson moved swiftly on.
'Okay then, let's see who else we have here tonight,' he said, shutting his eyes, listening for the voices. 'Mark, Mark C? Your mother says that you should take the job. She knows that it is far away, but she said, 'take it'. She thinks that you don't want to move away because you'll be letting people down, but you have your own life to lead, son, she says.'
Mark C stood up and began explaining to the crowd that he had been offered a job in Dubai. He felt that if he took the

job, his father would be left on his own. 'That is enough confirmation for me,' Mark said. 'I'll take the job.'
Jeremy clapped loudly, shouting, 'Good decision. Well done.'
Duncan R. C. Davidson passed a message to a girl whose brother had been killed in Iraq, then to a man who had lost his wife in a house fire. Jeremy waited eagerly for news of Kira, but, once again, there was nothing for him.
As soon as the meeting was over, Jeremy ran past everyone, apologising as he bumped into them. It was of the utmost urgency that he made his way quickly upstairs to the rooms where the private readings took place. Leaping up the stairs two at a time, he was met at the top by a gentleman in a burgundy velvet jacket. 'Are you here to see Claire?' he asked, with a clipboard in his hands.
'Yes, my appointment is at eight.'
'Name?' the man inquired.
'Jeremy Ward.'
'Take a seat, Mr. Ward. Ms Voyant is with a client at the moment, but she will be with you shortly.'
Jeremy sat in one of the three high backed chairs which had been placed outside the door for early arrivals. He was disappointed that he didn't get a message from Kira at the meeting but there were a lot of people there, perhaps all the spirits couldn't be heard in a one-hour session. *She may get through next week,* he thought, making a mental note to check the notice board for the up and coming events.
Whilst he sat waiting outside Ms. Voyant's room, his knees began bobbing up and down, as they always did when he became nervous. Instinctively, he leaned his elbows down upon his legs to prevent the reaction. A tearful couple

emerged from Claire Voyant's room. *Stop your bubbling and get the hell out, there's other people waiting here,* he thought, when he saw them. Glancing up at the usher in the velvet jacket, he noticed that he was pressing on his ear, nodding. Jeremy realised that he was wearing an earpiece. The man then walked over to him announcing dramatically, 'Ms Claire Voyant will see you now.'

With a little trepidation, Jeremy took a few steps into the darkened room. There were candles in holders placed all around. Claire Voyant sat at a table facing him as he entered.

'Have a seat, Jeremy. It is a pleasure to meet with you.'

The nerves really began to kick in as Jeremy sat down on the seat opposite Claire, knees trembling uncontrollably.

'You are a very, very troubled young man, Jeremy, are you not?' she asked.

'Yes, I am a troubled man,' he answered, quietly.

'You crave to hear a certain voice from the grave. Is that right?'

'Yes, I do.'

'You hope that by hearing this voice from the other side, you will be able to understand things, make sense of the situation you have found yourself in. Does this sound familiar to you, Jeremy?' Claire asked, closing her eyes.

'I suppose it does,' he admitted. 'I am looking for answers.'

'You always feel the need to be in control, Jeremy, but you are not in control right now and you don't like it. You feel adrift, you feel as though your life is unravelling like a ball of string rolling down a steep hill. Am I describing what you are feeling?' she asked, with her eyes still closed.

Jeremy broke down. 'Yes, that is exactly how I feel. I can't seem to pull things back together.' He rested his head in his hands in despair.
'You've lost someone dear to you and you are filled with regret. I see an image of an engagement ring. Is it your fiancé that you have lost?'
'Yes, she was my fiancé. She disappeared.' Before he entered the room, he made a vow to himself that he would not divulge anything about the disappearance, but he couldn't help it. It simply slipped out.
Claire Voyant suddenly realised who Jeremy was. A memory of a story some time ago, on the front of the newspaper returned to her. There had been an unposed photograph of him, glaring angrily outside his front door. The image of him was dishevelled but it was definitely the same man who was sitting in the seat before her. The article had given all the facts of the disappearance. It went on to say that Jeremy Ward, the missing girl's fiancé, had refused to take part in the press conference. After reading the story, Ms Voyant had been left wondering whether he had been involved in his fiancé's demise. However, seeing this young man so burdened with sorrow, left her in no doubt of his innocence.
'Ah! So, you believe that if she contacts you from the other side, she may give you information about what happened to her? Does this sound accurate, Jeremy?'
'Yes, that is what I was hoping for. I'm desperate.'
Taking Jeremy's hands in hers, she bowed her head slightly for a few minutes.
'She will never come to this establishment to reveal these answers, Jeremy,' Claire announced with conviction.

Jeremy lifted head, staring Claire in the eye. 'Why not?'
'Because she is not dead. She is alive.' Claire leaned back in her chair, hands folded on her lap. A feeling of elation came over her after imparting this information to her client.
Jeremy smiled, 'Are you sure?'
'I've never been surer of anything,' she relayed theatrically.
'Where is she then?' he asked.
'Jeremy, I don't know. There are limitations to my gift of foresight. She is alive, but I can't see where she is.'
'No wonder I wasn't hearing anything at the spiritualist evenings. Can you give me any information about her disappearance?'
Claire sat motionless for a moment, her eyes flickered shut. 'I have nothing concrete to give you, but I will say that it is all in the names. Consider the classics and it will become clear.'
She then stood up to indicate that his time was up. Reaching for Jeremy's hand, she shook it limply.
Jeremy was ravenous for more information, but he was ushered out of the door where two more desperate customers were sitting on the early arrival seats. In a daze, he walked down the impressive staircase as Claire Voyant's parting words circled around in his head. *What's she talking about*? he mouthed to himself as he left by the main door. *It's all in the names. Consider the classics and it will become clear. What does that mean and what does it have to do with Kira?*

Chapter 16

Celia walked around the back of St. Mary's Cathedral. A small gathering of people stood together around the door of a prefab hall. Nervously, she walked towards the group that had gathered for the evening's meeting.

An elegant woman wearing a turquoise suit left couple she had been speaking with to make her way over to Celia. 'Mrs Carmichael, it is so wonderful that you came. Don't be nervous, we don't bite! I am Lynette Cochrane, I put the card through your door.'

'I won't be staying long. I have other plans,' Celia told her coldly.

'That's fine Mrs Carmichael. It's great that you managed along at all. I will introduce you to everyone.'

That evening Celia Carmichael was the last to leave the church hall. The apprehension she felt on arrival, melted away within moments of listening to other parents talk of their missing children. For once, perhaps for the first time in her whole life, she felt a sense of belonging. She could happily have remained there all night. These people were going through exactly what she was experiencing. They were all dangling on a cliff-hanger with no concluding chapter.

Hearing everyone's story made her feel less alone. Ramsay was on an investigation mission, locking himself away from the world. To him, her only purpose was to bring him food and cups of coffee. Ramsay only surfaced from his office to pee, shit and sleep, and even then, he made no attempt to make conversation with her. A sense of isolated hopelessness had consumed her, until now. This meeting had given her a new group of friends that she could relate to. They had a

common bond which no one else could truly understand. It was an exclusive club where the members all needed the same sad credential in order to join.
After several months of segregation, Ramsay Carmichael had penned page upon page of information. Sadly, everything he had written had been simply copied, word for word, from the internet. He hadn't uncovered anything relevant in his extensive time of trawling, but he kept on going, carefully copying every detail from the screen in front of him. He wrote about all the missing girls in Scotland, he then wrote about missing girls in England, Wales and Ireland. When that task was completed, he moved on to missing girls of a similar age to Kira throughout Europe. When that line of investigation was exhausted, he wrote down information on missing boys in the United Kingdom and in Europe. With nothing left to explore in that section, he then moved on to backpackers who had been reported missing across the world in the previous ten years. There was absolutely no stopping him, he just kept on writing. Deep down, he knew that it was all a waste of time, but at least he was doing something. It somehow gave him a purpose, a reason to get up out of bed each morning.
Celia continued to bring him consumables, oblivious to the worthless content of his research. When she saw how much he had written, she was alight with hope. *He must be close to finding her. He has worked so hard piecing everything together, following every lead. It will all be laid out in black and white for the police to simply swoop in and rescue Kira.*
Ramsay had a way of fixing everything. Celia had to admit that sometimes Ramsay's 'ways' were not always legal, but he got the job done by making everything right. *When he*

discovers who has taken Kira, he will bring her back to the arms of her loving family. As soon as she is home safe and sound, I'll book that beautiful 'Pennyghael House Hotel' in Mull for us all to have a relaxing break together.

Celia made the decision not to cancel the Prestonfield Hotel as a wedding venue for the simple reason that Kira would be back by then. If she cancelled the booking, they would miss out. It was such a popular place to hold a wedding. In the past week, Celia had even wandered into a few wedding dress shops to get an idea of the latest fashion for brides. The mother-of-the-bride outfits that she had taken the liberty of trying on, were fabulous. *Would it be too extravagant to change into a different outfit for the evening celebrations of the wedding?* she asked herself. *Not if the photographers from 'Hello' magazine were there; anyway, I'm the mother-of-the-bride, I can do whatever I like.*

A rare smile appeared on Celia's lips as she sat reminiscing about the night the love birds got engaged. Jeremy had already shown them the beautiful ring with its three substantial diamonds. Secretively, he had announced to them that he was going to put it on her finger at precisely 7.15 pm. They were invited round to the house, along with his parents at 7.30pm. Both sets of parents had arrived on the doorstep at exactly the same time. By pure chance, the couples had brought with them identical bottles of Bollinger champagne. Celia had been glad that she had gone a step further, turning up with a handful of helium balloons with the words 'Congratulations' and 'Just engaged' written in large, silver lettering. It had been obvious that Jeremy's mother's nose was out of joint with this addition to the celebrations. They had been told not to ring the doorbell, just

to wait on the step outside. Jeremy furtively let them in before leading the four of them through to the front room where they all shouted, 'Surprise! Congratulations!'
Ramsay had noticed the solemn look on Kira's face as she stood before them in the hallway. He joked, 'Cheer up, it may never happen!' They had all hooted with laughter. Perhaps she had been a little overwhelmed by the attention that night. It was not in her nature to court the limelight. It was Celia's hope that her husband's joke that night were not words of prophecy.

Chapter 17

The ceiling in Jeremy's bedroom was corniced with a repeated pattern of fruit bowls. He stared up at the plastered grapes and apples, thinking over Claire Voyant's words. 'Consider the classics,' he said aloud. A-level Classics had been one of his chosen subjects when he boarded at Fettes College. It had been an incredibly challenging subject, and boy had the teacher been harsh. By the end of the year, he barely managed to scrape a pass. His school days had been a miserable time for him. Bullied relentlessly from boys in the year above, he had suffered day in and day out. The trouble with a boarding school was that you could never escape it. Every turn of the corridor or trip to the bathroom was a potential minefield. It caused him great angst over the years as to why he needed to board in the first place when his parents lived two streets away. On many occasions, he would wave to his father in the morning as he drove past the school gates on his way to work. He supposed that it was just how things were in upper class families like his. His father and grandfather both boarded at Fettes, as would his own son, when the time arose. It was tradition. His mind returned to the subject of the classics. *Consider the classics,* he thought. Latin and Greek? How could that be connected to Kira's disappearance. *Disappearance, now what is the Latin word for disappearance? Ah, 'exitum',* he remembered. What about the Latin word for 'vanish?' he wondered. He couldn't recall, so he switched the bedside lamp on and reached for his phone. 'Latin word for vanish' he punched in. 'Praetervolo' came up as the answer. *'Volo', could that be*

something to do with a Volvo?' he questioned. *Could praetervolo be an anagram, parter, retrap, vapor, travel, Peter, repeat…'*
He was driving himself crazy as he lay there desperately trying to figure out what Claire Voyant had meant. 'It's all in the names,' he repeated to the empty room, 'consider the classics.' He soon fell asleep with the lamp on, phone in hand.
Awakening at 3.15am, the first words to enter his head were, 'consider the classics' and 'It's all in the names.' Torment consumed him, spurring him to get up and make himself a hot drink. His mind was wide awake, his body fatigued. Sleepily, he stumbled downstairs to the kitchen and poured milk into a mug. *Consider the classics,* he thought, putting the cup in the microwave. *It's all in the names.*
Clambering up on the tall stool at the breakfast bar in the middle of the well equipped kitchen, he concluded, *I have to clear my mind. Start from the beginning.* He knocked on his skull with his fist. What did he know to be true? Kira drove to an appointment at Regent Terrace. She was meeting Mr Darcy… *hold on,* he thought, *Mr Darcy was one of the main characters in Pride and Prejudice. Pride and Prejudice was thought to be one of the classics. Remember the classics, it's all in the names.* The realisation hit him head on, full force. It was nothing to do with Ancient Greek or Latin, it was the literary classics. A sudden urgency came over him; he needed to see Kira's office diary. He had a hunch, and he was going to act upon it.
The kitchen clock said that it was 4.30 am. It was very early but what the hell, he decided, running through to the shower to freshen himself up. For the first time in months, he felt invigorated; he actually had a lead.

By 5.05am he was showered, dressed and eagerly waiting for time to pass. By his calculations, Ivan Cole probably arrived at the office around 8am. So, he would sit in the leather wing chair at the window until 7am. As soon as it reached that hour, he would head across town to the area of Bruntsfield where the estate agency office was situated. This would be the first stage in his investigation. A strange excitement bubbled within him. *And so, it begins.*

Jeremy watched the digits click onto 7.00 on his phone; the alarm resounding in the room. Bolting off the chair, he ran with haste to the front door. His car was parked outside, so he pressed the central locking system to get in. *I won't drive fast,* he decided. *I will take my time, keep my mind focused. I don't want to get there too early, timing is everything.* Switching on the radio, he tuned in some soothing classical music. There was a tautness around his neck and across his shoulders, probably brought on by endless tension. Down at his lefthand side, he reached for the built-in seat massage button. 'Oh, that feels soooo good,' he moaned aloud.

When he reached Bruntsfield, he kept driving along the main street until he reached the Estate Agency. Fortunately, he managed to get parked directly opposite the door. The office was still in darkness, but he knew it was only a matter of time until Ivan arrived. He was feeling somewhat agitated. *What if it turns out to be nothing? It doesn't matter, it's worth a shot. Everything is worth a shot to find Kira.* He reached down to lean on his nervously bobbing knees.

Twenty minutes had passed, and he was still sitting in his car, staring across at the unlit office. 'Where the fuck are you, Ivan? Get a bloody shift on, you stupid bastard. Ivan the

fucking terrible. Is this any way to run a business?' he remarked, thudding several times on the steering wheel.
Thoughts of Ivan back in their school days entered his thoughts. Oh, how desperately he had wanted to be Ivan's friend, but Ivan had no time for him, that was obvious. Ivan was one of the popular boys. Everyone liked him, he liked everyone. Jeremy was reminded of a time when a parcel of sweets arrived in the post for Ivan from his mum. He stole the sweets then confided in Ivan that he had seen Bobby Aiken taking them. 'Why don't we wait for him in the showers and force him to confess?' Jeremy had suggested. Ivan reluctantly agreed. They cornered Bobby, then sat on him until he started to cry. Ivan felt sorry for him saying it was okay. Jeremy punched him hard in the stomach before they let him go, just to show Ivan how loyal he was as a potential best friend. That night, Jeremy ate the sweets, enjoying every last one of them.
As if by magic, the Ivan Cole Estate Agency was suddenly illuminated with bright lights. Jeremy saw Ivan walking around switching on computers. *What the bloody hell?* he thought, getting out of his car. *The bastard must have been in there the whole time.*
Only when Jeremy pushed heavily on the door of the office did he realise that it was still locked. He gained Ivan's attention by knocking on the window. Ivan acted genuinely pleased to see him, as he headed towards the door to let him in.
'Jeremy! How are you? It's good to see you. Come in.'
'Thanks Ivan. I need to see the office diary that Kira wrote her appointments in.'

Ivan was a little taken aback by the state of Jeremy's appearance when he stepped into the light. Alarm bells pealed, albeit gently at first, as he began to notice his slightly manic behaviour. 'No problem, it's over here on the desk by the window. Take as long as you like.'

Jeremy turned the large pages back to the day Kira disappeared. From that Thursday in April, he scanned every appointment, working his way backwards, one day at a time. The Thursday before she disappeared, he saw that she had an appointment at 4pm with Mr Rochester. Thinking about the name for a moment, he took out his phone to google search 'Mr Rochester'. Straight away the name Jane Eyre came up. Jane Eyre was a classic novel by Charlotte Bronte. Nothing untoward showed up until the Thursday before Mr Rochester, where he noticed a 4pm appointment with Mr Nickelby.

'Ah ha! Bingo!' he announced, the penny dropping that Nicholas Nickleby was a Charles Dickens classic. Going back further still, he found Mr Copperfield. Then came Mr Heep. 'Well, looky here, Good old Uriah!' Uriah Heep was closely followed a week earlier by Mr Brocklehurst, Mr Fagin, Mr Haversham. 'Actually, it was Miss Haversham, you idiot!' he said aloud, causing Ivan to look over in alarm. 'Mr Heathcliffe? Heathcliffe was his first name, you fuckin' clown!'

'Is everything alright, Jeremy? Are you finding what you're looking for? If you need a hand, just shout.' Ivan was becoming more and more concerned by the look on Jeremy's face. His tightly clenched fists had not gone unnoticed either. Beads of sweat were forming on his brow; his pallor had become quite florid.

Jeremy looked up at Ivan, his eyes fiery, his mood dark. 'I'm sorry about this Ivan but needs must.' Tucking the diary under his arm, he ran out of the door towards his car. Ivan shouted after him that he needed the diary for the day's appointments, but Jeremy screeched off at full speed. *No one uses a fucking diary anymore,* he said to himself. *I'm doing him a favour. It's time he got to grips with modern technology.* Glancing down at the diary on the passenger seat, Jeremy began to laugh uncontrollably. *No one on this earth is going to get in my way. If they do, then I shall mow them down.'*

Chapter 18

Six months before Kira disappeared

Kira breezed into the office wearing a cornflower blue dress with white daisies circling the hemline. Walking straight over to Connie's desk, she whispered in a quiet conspiratorial tone, 'Connie, could you do me a huge favour?'
'Sure, is everything alright?' Connie was a little unnerved by Kira's secretive manner.
'Yes, everything's fine. I've got an important appointment to go to this morning. I was wondering if you could show my 12.30 client the flat in Viewforth Road , then I can do your 4pm appointment. Does that sound doable?'
'Yes, no problem. That works out better for me because I can maybe slip away early. I'll write down the details of the property, it's quite local.' Connie took a piece of paper from her desk to jot down all the information she would need to know about the viewing.
Kira took the piece of paper, slipping it into her handbag. Leaning forward, she kissed Connie's cheek, informing her that she was the best. A taxi Kira had previously called, waited outside for her. No one in the office was given any information as to where she was going. As far as everyone, apart from Connie, was concerned, she was off to show a property somewhere.
Returning to Bruntsfield later that afternoon, Kira bought a latte from Costa Coffee. The tall young barista with the long

hair, served her, engaging her in a little small talk. He managed to glean plenty of useful information about her by using some clever conversational techniques that he had used many times in the past. There had been other girls that he had taken a shine to but this girl, with her pretty dresses and blonde hair, was his favourite. The first time he fell for her was when she came into the shop acting all chatty. As soon as she had left, he ran to the window to watch her walking away. By sheer luck, a gust of wind encircled her, blowing her skirt up to her chin. He had never seen anything like it. She had white lacy knickers on, her flesh was firm and sumptuous. How many nights had he lain in bed replaying that scene, over and over. From then on, he waited for her to return to the coffee shop. Pushing the other assistants out of the way, he made sure that he got to her first. She was his dream girl, the centre of all his fantasies.

As time went on, he became a little more daring. On one particular occasion, he joined her at the booth where she was sitting. Without losing eye contact, he reached his phone under the table, clicking his camera at that beautiful flesh under her dress. When the job was done, he wrapped up the conversation, before hurrying straight into the gents' toilets to get a really good look at his spoils. He wasn't disappointed with the photo because there was some bare thigh and a flash of pink lace, but he felt that he could do better. The next time he would drop his phone near her feet. When he bent to pick it up, he could move in close to her privates.

Kira drained the last drop of her latte, it was time to leave. With her handbag on her knee, she rooted around for the piece of paper containing the details of where she was to be

at 4pm. Waving goodbye to the friendly young gentleman with the long hair, she made her way back to her car before heading off in the direction of Connie's appointment in Spylaw Road.
As soon as she turned into the road, she saw the bold Ivan Cole 'for sale' sign, halfway down the street. The property was a top floor conversion of a large Georgian style house. The streets were quiet, and it was now four o'clock, on the nose. The client's name had slipped her mind, so she took another look at Connie's scribbled details. The sound of a car could be heard approaching, which alerted her to look in her rear-view mirror. A black sports car had pulled up behind her. *This must be him,* she thought, getting out to greet him. With a quick glance at the scrap of paper, she saw that his name was, 'Mr Jackson.'
Mr Jackson got out of his car at the same time she did. They stared at one another as they stood transfixed to the spot. It was unbelievable, joyous and painful. Kira started to cry as Fraser Jackson, her true love from university, ran full speed towards her, scooping her into his arms. It was as though no time at all had passed between them. The two became emotional, holding one another urgently.
'Kira, I can't believe it's you!' Fraser Jackson said, reluctant to put her down.
Kira cried, hugging tightly around his neck with both hands.
'I didn't think I'd ever see you again. I've thought about you every single day,' he told her.
Kira loosened her grip on his neck, looking straight into his face. 'Why did you leave me then? You broke my heart.' She cried again as her grip on his neck tightened.

'What did your parents tell you, Kira?' he asked, suddenly turning very serious.
'My father told me that he had offered you money to leave me. He never dreamt that you would take it because he thought you loved me.' Now crying bitterly at the painful memory, she continued, 'Then... then he said that you nearly chewed his hand off to get the money. In fact, he said you asked for double the amount if you promised to stay away for good.'
A look of fury flashed across Fraser's face. 'Let's go in, we will look at the property, then I'll explain what really happened.' They walked together in silence along the path to the side entrance of the conversion. With her trembling hands, she took the key from her pocket and opened up the door to the property. They walked up the stairs which led into the hallway. Fraser took her in his arms, holding her close without saying a word. The chemical attraction between them was almost tangible as they stood, burning with love, full of desire for one another. Kira would have stood in the embrace for longer, but she needed to hear what Fraser had to say about their breakup. Her mind was spinning, as the trauma of the separation returned to her. The depression she had suffered, the tears she had cried and the pain, the unbearable, agonising pain she had endured after he left.
They sat down together on the sofa, in the clinically tidy lounge. Fraser gripped Kira's hand and began piecing together the order of events of that horrendous period in their lives. 'Your parents invited my mum and dad out for dinner. They said that it was time they met up as we had been dating for some time. I was suspicious because I knew

that they had forbidden you to see me. Do you remember how you climbed out of your bedroom window and down the trellising on the wall, in order to meet me?' he laughed.
'I know. I could have been killed but you were so worth it,' she said, stroking his cheek.
'Anyway, my parents got dressed up.' Pausing for a moment, he recalled the details to his mind. 'My mum had actually bought a new dress, then visited the hairdresser's. Anyway, they met your parents in a restaurant in the city. It turned out that my dad had been in a bit of trouble with the police a few years before I met you. It was nothing major and it was his own stupid fault. He paid the price for it and has regretted it ever since. Anyway, I don't know how he managed it, but your father got a hold of the police report and threatened to turn it into a scandal for the newspapers. He said that he had many connections in the tabloids.'
Kira interrupted him to confirm. 'He does have connections. Connections in the police force, the media, everywhere!'
'He told my parents that he wanted me to disappear out of your life or he would bring so much shame upon our family. He said he would ruin my father's business and they wouldn't be able to pay their mortgage, so they could lose their house as well as their reputation. Basically, he told my father that he would finish us all. So, when my father explained everything to me, I just packed a bag and travelled across Europe. I got home a couple of years ago and started a business which, fortunately, has been successful. My father is retired now, but he never got over that meeting with your parents. Part of the deal was that I couldn't say goodbye to you. I simply had to vanish.' Reaching over, he held her pretty face in his hands. 'It was the most painful, unhappy

time of my life. It took me so long to get over it. I'm still not over it!'
'I'm still not over it. I never stopped loving you and thinking about you. I cried every day and every night.' She wrapped her arms tightly around his neck again. 'Fraser, I am so sorry that this happened, I knew nothing about it. I just accepted everything that I was told. I can't believe my parents did this to you and your family. I can never forgive them.'
'Well, we've found each other now. Let's put all of that behind us. It is really funny how we were separated and yet we somehow gravitated back to one another. Why don't we go out for dinner tonight?' he suggested.
Kira flinched at this comment. 'Things are not as easy as you think, Fraser.' She held her hand out in front of him, showing him the ring with the three oversized diamonds. Instinctively, he pulled back from her.
'Who is he?' he asked, feeling unjustified jealousy.
'His name is Jeremy Ward. His mother and father are friends of my parents.'
'Do you love him?' Fraser asked.
'No, I've only ever loved you. I am in this relationship and I'm too frightened to get out of it. He didn't propose to me. He put the ring on my finger, then two minutes later both sets of parents arrived with champagne. I was never asked if I wanted to marry him but if he had asked me and I had said no then I would have suffered for it.'
'Tell him tonight that it's over,' Fraser said adamantly.
'You don't understand anything. He would kill me and when I say 'kill', I mean murder. I am terrified of him. You have no idea what he is capable of. My parents think he's

wonderful.' She trembled as she explained how things were with Jeremy.
'Well, we'll meet in secret for a while until we decide what to do next. That'll be exciting, won't it?' he suggested.
'Fraser, you're not listening to me. He has a tracker on my phone and on my car. I had an appointment this morning that I didn't want him to know about, so I took a taxi and left my car outside the office. I also needed to leave my phone in the drawer of my desk. He checks my phone every night for calls and texts. He scrutinises my bank statements to see what I spend. I am only allowed to wear dresses, he simply forbids me to wear jeans or tracksuit trousers. Fraser, I don't have a friend in the world. And that is only a fraction of the control he has over me. You have no idea. He's a very dangerous man and I can't get free of him.'
'I'll see to it that you get free of him. Now that I've found you, I'm never going to let you go,' he said, holding her close to him, stroking her soft familiar hair.
They made passionate love in the house in Spylaw Road. Before leaving, they pledged that this time they would be together, forever.
When the house was locked up, they walked hand in hand out on to the street where their cars were parked. As Kira climbed into her car, she asked jokingly, 'So, Fraser, do you want to buy this wonderfully bright and spacious conversion?'
'No, I'll have to keep looking. I'll be booking another appointment next week to see some other property.' He laughed as a plan began to formulate in his mind.

'Please don't give your real name just in case someone finds out. We have to keep this so quiet,' she warned, feeling truly terrified that Jeremy might suspect something.
'I will book under a different name,' he told her.
'How will I know it's you.'
Leaning his head in the car window, he kissed her gently. 'Don't worry, you'll know.'

Chapter 19

Pure, undiluted joy bubbled away within Kira. The smile would not leave her face. Fraser was back in her life, and she loved him more than ever. That very morning, she had felt so unhappy and alone, now life had offered her another chance and she was taking it. In a matter of hours, a path of hope had magically appeared through the mire around her life. *I am the luckiest girl alive. If I hadn't taken Connie's appointment, I would never have met him. Fate has really shone down on me. Oh, thank you, thank you, thank you.*

The joy soon dissipated when she reached her house in Palmerston Place, suddenly remembering what she would have to endure when she walked in the door. The sound of the key going into the lock would draw Jeremy out of his lair to greet her, a predatorial look burning in his eyes. Most days she could take her mind to a better place, but not today. Not even the thought of her true love, Fraser, could help her endure the violation.

Sure enough, one step over the threshold, he pushed her face first against the wall, tore off her lacy knickers before ramming her furiously from behind as she screamed. After all, this was his fantasy, whether she liked it or not. Jeans or trousers would have ruined everything for him.

That evening Kira and Jeremy sat eating a wonderful dinner together. Jeremy had enrolled Kira in evening cooking classes the previous year. He had arranged this because he was sick and tired of eating the muck that she dished up to him. On occasion, he would sample the first bite of his meal, pretending to like it. With relief, Kira would exhale, but he was only being cruel. Rising to his feet, he would take his dinner to the pedal bin next to the sink. Holding the plate up high, he would press the pedal with his foot, keeping his eyes fixed on her as he tilted it. The food would slowly slide off, slopping into the bin. More often than not, the contents missed the bin, landing on the floor; Kira was sure that he did that on purpose. Before leaving the room, he would warn her, 'You are going to have to do better. I don't want to get tough on you, but I will. Now get it cleaned.'

In the early days of their relationship, Kira cried when Jeremy was unkind to her, but time soon toughened her shell. Life for her had become an existence of physical, mental, emotional and sexual abuse. Defending herself made life even more intolerable. She had read an article once about a survivor of domestic violence. The woman had described how she learned to cope with the cruelty by taking her mind to a tropical beach or busy, vibrant city. Kira first tried this strategy when he kept her awake by 'teaching' her how to keep her wardrobe tidy. That night, she had escaped from her body to walk along 'The Great Wall of China' in her mind, it was beautiful. Several times a day, she thought of leaving but where could she go? What did it matter, anyway; he would hunt her down, he would find her. He had total control of her money and her passport. There would be no help available from her parents as they believed that she was unworthy of a wonderful man like Jeremy. To be fair to her parents and their abominable judge of character, they had only ever seen the believable, charming side of him. To any onlooker, she was the luckiest girl in the world.

Now that Fraser had come back into her life, she had to act normally at home. Jeremy had a way of seeing straight through her, reading her mind. No phone calls, no unnecessary journeys in her car to see Fraser. The amount of money she spent had to remain the same each day, no extras. Over the past few months, before Fraser arrived back in her life, she had found it necessary to 'borrow' money from Ivan's petty cash box to pay for a taxi to her own private appointments. Jeremy would have interrogated her about where she had been. Attending her appointments no longer mattered now because Fraser had assured her that there was a way for them to be together safely, forever. Having Fraser back in her life was all she cared about in the world. She had no choice but to trust in him completely, he would never put her in any danger. Knowing now of the suffering her parents had inflicted on Fraser's family, made Kira mentally disown them. If she never saw them again, she would not shed a single tear. How must the Jacksons have felt when they were told that their son had to disappear? They were good people; they didn't deserve to be treated that way. When the break-up happened, she had been distraught, but her parents had supported her through that terrible time. They had witnessed, first-hand, how much pain she was in, how many tears she had cried. The truth was that they had engineered the whole thing for 'her own good'.

How dare they! she thought. *Causing so much suffering to so many people. How could they?* As if that wasn't bad enough, they then set her up in a life controlled by a monster. It was unforgivable; she felt no love for them.

Chapter 20

Kira had waited patiently for word from Fraser. The last thing he had told her was that he would book an appointment under a false name, but she would know without a doubt that it was him. Every day for a week, she had scrutinised the appointments in a hope that something would strike a chord.

The traffic was heavy on a Thursday, but she was still first to arrive at work after Ivan. Breezing through the agency door, she shouted to her boss in the back office, 'Hi Ivan, it's just me.' She switched on her computer to check if any more appointments had been added online. It was common practice to copy the extra viewings to her large desk diary.

10 am Mr and Mrs Reid viewing the property in Blinkbonny Terrace.

12.45pm Mrs Kerbyson and her daughter viewing the property in Haymarket Terrace.

2pm Mr and Mrs Clark viewing in Abercorn Avenue (new to the market)

4pm Captain F. Wentworth viewing the property in Alnwickhill Terrace.

The name Captain F. Wentworth caught her attention. Something about it was highly familiar. Who was Captain Wentworth? Gazing out of the window, she searched through the recesses of her memory. Where had she heard that name before? A light bulb illuminated in her mind. Of course, Captain Fredrick Wentworth was a character from the Jane Austen novel, Persuasion. She loved that book, and Fraser knew that she did. Captain Wentworth had been a kind gentleman who had become separated from his love.

He was reunited with her years later, winning her heart with a letter. A laugh escaped her when she realised that it must be Fraser who was viewing the house. It was a personalised, romantic gesture. Oh, how she loved him for it. *Four o'clock is too long to wait. How will I get through the day? Oh Fraser, I can't wait to see you.*

All the properties on the day's itinerary were shown to the viewers with faked enthusiasm. There was only one thing that got the juices of excitement flowing for Kira and she was meeting him at four o'clock. Getting to the house in Alnwickhill Terrace to be alone with Fraser was all she could focus on. She physically ached to hold him, kiss him, feel him inside her.

Fraser's black sports car was the first thing she saw when she turned into Alnwickhill Terrace.

Having arrived half an hour early, Fraser had been sitting in his car willing Kira to drive around the corner.

The moment he spotted the pink mini, he leapt from his car, leaving the door ajar. His heart trilled with adrenaline as he raced over to open Kira's car door. 'I missed you,' he said, reaching in to hug her. 'I was so tempted to text you to say goodnight or I love you or anything.'

'No, no, you must never do that, Fraser. Please, it would be really bad for me.' She stiffened in terror at the thought of what would happen if he had done this.

'I know, that's why I didn't. Don't worry, I will never do anything that will put you in any danger,' he promised; feeling alarmed by the level of fear that she had for this man. Feeling that he had ruined the moment, he tried to pull it back. 'I've been sitting here twiddling my thumbs waiting

for you for nearly half an hour. What kind of estate agent are you?' he joked with her.
'Okay, Captain Frederick Wentworth, would you like to see around this house that you have no intention of buying?' she asked him.
'Yes, show me the upstairs first.' Grabbing her by the hand, they ran together to the front door. He kissed her neck all over as she tried to get the key in the lock.
The couple had a passionate sexual encounter in one of the upstairs bedrooms in the house. They satisfied each other's flesh, enjoying every moment of it. When it was over, she lay staring at his profile as he lay on his back. The sheen on his hair made her reach over to stroke it. Memories of their university days filled her thoughts. They had been so happy together, inseparable. His almost black hair had been shoulder length back then, she loved it.
'How do you get your hair to look so shiny?' she asked him, running her fingers through it.
'I wash it every day using a mild shampoo,' he said, adopting a feminine voice.
She laughed at him. In fact, she laughed at everything he said because he made her so happy.
'I wish we could stay like this forever. I don't want to go home.' A feeling of repulsion came over her knowing she would have to go through Jeremy's fantasy ritual at the front door. The very thought of him anywhere near her made her sick to the stomach. Fraser returning to her life was not the cause of her loathing towards Jeremy, he had earned it with his vile treatment of her. Now she yearned to be free from the constraints of both her fiancé and her family. Fraser was the only good, pure thing in her life.

They lay together laughing, reminiscing, basically discovering each other all over again. They made love one more time before Kira announced that she had to leave. Lifting her clothes from the floor, she got dressed in haste. 'By the way, sir,' she said, 'do you want to buy this house, or do you want to keep searching?'

'Definitely keep searching!' he laughed. 'I'll book an appointment for another house as soon as I can.' He reached for her at the front door, pulling her into his arms. 'Kira, I love you and I am going to take care of you forever. I just need to work a few things out, you won't need to wait too long. Okay?'

'Okay, I trust you,' she said, wrapping her arms around his neck.

'Now, let's see your sweet smiling face.' He held her face up by the chin, she responded with a wide smile.

'That's my girl. Stay strong.'

A churning motion in Kira's stomach made her want to be sick, as it always did when she headed home. The magical time she had spent with Fraser only served to magnify the horror of her life with Jeremy. Her repulsion for Jeremy began to fester, gnawing away at her like a disease. Playing the dutiful, obedient partner became more and more untenable.

She approached the doorstep with her key in her hand, reconciling herself to the fact that there was nothing she could do. If she did not let him have his way with her, he would suspect that something was going on. Could it be possible that he wasn't standing behind the door today. *Please, please,* she pleaded silently. *Please don't be there today. I can't do this anymore.* She wasn't hopeful.

As sure as day follows night, there he was standing in wait with that familiar wild look on his face. Licking his lips, breathing heavily, he prepared to pounce. A sickening thought occurred to her, as she looked at him. *He actually thinks I enjoy this.*

When the assault was over, he zipped up his suit trousers, walking away. Remaining against the wall for a moment, Kira tried to compose herself, to recover from the act of rape that had just occurred. As she pulled up her torn underwear, she affirmed to herself, *I have to act normal. He must not suspect a thing*. Tears soaked her cheeks, so she wiped them dry before joining her fiancé in the kitchen.

'How was your day, Jeremy?' she asked him sweetly.

'Good,' he answered. 'I picked up two lucrative contracts today that are going to make us very rich. Or should I say, even richer.' He threw his head back, laughing loudly.

'That's great,' she replied, thinking how little she cared for money. It meant absolutely nothing to her. The expensive house they lived in was never her choice. All the holidays they had been on were chosen by Jeremy, and she despised spending two full weeks with him. Shopping for nice clothes for herself was not an option, he had to go with her. His say was final in everything she wore. He insisted on short, chiffon, flowery dresses, regardless of the time of year. In winter, when frost covered the ground, her legs were so cold she could see a bluish hue on them. She could even swear that they had grown an extra layer of fat around her calves and ankles to combat the cold.

'How is your secretary Lucy doing?' Kira asked, making small talk.

'Why?' he asked suspiciously.

'No reason. I like her and I haven't seen her for a long time.'
'You're acting a little odd this evening, Kira. What's going on?'
'Nothing. I was just curious.' Beads of sweat formed in her armpits, her face burned. 'I just wanted to know about your life, Jeremy,' she stuttered.
He started to laugh at her. 'I get it,' he said snidely.
'What?' she asked, wishing that she could leave the table, the kitchen, the house, her life.
'You're jealous of Lucy, aren't you?'
'No.'
'Yes, you are. You can't stand the thought of sharing me with anyone else,' he smirked.
His assumption was the furthest end of the spectrum from the truth. 'Well, she is very attractive.' Kira said, thinking how happy she would be if he left her for Lucy, although she wouldn't wish him on anyone.
'Silly girl. I gave you that beautiful, expensive ring for a reason, so you need to trust me the way I trust you. It's a two way street, Kira. We have chosen a life together, so don't go spoiling it with your schoolgirl jealousy.'
'I'm sorry. I do trust you,' she told him.
'By the way, I've ordered a running machine for you, Kira. I noticed that your legs are looking a little beefy.' He ruffled her hair as he headed upstairs to the shower.
Kira felt a yearning within her to send a message or make a phone call to Fraser, but she would never do that. Any unknown numbers showing up on her phone records would be fatal at this time. Jeremy had a way of finding everything out. She couldn't possibly run the risk of him becoming suspicious. Besides, she didn't have Fraser's mobile number.

It was better to keep the temptation out of her hands. Sitting alone in the kitchen, thoughts of her beloved Fraser and his shiny black hair, entered her mind. As she rubbed her fingertips together, she could almost feel the softness of it when she closed her eyes. What was he doing at this very moment? Could he be thinking about her? Was he devising a plan for the two of them to be together? How much longer could she live in the same house as Jeremy, tolerating his cruelty? How much longer could she talk weddings with her mother?

Her mother wanted to view the Prestonfield Hotel as a venue for the big day, but it was only to impress their friends and Jeremy's business associates. There wasn't going to be a wedding. Even if Fraser hadn't come back to her, there still was never going to be a wedding. Ending her own life was more favourable than walking down the aisle with that wretched human being. *Why was I so weak?* she questioned. *How could I have allowed myself to get into this position in the first place?* She had a university degree, yet she said nothing when he bullied her into working in an estate agency. She took her father at his word when he told her that Fraser accepted money to leave her. She knew Fraser, she knew the love he had for her, so why did she, so readily, believe this explanation? What was wrong with her? She has been nothing more than a pushover to everyone in her life. Fraser was going to change everything for her. With him by her side, she would fight to the death to have freedom from Jeremy.

Her thoughts were interrupted by Jeremy shouting down from upstairs.

'Kira, come up and try on this little black lacy playsuit I bought for you. I think you're going to like it. I know I will.'
Kira gagged. *Put the bloody lacy playsuit on yourself if you like it so much,* she thought.
'I'm just coming!' she answered dutifully. *Keep him happy at all costs. It won't be for much longer.*

Chapter 21

A knock at the door on the Saturday morning got Kira up out of bed. Rising early on her days off was no hardship for her, it ensured that she didn't lie next to Jeremy a moment longer than she needed to. This meant she avoided being the target of his searching hands under the duvet. He got angry with her if she rejected his abhorrent advances, so it was best if she separated herself from the situation. On opening the front door, she was surprised to see her mother standing there with her hair freshly shampooed, set and sprayed into a solid mass.

'Hi mum, your hair is lovely. Have you just come from the hairdresser's?'

'Oh, thanks. Yes, it was Stefan that did it today. I'm really pleased with it. I'm going to request he does my hair from now on. I just stopped by with these wedding brochures. They have some wonderful ideas on how to make your special day a little bit more special.' She made her way into the house carrying four glossy magazines.

'How lovely!' Kira told her, kissing her cheek as she passed. 'I will get a good look at these tonight.'

'I thought we could go through them together. There's no time like the present. The big day will be here before you know it.' She made herself comfortable in the front lounge.

'I'll make us coffee, then we can take a look.'

'Good girl. I will fold down the corners on the pages I think are relevant to us. Don't put sugar in my coffee, I have my sweeteners. I am watching my figure for the wedding. Small changes make a big difference you know. Perhaps you should think about that too.'

'Good idea,' Kira told her, snarling inside at her mother's tactless comment.
They discussed flowers, table settings, favours, cars and dresses, before moving on to the subject of bridesmaids and best man.
'I have asked your cousin, Ivy, to be one of the bridesmaids,' Celia Carmichael told her daughter. 'And I was thinking that you could also have that girl you used to be friendly with from school, I forget her name, but her parents were distantly related to one of the royals. Oh, another option is the daughter of your dad's friend, Irvine McGuire. She is about your age; very beautiful, you know. We want the wedding party to look just right. I was thinking we could have you in ivory, the bridesmaids in teal. What do you think, Kira?'
'I think that all sounds perfect,' she told her. *Fraser, please save me from this insane, superficial world I am living in.*
'I've booked us in for a wine tasting event in the city. It is very important to get the wine right for every part of the day. Champagne on arrival for everyone, of course! I am going to ask about booking St. Mary's Cathedral for the service, very handy for you!' she laughed. 'I simply must get the Prestonfield Hotel. I can't settle for anything less. I will get us an appointment to view it and if we like it, we will just book it there and then. Do you agree?'
'Absolutely!' Kira told her. *God, please help me.*
'Now, live musicians! Let's talk about what kind of music you would like for coming down the aisle and as background music during the meal. We will book a live band for the evening reception. I want a well-known band, someone that everyone knows. Of course, we'll keep it under

our hats until the event, then everyone will gasp when they walk in! We won't worry about cost. This is a once in a lifetime affair, it's got to be right. Anyone who is anyone will be there.'

Kira despised that expression. She also detested the way her mother was now saying, 'I want this, I want that'. Thank goodness this was not her real wedding because everything that her mother wanted, she definitely did not. Her cousin, Ivy, was not a particularly nice girl ,and she had no idea where her school friend Savannah Lyle-Jacobs was now, they had never kept in touch. As for Irvine's daughter, well that suggestion didn't deserve commenting on. It was now blatantly obvious that her whole life had been decided for her. She had been coerced into decisions that were not her choice. It was now time to take her life back, reclaim it as her own. All she needed in the world was Fraser.

Chapter 22

On Monday morning, Kira sat checking the list of viewings in the hope that an appointment had been made by Fraser, but there was nothing that resembled his secret code. Disappointment weighed heavily on her. It was too traumatic to imagine what her life would become if she never heard from him again. What if the mire grew over her path of hope; no, that was not a thought she would allow in.
Connie arrived at the office at around five to nine. Kira beckoned her over. In a barely audible whisper, she asked, 'Could we swap viewings in the diary again? I have another appointment that I must attend. I don't want to ask Ivan for time off.'
'Sure!' Connie told her. 'Just switch them around, then let me know where I am going, who I'm seeing and when.'
'Connie, you really are a good friend. I don't know what I would do without you.' It occurred to Kira that if she had been getting married then Connie was the only person she would have wanted as a bridesmaid. She was the closest thing she had to a friend.
Now she would have to wait until Ivan went out to value a property before she could pinch the taxi fare from the petty cash box. For some reason, she didn't feel bad about stealing the money because she deemed it a necessity. Anyway, she put in a lot of additional hours and always went the extra mile for the business; Ivan knew that. If he ever found out, he would totally understand. Well, it eased her conscience to think about it that way.
Kira called a taxi to take her across town to her appointment. 'Could you pick me up from the same spot in one hour?' she

asked the driver. 'If, by chance, I'm not out in an hour, could you please wait for me?' Into his outstretched hand, she counted out the fare in notes and coins.

By the time Kira returned to the office, a new appointment had been scheduled in the system for Mr J. Hawkins to view the property in Chamberlain Road, on Thursday at 4pm. Staring at the name Mr J. Hawkins, it began to strike a chord in her memory. 'John Hawkins, no, James Hawkins, no…Jim Hawkins!' she thought. *Treasure Island, I love it!* Her spirits soared as she wrote the details into her desk diary. Beside the name Jim Hawkins, she drew an asterisk, but soon thought better of it, scribbling it out. It would have been a mistake to highlight any of her meetings with Fraser. These appointments were secret, stolen moments with her classic characters in a stranger's home. No one must ever find out.

Ivan called a meeting with his staff on the Tuesday. Derek, Connie, Eric and Kira all kept their diaries free at lunchtime, making sure that they were all present. Ivan held meetings twice a week for updates on properties, but this was different; everyone was curious, perhaps a little concerned.

'I've called you all together to put it out there that someone here has been doing something that they shouldn't be doing in my employ. I'm not going to say too much about it, as I don't want to embarrass anyone, but it has to stop now. You know who you are, and you know what you've been doing, so, no more! Okay everyone, back to work.'

The staff returned to their desks deeply thoughtful. Derek knew that he had been burning the candle at both ends. He was hungover most mornings, so he would have a couple pints at lunchtime to make himself feel better. Ivan had been looking at him in a disapproving manner, even ticked him off a few times. This was the wake-up call he needed, he had to stop. His drinking had been excessive for some time now, but things were going to change. He loved his job, he would even go as far as to say he was damned good at it.

Filled with remorse, Eric knew that it was wrong to skive off early a couple of days each week. Last Thursday, he had been spotted by Ivan's wife, and she must have told Ivan that he wasn't where he was supposed to be. Eric's father was bedridden, he was his only carer. It deeply concerned him to leave his father all day on his own. The thought of his father having no one to talk to, no one to fix him food and drinks, was constantly on Eric's mind. From now on, he was going to have to make better provisions for him. Now that Ivan knew all about it, things were going to change. The last thing he wanted was to lose his job.

Connie felt thoroughly ashamed. She had lifted the odd little ornament or piece of jewellery from the houses she had been showing to viewers. She didn't know why she did it. It was not as if she needed any extra stuff, her house was a hoarder's paradise, full to bursting. Perhaps one of the houses had security cameras in the rooms. That was mortifying, she was so grateful to Ivan for not embarrassing her. Starting right now, she was going to do her level best to stop it. If she couldn't, then she would need to seek help. Her position was one of trust and it was morally wrong to betray the people she was working for. She would need to fight these terrible impulses, she owed it to Ivan, the clients and herself. What if someone, someday, decided to press charges? It didn't bear thinking about.

Kira squirmed as Ivan talked about someone doing something they shouldn't be doing. Having wild passionate sex on a bed in someone's house every week, sometimes twice, was definitely wrong. To her credit, she thought, she did always choose a bed in what seemed like a spare or guest room, rather than the owner's master bedroom. What else could she do? For now, it was the only way, she couldn't possibly give it up, but she would try to be more discreet.

Knowing he had a dishonest employee; Ivan had phoned a security company to ask them to install a hidden camera in his office. He needed to know who was stealing small amounts of cash on a regular basis. The last person he would have suspected was Kira. If he had to put a bet on it, he would have ranked Derek first, then Eric, followed by Connie. Kira wouldn't even have made the list.

Chapter 23

Normalcy was Kira's main focus in the days that followed. In the office, each day, she was the ever-eager estate agent, hungry for a sale, closing the deal. In the home, she was the dutiful fiancé who was always happy to accommodate. Outwardly, she functioned on autopilot, inwardly, she thought only of the classic meetings with Fraser. An electrifying thrill of excitement ran through her body at the thought of her impending meeting with Jim Hawkins on Thursday.

Derek arrived in the office minutes after Ivan on the Wednesday. His face was freshly shaven, his shirt was ironed all over, not just the collar. Ivan faked a double take look for effect when he saw Derek.

'Derek, you're here? Early,' he said, looking at his watch, noting that it was before 8am. 'What's going on?'

'Nothing. I just wanted to get an early start, you know, be ahead of the game.'

'Good to hear, Derek,' Ivan told him, walking into the back office.

'Hey boss?' he shouted, following Ivan. 'Thanks for not embarrassing me in front of everyone. I took your point; things are going to change. I've decided to give up going to the pub through the week.'

Ivan wanted to smile but instead feigned a serious face. 'You've made the right decision, Derek. It was becoming a bit much.'

'I know boss, I'm only going to get drunk at the weekend from now on.'

'Wise decision, Derek, very wise decision.'

Kira arrived shortly after. She sat chatting for a while with Ivan and Derek before the start of business. She couldn't quite believe the change in Derek. Apart from the fact that he was early, he had really cleaned up his act: combed hair, smart shirt, the works. *He must have met a girl,* she thought, there was no other plausible explanation. Connie walked through the door shortly after, heading straight over to her desk. Taking out her compact mirror along with her items of make-up, she began her usual ritual of painting her face. Waving her mascara in her hand, she said, 'Hey guys, it's my birthday today. Does anyone fancy going for a drink at Montpelliers after work?'

Ivan came through to the front office and kissed her cheek. 'Happy birthday, Connie. Yeah, I'll come for a drink after work.'

Derek said, 'Happy birthday Con, I'll join you. But don't go trying to get me drunk so that you can seduce me!'

'Oh, Derek, you've caught me out. How did you know that I was planning that all along. There's no point in going now.'

'Eh, Derek, I thought you didn't go out for a drink on a weeknight anymore?' Ivan asked.

'This is the last ever time. After tonight, never again. Promise.'

Connie looked at Kira, 'How about you, Kira? Can you come? I need you to even up the girl boy ratio.'

Kira would dearly have loved to go for a drink after work with colleagues, but she couldn't. Jeremy would never allow it, and he would make her life hell on earth for asking. Even if she had been tempted to risk it and suffer the consequences, she couldn't because of the situation with Fraser. Staying on her best behaviour with Jeremy was all

that mattered. Anything out of character like going for a drink with friends could jeopardise everything.
'I'm so sorry Connie, I can't. I have wedding stuff to organise with my mum after work.' It was a lie, but she knew that they would buy it. Looking at them joking and laughing about going for drinks made her feel left out, abnormal almost. Why did she accept these rules from Jeremy? She questioned herself again. It was normal to go for a drink after work with your workmates. Why had she allowed the leash around her neck to be pulled so tightly? More pointedly, why did she accept a leash at all? Jeremy had complete control over every aspect of her life; she had become no more than a dim shadow of herself.
The following morning, Kira was up and showered early. It was the day of her appointment at 4pm with 'Jim Hawkins' from Treasure Island. She chose a jade-coloured dress which suited her long blonde hair. Normally, she would put her hair up with a clasp, but not today. It was left loosely lying on her shoulders. Searching through her drawer of perfume bottles, she decided on the scent of Black Opium. It was the perfume she used to wear when she was dating Fraser at university. A little mascara was applied then she painted her lips with Yves Saint Laurent 'Rose Afrique' lipstick. She stood back looking at herself in the mirror. She liked the girl that looked back at her. The excitement she felt quashed her appetite for breakfast, instead she made herself a latte from the coffee machine in the kitchen. Butterflies flapped around in her stomach as she wondered how she was going to get through the day until four o'clock. The hot coffee settled her a little and as she sipped it, she let her mind drift to thoughts of Fraser. His soft black hair, his muscular physique, the way

he wore his shirts so tight, every muscle defined. *Oh, his hands,* she swooned. *His gorgeous, brown strong hands, touching me gently, then firmly…*
'Look at you!' Jeremy said when he walked into the kitchen. 'You look different. What's going on?'
'Nothing. What do you mean?' she asked nervously. Maybe she had overdone it a bit with her hair and the perfume.
'Are you dressing to impress someone?' he asked accusingly. 'Because it certainly looks like it.' He took several steps towards her. 'What is that smell?'
'I *am* dressing to impress someone, if you must know,' she plucked suddenly from nowhere. She fought to tame her pounding heart. Sidling up to him, she slipped her arms around his neck, kissing him passionately on the lips.
His tongue roved around her mouth, his hands began grabbing for anything tantalising.
Oh, no! she panicked, taking hold of his roving hands.
He was drunk with arousal.
'Tut, tut, tut…That's for later, cheeky boy!' She would worry about 'later' when it came, but right now, she was saving herself for Fraser. By the end of the day, she would have psyched herself up for the onslaught at the front door. The important thing was that she had led him off the scent by erasing all his suspicions. It had been downright dangerous making an extra effort for Fraser; Jeremy was no fool. From now on, she had to keep things the same, no changes to the norm.
Today's the day, she thought excitedly. Her body was out in the city, showing and selling houses, but her mind was locked in a private world where only she and Fraser existed. Unbridled excitement forced her to drive to Chamberlain

Road early, she wanted to be there when the black sports car arrived. But when she turned the corner into the road, he was already waiting. His handsome face broke into a wide, winning smile when he spotted her. Stepping out of the car, he ran to open the door for her. Without saying a word, he simply kissed her and held her for a few moments to soothe the ache his heart had felt for her. She studied his face, soaking up every detail, every contour. Kissing him all over his face, she laughed and laughed for no reason.

'Kira, I love you. I mean, I really, really love you,' he told her.

'Fraser, I love you. I mean, I really, really love you,' she repeated back to him, still laughing.

'I 'till death us do part' love you,' he told her.

'Me too,' Kira said, more seriously.

'I'm already working on a plan for us, Kira. I won't tell you about until the time is right. It's best that you don't know anything, just in case. Now take me into this property and show me the bedrooms!' he joked, lightening the tone.

The lovers undressed each other, exploring every inch of each other's bodies. They were ravenous for one another, which heightened the passion in their love making. Afterwards, they lay naked, talking about life and the past. Whenever Kira brought up the future, Fraser told her, 'Shhh. Don't ask, just trust.'

They lay together until the last spare moment, then Kira got up and dressed. It was becoming more and more difficult to tear herself away from him. The time she spent without him was an existence of constant painful craving.

'So, are you interested in putting an offer in for this property, sir?' she asked him, as they got ready to leave.

'Let me think about it... Nay, Jim lad!' he answered, in the style of Long John Silver.

Chapter 24

Every Thursday around four o'clock, Kira 'showed' properties to Mr Rochester, Mr Copperfield, Mr Nickelby, Mr Haversham, Mr Brocklehurst and Mr Heathcliffe. There had been worrying moments when her classic character had been entered into the system under Connie's appointments, but Kira managed to switch things over in time. Her classic gentlemen callers viewed a whole host of properties on Ivan Cole's books. The more time they spent together, the more painful the separation. Kira continued to keep all of her own, private appointments, travelling in the usual manner. Leaving her car at the agency, she sneaked money from the petty cash box to pay for a taxi. It was so fortunate that Ivan had never noticed the missing money.

After spending a wonderful time with Fraser as Mr Heathcliffe, he left her with the parting words, 'Everything is in place. Be ready to leave the next time we meet.'

There were so many questions she wanted to ask, but he told her that she would find out when she needed to know. Her mother had turned up the pressure for dress fittings, cake viewings and wine tasting events; it was becoming overwhelming. Jeremy was even more demanding sexually, his criticism of her even more cruel. The collar and lead that he had put around her neck all those years ago was slowly choking her.

Her father continued to tell her how lucky she was to have a successful young man like Jeremy. 'You don't know how fortunate you are, Kira. If things had been left up to you, you'd be in some rundown council scheme somewhere with a brood of children.'

On Monday morning, she checked the diary for her classic character but alas there was no appointment made with any such person.
Tuesday came and went with no word from the classics.
By Wednesday, she was ready to hit the panic button. What if her father had found out and got to Fraser and his family again? What if Fraser had taken cold feet and run off to find someone who was baggage free? How could she possibly stay in this Godforsaken life without him? *No, stop it,* she told herself. *The love between us is true, Fraser is the real deal, I just have to trust him.*
Thursday morning, she checked the diary. 4pm, Mr Darcy viewing Regent Terrace. Voila! Laughter escaped her when she saw it, picturing Colin Firth emerging from the water, his white shirt soaked through. *Regent Terrace*! she thought. *Wow, that's a property worth a shilling or two. Impressive!'*
Wearing what she called her 'Pretty Woman' spotted dress and a diamante clasp in her hair, she carried out her daily duties in a daze. Back to the office for the lunchtime meeting, she parked in a side street then strolled over to the agency. As she walked past Costa Coffee, she heard knocking on the glass from inside the shop. Glancing furtively around, she saw the tall young man with his hair tied back in a bun. He was banging furiously on the window to get her attention. This was a little embarrassing, her first reaction was to ignore him, but she decided instead to flick her hand up in a semi-wave. *Thank goodness I don't need to see that guy ever again. He's becoming a pest.*
It was 3.45 when she arrived at Regent Terrace, which gave her time to apply a little lipstick and fix her hair. In the distance, she could see the black sports car approaching.

What has he planned? she thought. *What's going to happen*?' Somersaults turned in the pit of her stomach; her heartbeat resounded in her ears. Today was the day of the new beginning, she felt no fear, only excitement. Wherever they were going was perfectly fine by her. A tent in the wilderness would make her happy, as long as she had Fraser.

Fraser ran from the car to meet her, the expression on his face was serious, no trace of a smile. In his hand was a large, black leather holdall.

'Kira, you need to really think about what we are about to do. I'm afraid that there will be no turning back once we've made the decision to go ahead. Do you want to leave here to start a new life?' he asked, looking directly into her eyes.

'Yes, without a doubt,' she answered.

'You won't see your parents or friends again. Do you understand this and are you agreeable to it?' he questioned.

'Fraser, this is all I want in the world. I am appalled by my parents, my only friends are work colleagues who, much as I like them, I can live without.'

'Great, now here's what I want you to do. Open the door to the house, stand in the hallway. I won't come in. I brought you jeans, a jumper size 12 and some trainers size 6, right?' he asked, making sure he had got the sizing right. 'Get changed and walk away. Leave your handbag with all its contents in your car. Take nothing.'

Removing her 'Pretty Woman' dress, she then pulled on the faded Levi jeans and arran jumper, before wriggling her feet into the trainers. All of the items of clothing were exactly to her taste, in fact, she had a memory of wearing the self-same outfit at university. This made her smile. *This is how he remembers me.*

Fraser's face beamed when she emerged from the front door, looking like a completely different woman. 'Oh, Kira!' he said, clutching his heart. 'You are amazing!'

'Have you any idea how great it is to wear jeans and trainers again? I am so tired of wearing short dresses all the time. I hate this thing!' Using all her strength, she tugged at the fabric of the dress, ripping it down the front. The ritual was cathartic, she tore at it again and again.

'You will only have to wear one more dress in your whole life,' he told her, watching her tearing away at the cloth. 'And it will be long and white, and you will wear it with a veil.'

She took the shredded garment to the back of the house where she stuffed it deep into a wheelie bin. Then holding her high heeled shoes in the air, she lobbed them one at a time into the shrubbery of the nearby woods. Her handbag with her bank cards and personal items were still sitting on the passenger seat of her car, she did not return to collect them.

Like Bonnie and Clyde, they ran hand in hand to the black sportscar. Fraser opened the car door, smiling reassuringly at her. Seats belts on, they sped off in the direction of the M9.

On the motorway, approaching the town of Falkirk, Fraser looked down and saw that Kira was still clutching her mobile phone. 'Kira,' he said, slowing the car, 'roll down the window.' She did as she was told. 'Now, throw your phone out.'

Kira hurled her phone as far as she could onto the boggy verge at the side of the road. They drove on for a few hours

with the radio playing, both feeling euphoric about the brand new start that lay ahead of them. The old life that Kira had lived was now symbolically in the bin, shredded, just like the Pretty Woman dress.
Fraser turned off the motorway, into a layby which was tucked away from view. It was imperative that there were no sightings of them at this early stage.
'Kira, you stay in the car and keep your head down. I'm going to get us something to eat.' The garage along from where he parked sold sandwiches and snacks. 'What would you like me to get for you?'
'I don't mind, I like everything.' She was so happy, she didn't care what she ate.
'I would love to have taken you to a top class restaurant somewhere but we just can't. We are now officially in hiding from the world.'
'That suits me fine,' she told him. 'I don't need top class anything. I just want you. Can you tell me where we are going now?'
'No, it's a surprise. Just trust me that you will love it.' He had been planning this day for weeks, he wanted it to be perfect. He reached over to take her hand, saying, 'I can't wait to sleep beside you tonight.'
'Oh, great, I forgot all about that!' she told him, clapping her hands in glee. 'I warn you though, I can look a bit of a fright in the mornings.'
'Oh, now you tell me,' he laughed. 'Actually, I'm no Michel Angelo's David myself in the morning.'
Fraser was in ignorant bliss about the fact that there was a dark cloud looming over the future of their happiness. Kira had not been honest with him. An impossible decision that

she had made before she left was now troubling her conscience. Perhaps it was something she should have discussed with the man she was going to spend the rest of her life with. Sadly, she knew that it was a conversation that had to take place eventually. But she was far too happy to have it now.

Chapter 25

Jeremy drove recklessly through the traffic to get home to Palmerston Place. The diary that he had taken from Ivan Cole's office changed everything. Ivan had been nothing short of furious with him for taking the appointments book without asking, but Ivan had to understand that he needed the information that lay within those precious pages. Covetously, he stroked the cover of the large diary on the seat beside him, trying to focus on the road. This book held the key to Kira's vanishing, and as he was the Sherlock Holmes of this case, he was going to unlock every mysterious detail. As he drove past the Sir Arthur Conan Doyle centre near his house, he banged heavily on his car horn. It was a small gesture of acknowledgement for the help he had received from them. 'I couldn't have done it without you!' he shouted, in passing. *Credit where its due,* he thought earnestly. *Credit where its due.*

Tingling with anticipation, he pulled on the handbrake, tucked the all-important book under his arm and ran with it. The keys fell out of his hand twice as he fumbled with them in the lock. He had worked himself into quite a state. In the end, he decided to put the diary down on the step to free up both hands to open the front door. *Here we go,* he thought, entering the house. He ceremoniously carried the diary with outstretched arms into the formal dining room. In his mind, he had already decided that this was the best place to peruse the diary for information as he could sit on one of the high-backed chairs with the book on the table in front of him. Retrieving a note pad and pen from the sideboard drawer, he wrote the heading 'Kira's Appointments'.

He started with the day of her disappearance, her 4pm appointment was with 'Mr Darcy'. Working backwards from that day, he scrutinised every entry in the diary with a very keen eye. The day before Mr Darcy, he saw an appointment with a Mr Skinner. Laying his pen down, he picked up his phone. He searched for, 'Novels containing the character Mr Skinner'. When the list of results appeared on the screen, he saw that there was a series of books by Quintin Jardine with the main character called DCC Bob Skinner. They were modern day detective novels, so Jeremy ruled it out as it did not fit the modus operandi of the other suspicious appointments. Methodically, he scanned each appointment for a name that fitted with the names of characters from classic books. His phone aided him in researching any dubious surnames that he may not have heard of. It was a full seven days in the diary before the name Mr Rochester appeared and the appointment was of a similar time to that of Mr Darcy. Knowing that Mr Edward Rochester was a character from the novel Jane Eyre, he made an entry in his notebook. He scanned systematically through each page until he reached seven days prior to Mr Rochester. Mr Nickleby appeared again at a similar time to the others. A definite pattern was emerging.
He continued with this method until he had several weeks-worth of meetings with possible characters from the classics. They all tended to be on a Thursday at around four in the afternoon. The week before Captain Frederick Wentworth, there were no suspects in the diary. Jeremy asked himself why it started out of the blue with Captain Wentworth. Did Kira know this man, or did he wear a disguise each time? Was it one man or a group of men masquerading as classic

characters? There were so many unanswered questions about the whole curious affair. Suddenly, he was reminded of the day that Kira rose early for work. From memory, he could see her wearing a jade dress, her hair was lying on her shoulders instead of in a clasp or up in a ponytail. He recalled that she had on a little more make-up than usual, her perfume was different to anything he had ever smelled on her before. His suspicions had been aroused that day, but she had become sexually flirtatious with him. Racking his brains, he tried desperately to remember what day of the week that had been. If it had been the Thursday, then his instincts had been correct. All he could remember was that he had met with the law firm, Darnley and Tod, first thing that day. The memory was clear because Kira had excited him, which had distracted him at the meeting. His head was filled with thoughts of what he would do to her when she came home later that day. Had it been a Thursday? He simply had to know. Reaching for his phone, he called his secretary, Lucy, at the office.
'Hello Lucy, I would like you to do me a favour. Look back in my diary, let me know what day of the week I met with the partners of Darnley and Tod, last year.'
'Oh, you've remembered that you work here. Do you have any idea what kind of mess this company is in? You could not possibly comprehend the extra work that I have had to put in and the decisions I have had to make on your behalf...' she ranted, until she was interrupted.
'Just do it!' he snapped.
'But I feel you should know...'
'Did you hear me, bitch? Do it.'

Turning the pages and looking back in the diary, she told him it had been on a Thursday she had met with the law firm. She then added, 'I quit.'
'Good, I couldn't stand you anyway.' When he ended the call, he did not spare a thought for the loyal, hardworking secretary who had been by his side as he climbed his way up the ladder of success.
Starting at the beginning, he thought through everything he knew. The only conclusion to be reached was that it was only one man, and she knew him. They were meeting every Thursday at various properties because she knew that he tracked both her and her phone. He turned back in the diary to the week before the meeting with Captain Wentworth. She must have met someone by chance that day, then arranged to meet every Thursday thereafter. Scanning the list of clients, there was no name that leapt out at him from the page. However, there was a score through one of her morning appointments, with the words 'swapped for Connie's 4pm' scribbled in pencil. This was a vital line of enquiry that he knew had to be pursued, all leads must be followed.
Jeremy picked up his phone again, this time calling the Ivan Cole Estate Agency. Disguising his voice slightly, he asked to speak to Connie. The last thing he wanted was a tongue lashing from Ivan. It was best all round if he kept the situation calm. No point in escalating matters by upsetting people, it would only hinder his investigation.
Moments later Connie was on the line.
'Hello, Connie here, how can I help you?'
'Hi Connie, it's Jeremy. I need a favour,' he told her.

'Hi Jeremy, what can I do for you?' Connie asked cautiously. Ivan had discussed the earlier events of Jeremy's behaviour with the staff.

'Could you look up a date in your diary for me. On Thursday 17th of January, last year, you swapped appointments with Kira on that day. You took her morning appointment, she did your 4pm. Could you tell me the name of the person that had originally booked the appointment with you?'

'Jeremy, I'm going to have to phone you back with that information. It's a long time ago now so I will need to search through to the beginning of last year. We are very busy today. I'll call you when things have calmed down a bit here. I'm sorry.' Connie's tone was abrupt.

'That's fine, Connie. I'll just sit by the phone and wait,' Jeremy said, hoping to gain her sympathy.

Connie came off the phone feeling agitated. *I really don't like that man,* she thought. *On the other hand, if he has found a lead in discovering what happened to Kira then I'm happy to help him all I can.*

From what Connie had heard from Ivan, she suspected that Jeremy was beginning to lose a grip on reality, which was understandable after everything he had been through. *I have an appointment in half an hour and a few things to do right now but will find the information Jeemy needs after that,* she decided.

Jeremy sat at the dining table staring at his phone. 'Come on Connie! What the hell are you waiting for, you dumb cow?' he bellowed aloud. Talking to himself had become commonplace in the past year. 'I need that fucking information, now! Stupid tart.' There had also been a marked increase in the level of rage within him. In truth, it had

always been there, but he now seemed to have lost the ability to hide it from the world.
Completely lost in thought for how long, he had no idea, he was given a jolt when there came a loud knock at the front door. Concerned that Connie would call when he left the room, he clutched the phone to his chest and rose shakily to his feet. When he opened the heavy storm door, he saw two gentlemen in raincoats, standing on the step. He stared at them.
'What?' he said grudgingly.
'Mr Jeremy Ward?' one of the gentlemen asked.
'Who wants to know?'
'We are here from the Bank of Scotland. We have tried to contact you on several occasions by phoning and sending reminders, but we have been unsuccessful. We need to speak to you urgently about how you have reneged on your mortgage payments over the past few months. You also have a substantial business loan with us for which no payments have been made for some time now. Could we come in to discuss possible solutions to this situation, Mr Ward?'
Jeremy looked from one man to the other. 'Fuck off!'
Banging the door shut, he left the men standing on the doorstep. There were far more pressing things to worry about. For a start, he was making serious headway in cracking a case that had lain unsolved for well over a year. Interruptions at this time would hinder his investigation.
'Come on, Connie! How long are you going to keep me fucking waiting here?' his voice echoed throughout the empty room.

An hour later, Jeremy physically jumped in his seat with fright when his phone began to play the William Tell Overture.
'Hi Jeremy, it's Connie. I've been through the dates from last year's diary and the client Kira was meeting on that day was a 'Mr F Jackson'. That's all I can tell you about it. Kira didn't mention anything about the viewing when I saw her the following day. Jeremy, Jeremy, are you there, Jeremy?' There was silence on the other end of the line.
Jeremy had ended the call as soon as he got the all-important name from Connie.
'Mr F. Jackson,' Jeremy said over and over to himself. The name didn't mean anything to him. Google search told him that he wasn't a classic. Perhaps it was time he paid a visit to Kira's parents. It wouldn't do any harm to run the name past them and see if they could come up with something.

Chapter 26

Fraser continued driving in the direction of the north of Scotland. They passed Inverness on the left, then drove on until they reached the town of Tain, which sat on the south shore of the Dornoch Firth. Entering the town, Fraser told Kira that it was the oldest burgh in Scotland. Pillars at the entrance to Tain displayed the date of 1066. He nudged Kira, who was looking in the opposite direction, to show her the how old the town actually was. Fraser told her all about the caravan holidays he enjoyed there when he was a boy. The thought of settling here one day had always appealed to him. Going on the run with Kira seemed like the perfect time to make the move. They drove along Tain's quaint main street with its bakeries, gift shops and boutiques. Bunting on the lampposts still remained from the summer gala although the flowers in the town's hanging baskets had now withered.
It wasn't long before the landscape around them turned from the grey stone of the Tain buildings to plains of flat countryside with occasional farm steadings dotted across the fields. The road they now travelled was long and straight. They passed a turning on the left for the small town of Inver which sat on the south east shore of Inver Bay. From the road, Kira could see the rows of terraced houses, a school with a playground and a large cross on the roof of a small building. The oversized cross made her think that perhaps God was more important to the community than the church building they worshipped in; she liked that idea. The unspoiled scenery around them was so appealing to Kira, not only was it beautiful but it was far, far away from the people who had hurt her. An odd sensation came over her, it

was the feeling that she was returning home, home to a place that she had never been to.
Fraser reached over to take her hand, telling her that they would be there soon. The further they travelled north, the narrower and more winding the road became. 'A few more minutes,' he assured her, 'I think you are going to love it.'
'I can't wait,' she said, squeezing his hand. 'Oh, look at all these pigs. I have never actually seen a pig in the flesh before,' she laughed.
'That's the local pig farm. It stinks a bit, but they are cute, aren't they?'
'Yeah, they are so cute. I always think that pigs look bare, you know, like they should be wearing clothes.'
Fraser laughed at this suggestion. 'Ah, now there's an idea that would keep you busy while I'm working. You could design a range of fashions for pigs. That will keep you out of mischief.'
Kira took a sharp intake of breath as they reached the top of the hill. A panoramic view of their new hometown was there, laid out before her. 'Wow!' she said wide-eyed. 'It is unbelievable.'
'Welcome to Portmahomack!' Fraser announced, delighted by her reaction.
The historic fishing village of Portmahomack was built with houses in tiers on the hillside. This ensured that most of its residents got a sea view. The harbour, with its many colourful boats, decorated the waters of the Firth. Fraser stopped the car to allow Kira to take in the picturesque scene.
'Fraser, it's perfect, absolutely perfect.'

'I'll drive down to the harbour to show you the town before I take you home to your new house.'
She laughed loudly, covering her face with her hands in excitement.
Fraser smiled as he looked at her animated response. *I can't believe how much I love this girl,* he thought, shaking his head.
They left the car parked on the main street to go down to the harbour's edge.
'Can we sit on the seat and just look out to sea for a while?'
'Of course we can,' Fraser laughed. 'We have all the time in the world.'
The woven sails on the small boats flapped in the breeze. Kira filled her lungs with the salty sea air which was blowing in across the water. A creaking noise from the quiet main street behind her made her turn to investigate. She saw that it was wooden sign, hanging horizontally, swinging back and forth on chains. 'Look Fraser, there is a sign for The Oyster Catcher Hotel and Restaurant. Is that what an oyster catcher looks like?' she asked, pointing at the black and white bird on the sign.
'Yes. They're nice aren't they. When the tide is out, you usually see them pecking in the sand for worms.'
'I'll look forward to that,' she told him. 'Hey, look at that ice cream shop. I'm not hinting or anything, but I could really fancy some ice cream.'
'I have reason to believe that you are hinting but sit here and I'll go and get us some.'
He returned soon after with two tubs of ice cream with flakes and sprinkles. Kira laughed when she saw them. She couldn't remember ever laughing during her time with Jeremy, now she couldn't stop. Everything made her happy.

Council bins sat every few metres along the harbour front. Kira took Fraser's empty tub and scoop from him, pushing them into the bin with her own. They walked arm in arm back to the car to head home to their new house.

The house was situated in a row of five new builds at the top of the hill. The front of the property faced the sea, so the back door was the most accessible for entering. Parking was also at the rear of the house. Fraser told her to close her eyes as he led her into the kitchen.

'Okay, you can open them now.'

No words would come to her as she stood staring with her hands over her mouth. The open space she was looking onto was a bespoke kitchen which led out to a tasteful lounge. What captured Kira's attention was the ceiling to floor picture window that framed the Dornoch Firth. Rooted to the spot, she took in the detail of her surroundings.

Fraser knew from her response that she loved it, but he waited to hear her say it.

All Kira could do was cry. What had she ever done in this life to deserve so much happiness.

'Oh, Kira, don't cry,' Fraser said gently, his heart sore with love for her. 'Let's just sit down and admire the view before I show you the upstairs. Can you believe that I'm showing you a house for a change.' He led her over to the elegant sofas which were angled towards the extensive vista of the sea.

'I can't thank you enough for everything that you've done for me,' she told him through her tears.

It was Fraser's turn to well up. 'I did it for us. I love you and I want to make you happy. Looking at you right now, I think I've failed in that mission.'

Kira laughed again; it didn't take much.
The upstairs was as inspiring as the rest of the house. The king sized, oak bed also faced the sea. Fraser thought that it would have been a crime to waste such a valuable asset. His study was located along the hallway, next to the shower room. It had been kitted out with all the office equipment he would need to carry on his business from home. The window of his study led out to a small balcony, which had the alternative back view of the fields.
'This is the most spectacular house I have ever seen,' she told him. 'How on earth could you afford it?'
'This house cost less that a flat in the city of Edinburgh. Trust me, I'm getting off cheaply.'
'I love the town and I love the house, but I could have gone anywhere with you and been happy.'
Without saying anything, he pulled her close, holding her tightly for a while, just to cherish the moment.
'Now, we have to discuss some important stuff,' he told her. 'I bought you some clothes to use for now, but you'll need to do your shopping online. I also picked you up a brown hair dye because we need to change your look. I don't know how much of a stir your disappearance will make but there will be people looking for you and if your fiancé is as unhinged as you say he is, then he won't give up until he finds you.'
He then asked, 'Do you think that you'll miss your parents?'
'Not in the least. I feel free for the first time. My whole life has been under their control. When I left home, I went straight under Jeremy's iron thumb. I am so happy that I can now make my own decisions and be with you. That's all I ever wanted.'

'Was Jeremy ever violent towards you?' he asked, slightly worried about his own reaction.
'Many times. He was violent and cruel, but it was the mental abuse that was the worst. He would humiliate me, make me feel that I was rubbish. I had nowhere to turn. I tried telling my parents once, but they didn't want to know. They told me that love didn't always run smoothly and sometimes we have to turn a blind eye to the bad things and just focus on the good. The sad thing was that there was nothing good in the relationship to focus on.'
She winced at the memory of the misery. It had been a dark secret that she had kept hidden deep for years. It felt rather healing to unlock it.
'No one can ever hurt you again. I am going to keep you so safe. In fact, I've got this great big roll of cotton wool to wrap around you,' he joked.
'Hey, that sounds great.'
'Right, you go and dye your hair, I'll go out and forage for some dinner for us.'
'Deal,' she told him. Lifting the hair dye from the kitchen table, she made her way up to the bathroom to transform her look. She didn't know when the right time would be to tell him the whole truth, but she decided to hold on to it for now. *I'll wait until we are settled into our new life. There's too much to think about at the moment,* she thought.

Chapter 27

Jeremy wrote down the name Mr F. Jackson and jotted down one other name from the diary, which was S. Marsden. He didn't know whether S. Marsden was male or female, it hadn't been the usual 4pm appointment but he wanted to have more than one name to take to Kira's parents.

Completely focused on his mission, he drove along the tree-lined drive of Kira's family home. It was a charming Georgian house on the outskirts of the city. He had the utmost admiration for the Carmichael house as it stood on its own, upon manicured sprawling grounds. The symmetry of the building appealed to him, as did the doorway which was flanked with Roman pillars. It really smacked of wealth and prosperity, which were two of the most important things in life, as far as Jeremy was concerned.

The wheels of his car crunched to a halt on the gravel at the front of the house. A fountain sat elegantly positioned in the centre of the gravelled carpark, and Jeremy dabbled his fingers in the water as he passed. *This is a touch of class,* he commented to himself. *When Kira gets home, we'll look for a property just like this, only bigger and better with a grander fountain.* He pressed hard on the doorbell, which he remembered being told was the original bell from when the house was built in 1769.

Celia came rushing down the curved staircase, sliding her hand down the polished oak banister.

'Jeremy!' she gushed, as she stood aside to let him enter. 'How perfectly wonderful to see you. Ramsay will be delighted that you've come. Ramsay! Ramsay! Guess who's here?' she shouted in the direction of the upstairs. 'Come

through to the kitchen, I'll make us all some coffee, perhaps I have some blueberry muffins in the pantry.'
Jeremy followed her through to the kitchen where she pulled out one of her newly upholstered chairs for him to sit at the table.
'How have you been, Jeremy?' she asked him.
'I've been coping. I have started to attend the spiritualist church where I live, and I have found great comfort in it.'
'That's wonderful, Jeremy. I too have been attending meetings at a church, in fact it's the big church which is on your street. I must drag you along sometime. It has been a Godsend for me over the past few weeks. You see, Ramsay has been working on solving Kira's case. He goes into his study early in the morning, he doesn't come out until bedtime. I swear that he is so close to cracking the case; in fact, it could be any day now,' she explained, as she poured hot water from the kettle into three mugs.
'That's great news, Celia! It would be fantastic to have Kira back safe and sound,' he said, humouring her.
Celia then lifted the postcard with the picture of Mull from the shelf.
'Jeremy, look at this pretty painting of Mull. I had such a lovely idea when I saw this picture. I decided that when Kira comes back, we will all go to Mull for a holiday. We went once when Kira was small. We stayed in a beautiful five-star country house hotel in Pennyghael. It was a truly wonderful time. I think that it is exactly what we will all need once this is over. Don't you agree?'
'Yes, that sounds just the ticket.'
Ramsay appeared at the kitchen door. 'Jeremy, how are you old boy?'

'Oh, you know, plodding along, day to day. How are you? I hear that you've been working on Kira's case?'
Ramsay pulled out a chair from the table and sat down. 'Yes, Jeremy, I've been working flat out. Researching, cross-referencing, investigating and following every possible clue. It hasn't been easy, I am exhausted,' he said, making an exaggerated gesture of being tired.
'Celia says that you're making a bit of headway,' Jeremy continued, curious to know what he had found out, if anything.
'I've made a lot of headway but it's all pretty confidential at this stage. I'm keeping a lid on it until I'm finished then, boom, I will blow the lid off the whole case. The Keystone Cops will be left with egg all over their inadequate faces.'
Jeremy gave a fake guffaw. 'Good for you Ramsay. Thank goodness you are here.'
Celia sat a tray of blueberry muffins on the table. Turning to Jeremy, she asked, 'To what do we owe the pleasure of your company?'
'I was really just coming round to touch base, check that you guys were doing alright, under the circumstances. I'm glad I came because I can see that you two have been keeping busy and staying positive.' He didn't quite know how to broach the subject of the names that he had intended to run past them.
'That was terribly thoughtful of you, Jeremy, because I know that it certainly hasn't been easy for you either. We are here for you whenever you need us,' Celia added, patting his hand gently.

'Yes, good point Celia,' Ramsay confirmed. 'We are here for you whenever you need to talk. We are all in this thing together. As far as we are concerned, you are already family.'
'Thanks folks. I feel the same about you two.'
They sat together, drinking coffee and eating blueberry muffins. Apart from Kira's disappearance, they had very little to talk about, but Celia kept the conversation going by telling them about the heartbroken people at her meetings who had lost a loved one. This was the first opportunity she had been presented with to actually talk to Ramsay. All the news of her meetings at St Mary's came as a surprise to him. He had no idea that she was even out of the house.
Jeremy was not remotely interested in Celia and her ridiculous meetings; after all, meetings never solved anything. He found himself becoming extremely irritated with her and although he nodded away with interest, he thought to himself, *Shut the fuck up, you pathetic woman.*
When Celia finally paused to take a breath, Jeremy stood up to leave. 'Sadly folks, I must head off now as I have so much to catch up on.' As he walked over to the door, he casually stopped, turning to face them, 'Oh, while I'm thinking about it, could you tell me if you recognise either of these two names, F. Jackson or S. Marsden?'
Celia and Ramsay stared at one another with a similar look of shock on their faces.
'Why do you want to know?' Ramsay asked, in a change of tone.
'No reason. They were just names that came up at my meeting at the spiritualist church. Are either of them familiar to you?' he probed, spotting some recognition in them both. *Ah ha,* he thought, seeing that he had hit a raw nerve.

'We make it a rule not to lift the name of Fraser Jackson in this house, thank you very much!' Celia said, with arms folded.
'Celia's right. It's not a name that we care to speak about. In fact, until recently we had managed to forget all about it,' Ramsay added.
'Could you give me a little bit of background on him? The last thing I want to do is upset you both but, trust me, I wouldn't ask if it wasn't important. Remember we are almost family and as you said yourself Ramsay, we are in this together,' Jeremy coaxed.
'Go ahead, Celia,' Ramsay encouraged, with his blessing.
'Well, it's a long story so I'll cut it short. Kira met a dreadful, common boy at university. He was not our cup of tea at all.'
'That's putting it politely, Celia,' Ramsay chipped in.
'Kira was sneaking out of the house to see him, even after we had forbidden her to have anything to do with him. It was a terrible time for our family,' Celia told him.
Ramsay laid his hand on Celia's back, echoing the sentiment. 'A terrible, terrible time, as Celia said.'
Jeremy could feel his knees shaking, his fists clenching.
'So, how did it end?' he asked, fighting to keep the rage tucked up inside him.
'We would rather not talk about that, Jeremy. Let's just say that we had to make him disappear; vanish if you like,' Celia admitted.
Huh, now that's ironic, Jeremy thought.
'Come, come Celia, you make it sound like we murdered him. We're not the mafia!' Ramsay said, putting the record straight.

‘So, where does Fraser Jackson live now?’ Jeremy asked, as casually as he could muster.
‘I have no idea. I can tell you where his parents live though,’ Celia said helpfully. ‘Although, I must confess that it is not an area that I would choose to frequent.’
‘Do you remember the names of any of her other friends from University?’ he asked, hatching a clever plan in his mind.
‘Oh, now there’s a question,’ Ramsay said, scratching his head. ‘My memory is not what it used to be. Celia, can you come up with any names of Kira’s friends?’
‘I remember the girl Robertson and George Roxburgh but that’s about it,’ Celia told them.
‘It doesn’t matter. It was just a thought,’ Jeremy said, finding it very helpful.
Ramsay stood up to walk Jeremy to the door. ‘Now, are you going to tell us what this is all about? You say Fraser Jackson’s name came up at one of your meetings. How is this connected with Kira? I don’t understand. Tell us what you have found out.’
Jeremy edged closer to the front door. He didn’t quite know how to explain this information away. ‘Listen Ramsay, it’s nothing. The clairvoyant mentioned many names when I asked for information about Kira. Perhaps this Fraser Jackson has passed away and was making contact from the other side. We’ll probably never know. If I find out anything, you’ll be my first port of call, I promise.’
‘Thank you,’ Ramsay said, resting his hand on his shoulder. ‘You are a fine young man, Jeremy. I will be proud to have you as my son in law.’
Jeremy gave him a bashful smile. *Idiot,* he thought, as he left.

Chapter 28

Fraser walked past the harbour towards the new house, laden with bags. There was locally caught fish with chips for their dinner and a bottle of red wine to wash it all down. There had been a small corner shop open, in which he had picked up toothpaste, toilet paper, soap, milk, bread and butter. A bucket containing bunches of fresh flowers had caught his eye whilst standing at the checkout. *I will take two of these bunches home to my girl,* he had decided. *She'll probably laugh when she sees them, she laughs at everything.* An image of Kira's happy face made him grin. The words of his Granny Jackson returned to his mind, 'What's for you, won't go by you.' How many times did she say that to him when he was growing up; countless. *Granny, if you are looking down on me now, let me tell you that you were right on the money.*

Kira's parents had gone to such lengths to split them up, but gravity had drawn them back together again. *Life is full of surprises. I have got to be the luckiest guy alive.* He whistled his way along the hilltop road carrying the supplies and the two bunches of flowers.

'I'm back, Kira!' he shouted. 'I've got us some dinner and a few essentials.'

Hiding around the corner of the door, she shouted, 'Don't get a shock when you see me!'

Appearing out from her hiding place, she walked towards him, revealing her new head of raven coloured hair. She no longer looked like Kira Carmichael.

Staring at her for a moment or two, his processed what he was seeing. 'I love it,' he announced. He didn't really, but he loved her regardless of the colour of her hair.

'How does this look?' she asked him, highlighting the grey tracksuit that she had found in the holdall.
'It looks great. You could wear a potato sack and you would look like a princess.'
'Fraser, I can't tell you how good it feels to wear baggy, comfortable clothes. I love these,' she said, rubbing the fabric. 'Now that I'm allowed to wear things like this, you'll never see me in a dress again.'
'Oh yes, I will. I've told you before, I will see you in a long white dress and veil soon enough.'
Together they sat at the dining table, eating fish and chips from the newspaper. There were no glasses in the house, but the wine tasted just as good from tumblers. They talked, planning their future as they drained the last of the bottle. After dinner, they moved through to the lounge where they sat watching the sun slide down below the horizon. They did not move from their seats until the remaining golden yellows of the sunset disappeared, and night took over. Eventually, all that could be seen in the darkness were the twinkling lights of Dornoch, the town across the water. It was agreed that an early night was in order, mainly because they were both excited to spend their first night as a proper couple, waking up together, side-by-side, in the morning.
Kira was awakened by the silence. Having only known city life where the traffic only eased through the night, the stillness was going to take a bit of getting used to. Sitting up in bed, she looked around the room which was lit only by the glow of the moon. When she saw the sleeping man beside her a rush of love caught her heart. It was difficult to believe that she was really here, in this small village in the north of Scotland, lying next to Fraser Jackson. *I wish it could*

stay like this forever. If only it were possible to ignore something to make it go away.

*

The rays of the morning sun on her face stirred Kira from her sleep. Reaching her hand over to touch Fraser, she felt only the soft pillow beside her. *Where is he?* she wondered. *Can I smell breakfast cooking?* The aroma of bacon brought her downstairs to see what was going on.
The sight of Fraser standing at the stove cooking made her laugh. Her phone lay on the kitchen table and she pressed it to check the time. 'Oh, my goodness,' she announced in horror. 'I can't believe the time. I'm so sorry. I have never slept this late in my entire life.' She fumbled with her tousled black hair.
'I'm happy that you lay in. We'll need to order you some slippers,' he told her, looking at her bare feet.'
'That would be nice. When did you get up?'
'I went for a run this morning. I picked up bacon and eggs on my way back. Oh, and I almost forgot, I saw a sign for something that I thought you might like,' he told her. 'Sit down and close your eyes.' From inside the porch, he collected the large box for Kira.
'Right, you can open your eyes now.'
'Oh, it's a very big box,' she said, laughing with excitement. 'What is it?'
'Look for yourself,' he told her, 'but be gentle.'
This comment made her throw him a curious look. She knelt down and slowly opened the lid. Two large, chocolate brown eyes looked up from within the box. To her sheer delight, she saw that it was a black and white puppy.

Ever so carefully, she lifted him into her arms. 'I have always wanted a dog of my own. I can't believe you got him for me.' She kissed and hugged the little animal.

'The sign caught my eye; it said, 'Puppies free to a good home'. He is just a little mongrel, half collie and half pointer, but isn't he cute? He's had all of his jags so we can take him out anytime. I thought he would give you something to do when I'm working through the week.'

'We'll need to order him a basket, a collar and lead. Oh, what do you think we should call him?' she said, hardly able to contain her excitement.

'I thought Darcy would be the most fitting name,' Fraser suggested. 'It came to my mind when I was carrying him up the hill.'

'Darcy it is,' she agreed, kissing and petting the new addition to their family.

'Kira, there is one more thing I picked up when I was out. I think you should see it.'

Fraser handed her the newspaper from the kitchen worktop.

The tone of Fraser's voice had changed; she sensed it immediately. Opening up the folded paper, she stared down at the picture of herself on the front page. The headline simply read 'Missing'. The photo was of her standing outside her house in Palmerston Place with a pretty dress on, a strained smile fixed upon her face.

The memory of the day the photo was taken instantly flooded back to her. She and Jeremy had just been to the lawyer's office to pick up the keys of the new house. There was no excitement on her part as she never wanted the house in the first place. Even with the very substantial amount of money that their parents had given them towards it, they still couldn't truly afford it. Jeremy had asked his accountant to 'cook the books' in order to make it look like they could easily manage the mortgage payments. The bank had been a little suspicious of Jeremy's exaggerated earnings, but Kira's father stepped in, had a word with them and, from then on, the bank was delighted to lend the money. She often wondered what offer or threat her father had made to the bank manager to make him become so obliging. Looking at the photo now, she relived the day that it was taken. Jeremy had told her to stand outside the house so that he could photograph her. As she stood waiting with a fixed smile on her face, he said, 'Move away from the house a little, I can't get the full extent of its size in the picture.'

On that day, she realised that he was not photographing a momentous, happy memory in their lives, he simply wanted to send this picture to people that *mattered* so that they could see how well he was doing.

That day had been so unhappy for her because the house joined them together by debt. It was the first shackle to be locked around her ankle. It was so typical of Jeremy to give this photo to the police. If he had looked closely at her face, he would have seen that her smile was fake. Every bit as fake as the love he believed she had for him.

Fraser watched her staring at the photo. 'Are you having regrets?' he asked.

'Are you joking! Quite the reverse. I am so happy to be out of that world and living in this quiet village with you and Darcy.'

'We'll make a point of not reading headlines or watching the news. It is better for us if we don't know what's going on in the outside world. Do you agree?' he asked her.

'One hundred percent. Whatever is going on back in Edinburgh, it will calm down. Soon they will all forget that I was ever alive. Now, can we take this little dog for a walk somewhere quiet?'
'Everywhere around here is quiet, but I'm going to show you a place that I visited when I was a boy. When we're ready to leave, wear the jacket that I brought for you. If we see anyone, you'll need to remember to pull up the hood and keep your eyes focused on the ground.'
They ate breakfast, played with the pup, then planned their day. Kira carried Darcy upstairs to stay with her whilst she got ready. It made her so happy to have a little dog, because it had never been a possibility in her previous life. Jeremy despised dogs, he presumed that she did too.
Fraser took Kira to Tarbat Ness Lighthouse, which was a short car journey from the village of Portmahomack. After parking in the carpark, they walked out onto the Tarbat Ness peninsula, feeling the bracing wind and the spray of the sea on their faces. Darcy walked alongside them until they reached the lighthouse where the land narrowed to a point. Seeing her little dog trembling, she picked him up and zipped him into her heavy jacket.
Fraser told Kira that they were walking on the North-East tip of Scotland. 'I will show you on a map when we get home. This is the recognisable jutting out part of Scotland.' He went on to explain that the spot they were walking on was originally the site of an old Roman fort which had latterly been used as a witches' coven. All kinds of demonic practices had taken place there according to the villagers' accounts in the history books.

Something in the sea caught Kira's attention. 'Look, Look!' She pointed at two seals poking their heads out of the water. 'I have never seen a seal before.'
'If you stand here long enough,' Fraser told her, 'you'll see fantastic sea birds and pods of dolphin too. It's quite a magical place. How's the wee pup doing?'
'Just fine. He's snuggled in like a baby, sleeping.'
Fraser put his arm around Kira's shoulder and told her that he couldn't be happier.
'Same,' she replied instantly.

Chapter 29

Jeremy kerb crawled along the street where Fraser Jackson's parents lived. He was looking for Number 14. The bungalows were so boringly boxy, he wondered how the residents even told them apart. They were identical in every way, apart from the odd one where the owner had been adventurous enough to add a dormer window to the roof. *How can people live like this?* he thought in disgust. *No wonder Kira's parents disapproved of her getting involved in this pitiful world. They can't even show the house numbers clearly; fools.*

After driving to the top of the road, then back down the other side, he eventually found number ten. On the presumption that the next house was twelve, then fourteen would be the one after that. Parking across the street, he scanned all over the property for a house number. Bingo! There it was, above the doorbell. Walking casually up to the house, he rang the bell twice. The outer storm door was already open, revealing a glass door with a deeply etched star-shape in the centre. An unremarkable looking woman, who he presumed to be Mrs Jackson, walked through from the back of the house. She displayed what he would describe as a welcoming smile, as she opened the door. Why wouldn't she? It wasn't every day that a man of his calibre would come knocking.

'Hello, can I help you?' she asked pleasantly.

Jeremy's face broke into an ear-to-ear smile. 'Mrs Jackson!' he blurted out, with exuberant enthusiasm.

'Yes,' she said, subconsciously adopting his vivacity.

'My name is George Roxburgh.' He thrust his hand out towards Mrs Jackson to shake. 'I'm a very good friend of

Fraser's. We went to university together. I'd love to have a catch-up with him. Can you tell me where I can find him?'
Jeremy's attuned senses detected a change in Mrs Jackson's demure. She appeared to cool off a little.
'No, I'm sorry. I have no idea where Fraser is at the moment,' she said, taking a step back into the house.
Jeremy moved towards her, while she edged back further. 'Look Mrs Jackson, I just want a word with Fraser. That's not too much to ask, is it?'
'I've told you that I don't know where Fraser is.'
She attempted to shut the door over, but Jeremy stuck his foot in the way, preventing it from closing. Mrs Jackson was finding him extremely menacing. The moment he said he was George Roxburgh; she sensed that she could be in danger. She knew George very well and this was not him.
Jeremy overpowered Mrs. Jackson, barging his way into the house.
'Could you please leave or I'm going to phone the police,' she warned him.
'Oh no you're not, Mrs Jackson. You are going to be a good girl by giving me the information that I have come for. I am not trying to frighten you, but I will get angry if you don't give me what I'm fucking looking for!' His voice raised to a shout as he pinned Mrs Jackson against the wall with his arm across her throat.
'I can't tell you what I don't know,' she choked.
'How about you have a really good think about it.'
His eyes narrowed, watching her blubber like a baby, so he decided to help her remember. Raising his clenched fist up from his side, he rammed it into her stomach, with the weight of his full strength behind it.

Screaming in pain, she bent over double. This man was truly terrifying, he was inside her home and there was no escape.
'Does that help you to remember anything, Mrs Jackson?' he asked her, oh so sweetly.
'I don't know where my son is, please believe me, I don't know,' she sobbed.
This time Jeremy curled his hand up into a taut ball. As quick as a flash, he smashed it into Mrs Jackson's face, causing blood to appear from a gash on her cheek.
'How about now? Remember anything? Need any more help with your memory or is it coming back to you?' he said with mock kindliness.
His focus moved to the semi-circular table standing against the wall behind Mrs Jackson. The mobile that rested upon it interested him greatly. Throwing Mrs Jackson to the ground like a discarded rag doll, he stepped over her to reach for the phone. Now this was something that could really help him.
'What is your security number?'
'There is no password on the phone. Just take it and go,' she pleaded, slumped across the floor.
'Anything to oblige,' he replied, taking a balletic leap over her whimpering body, saying, 'Whee,' as he went. Before he stepped out the front door, he turned to say, 'I think you should try to be more helpful to people in future. Now, don't worry, I'll see myself out.'
Mrs Jackson crawled through to the lounge, clutching her stomach. All she could do was wait for her husband to come home. The intruder had made it impossible for her to contact anyone when he took her phone. Even if she could get to a phone, she had not memorised any mobile numbers.

The frightening reality for Mrs Jackson was that this man was capable of anything, and he was now after her precious son. The only thing she could take comfort from was that the text messages from Fraser did not reveal his whereabouts. She had no idea where Fraser was, and she certainly didn't know what the hell he was involved in. Reaching for the tartan travel rug from the back of the sofa, she draped it around her shoulders. The shock had left her cold and traumatised. She remained shivering in the same position until she finally heard the sound of her husband's car pulling up to the side of the house.

A mischievous smile spread across Mr Jackson's face when he pulled into the driveway of his house. He reached over for the bag of prawns he had bought on impulse at the seafood market. The household cookbook had a recipe for spicy prawns, which happened to be his wife's personal favourite. The plan was that he would tell her to put her feet up, then surprise her by making the dinner; who knows, he may even do the washing up. The prawns came with their tails and heads on; they would be tastier that way. Saliva began to build up in his mouth at the thought of the spicy prawn dish. Perhaps he would open the bottle of Sauvignon Blanc that he had been saving.

'I'm home!' he shouted, walking through the front door. 'Have I got a surprise for you, lady.' Passing the lounge door, he headed towards the kitchen but was soon stopped in his tracks when it registered to him that his wife was sitting with her head in her hands.

'In the name of God,' he yelled, dropping his bag. 'What's happened?'

When she took her hands away from her face, he saw her swollen, bleeding face. 'Who did this?' he raged. 'Who the hell did this to you?'
Mrs Jackson cried uncontrollably when she attempted to tell her husband the events.
'You see, it was when he said that he went to university with Fraser and that his name was George Roxburgh, that's when I knew something was wrong. He looked nothing like Geordie Roxburgh. He was so angry. He was terrifying. He came into the house after he hit me and took my phone.' She began to cry again.
Mr Jackson stood up and announced, 'Right, we're getting the police involved. I'm going to call them.' When he picked up his phone, Mrs Jackson snatched it from his hand.
'No, we can't phone the police. Something is wrong, Bill. Fraser must be in trouble. His last contact with us was several months ago when he said that he could no longer be reached on his mobile. The message informed us that he would get in touch when it was safe to do so. Safe from what?'
Thinking back, Mrs Jackson had puzzled over her son's message, but she simply assumed that he was going travelling again. The visit from the unwelcome caller now made them both realise that there was a lot more to this than they cared to imagine.
'Do you think it could be anything to do with Kira Carmichael going missing?' Bill Jackson suggested.
'Well, I know he hasn't murdered her, if that's what you're thinking,' Mrs Jackson said, rationally. 'I don't know what is going on, but I don't want to get the police involved.'
'What if that man comes back?'

'I would be more prepared if he came back. I wouldn't open the door for a start,' she said, suddenly feeling braver and protective of her son. 'Wait, let me think what else Fraser said in that last text. He mentioned going to a place we took him to when he was a boy. I didn't think anything about that comment at the time other than, 'Oh, that's nice.' Where do you think that could be, Bill?'

Her instincts told her that regardless of Fraser's wishes, they needed to warn him that someone very dangerous was looking for him.

'Ann, I've been thinking about where we took Fraser was young. My guess is that he is up north in the area of Tain or Portmahomack, that was where we had our best holidays. He loved it there.'

'Yes, I think you're right,' Ann Jackson agreed. 'That horrible man will never find Fraser if he is up in Portmahomack, it's too remote. I hope he stays up there until it's safe.'

Chapter 30

Jeremy couldn't wait to get into the house to begin scrolling through the messages in Mrs Jackson's phone. He felt certain that there would be a clue of some sort to point him in the right direction. The progress he had made thus far was to be commended. It was not only his detective skills that stood him in good stead but his ceaseless perseverance that had assisted him greatly. *I am a cross between Sherlock Holmes and the Terminator,* he thought smugly. *After I follow the clues, I absolutely will not stop ever, until the job is done.*

Striding over the pile of final reminders that lay beneath the letterbox, he took Mrs Jackson's phone through to the dining room. He sat down purposefully on his designated detective seat. She had told him that no password was required. Sure enough, the stupid woman's contacts appeared on the screen; it was too easy. *Now, let's see what the golden boy's got to say for himself. Let's hope he's as thick as his mother.*

Starting with the first text from Fraser, he began reading through all the correspondence that followed between them.

Hi mum, held up with work stuff. Won't make dinner tonight.

Jeremy cringed at Mrs. Jackson's soppy reply of forgiveness, letting him off the hook completely. *What a pushover this woman is. Your son has obviously been made a better offer, mug.*

Happy birthday, mum. Have a great day. See you tonight.

Jeremy squirmed. *What a mummy's boy.*

Watched a great drama last night that I thought you would like. It's foreign with subtitles. 'Public Enemy'. Give it a go.

Jeremy shook his head. 'For fuck's sake! Who is this guy? He watches television programmes that his mother would like.'

How did you get on at the doctor's today? I hope you didn't play it down like you normally do!
'Stop pretending that you give a fuck,' Jeremy said aloud, despising Fraser more by the minute.
I'll be over about 6.30. Do you want me to bring anything?
'Yes, arsenic. Then drink it and give us all a break,' he responded.
Have I left my football boots at your house? Look in the cupboard in the hall.
'Look for them yourself, you lazy bastard.'
The texts carried on in that style for some time. Jeremy was unsure how much more of them he could stomach. *What could Kira ever have seen in a clown like that? A whole childhood in a boarding school would have sorted that guy out.*
The messages developed a different slant. Jeremy perked up.
Hi mum, I know dad is not one for texting so could you pass this message on to him too. I will be out of reach for a while. You won't be able to contact me on this phone. I'll get in touch as soon as it's safe to do so. Please don't worry. Love you both.
Jeremy read this with interest. 'Now we're getting somewhere.'
Fraser's mother replied, asking him where he was going.
I can't give you any details right now but think back to where you took me when I was a boy.
That was the final message to be sent from Fraser's phone.
Jeremy sat staring at the phone, thinking of a way that he could find out where the Jacksons took their son on holiday. Mrs Jackson must have an idea of where her son was, but he couldn't risk going to the house again to rough her up. She would be on her guard now and that was not the way he liked to work.

Holidays? he thought, attempting to conjure up images of places that he had been taken as a boy. *I can't remember any holidays. I have no memories of going away anywhere with my family.* Strangely, after all these years, the pain that he felt as a child, returned to him, causing tears to well in his eyes. Why did they always leave him behind while they travelled the world? Perhaps they didn't realise how lonely a vacated school was? *Man, those summer holidays felt like a lifetime. Even the matron saw me as an inconvenience. Who cares, she was an interfering old bag anyway.* There was one memory stored in his psyche which involved holidays, it was set in the formal lounge of his parent's home. Every solid surface in the room displayed gilt-framed photos of his mother and father standing beside various locations; the Leaning Tower of Pisa, the Empire State Building, Chichen Itza, the Taj Mahal, the list went on. The jealousy had gnawed away at him when he looked at their faces, tanned and happy. The only trips he ever went on were with the school; apart from that, he barely travelled further than the Fettes front gate. Another memory suddenly reared its hurtful head. He saw himself as a boy asking his parents if he could travel somewhere with them. Boy, had that given them a good laugh.

'Your school days are the best days of your life,' his father had told him once, when he had tried to explain how frightened he was of the older boys. 'It's time to man up, son. Your mother and I have sacrificed to send you there. It's high time you appreciated that instead of whinging about being bullied.'

This had been a most unpleasant trip down memory lane. He blamed the Jacksons for opening old wounds.

Back to the task in hand, he thought. 'Let me think,' he said aloud. He hadn't gone on holidays when he was a boy, but his parents had. How did he know this? Because there were framed photos of their happy trips displayed all around the front lounge. Could there be holiday photos displayed in the Jackson household? It was highly probable. There was only one way to take the investigation a step further; he would have to go back to their house, whilst they were asleep, to carry out a search of the property. If the Jacksons were not going to give out the information he required then he would have to go and take it for himself.

Chapter 31

Kira lay in bed a little longer than usual. It was so relaxing looking across the sea as she drifted in and out of sleep. It was only now that she was beginning to unwind from all the stress of the past few months, but it had taken its toll on her. Fraser woke her gently, placing pillows at her back to make her comfortable. Onto her lap he sat a tray of toast with marmalade and a cup of hot sweet tea, just the way she liked it.

'How are you feeling?' he asked her, pushing her hair back from her eyes.

'I'm absolutely fine. I think everything that has happened recently, has finally caught up with me,' she told him. 'I just feel exhausted.'

'Why don't you have a day in your bed?' he suggested. Darcy nosed his way into the bedroom, making a little yelping noise next to where Kira lay.

'No way, I'll eat my breakfast, then we'll take this little guy out for a walk. Take us somewhere else that you used to visit as a boy.'

'I have just the place,' he said, without having to give it much thought.

They had a leisurely morning pottering around the house, hanging out washing and generally tidying up. It was important to Kira to keep everything looking nice, mainly because she loved this house in a way that she had never felt for any other. The everchanging scene from the window brought her such joy. The weather or the time of day determined the colour of the sky, this in turn changed the

tonal shades of the sea and amidst all this, the pretty boats continued to bob away in the harbour; she just loved it.
During his morning run, Fraser had passed the local library. The sign on the window stated that books were being sold off for £1. He had gone in to select a few that Kira might like. He couldn't remember if she was a reader or not, but hopefully it would help to entertain in the hours she'd be left alone. His greatest desire would have been to spend every moment of the day with her, but the backlog of work had to be dealt with sometime. Their lifestyle was simple, but it still needed to be paid for.
After donning their outdoor jackets and footwear, Kira lifted Darcy's lead from a hook in the cloakroom. It made her laugh to see the little dog trying to contain his excitement while she fastened the leash to his collar.
'How do dogs know that you're taking them out for a walk?'
'Well, Kira, I think they make the association with the lead. They know that as soon as you clip the lead on, a walk will follow. It's not a highly intelligent assumption.'
'Okay, I agree but I still think it's clever that an animal can work that out. Now, where are you taking us today?' she asked, pulling on her hat.
'We're not going far. I'm going to take you to a place called Hilton of Cadboll. It's where the whisky 'Glenmorangie' is distilled. There is a lovely walk that takes you down onto the beach where we will hopefully see dolphins. I thought it would give Darcy a good run around.'
'That sounds nice,' she told him. 'I think I'll just hold Darcy on my knee for the journey.'
Although the sun was shining, the wind was unusually cold for the time of year. Closing over their jackets, they headed

down the tree lined path towards the beach. Hand in hand, they strolled with Darcy running to keep up. The trees hung over the path creating an archway to walk under. The arched pathway ended with the blue of the sea in the distance.
'Something very sad happened several years ago on this beach,' Fraser told her as they walked. 'Many porpoises were found dead one morning. They had been brutally slaughtered.'
Kira stopped on the path. 'That is so terrible. Who did it?'
'No one knew. It happened again weeks later. The people of the village were shocked that this could happen. They imagined all kinds of weird and wonderful theories but eventually they found out that the porpoises had been attacked and killed by dolphins.'
Kira's face looked shocked. 'Why would they do that?'
'No one really knows but it is thought that they became territorial.'
'Fraser, that's a terrible story! You shouldn't have told me that. I've always loved dolphins.'
'It was probably a survival thing. Maybe their food source was threatened and they needed to feed their young. Here's an interesting thing, did you know that there are many recorded cases of dolphins saving shipwrecked fishermen from icy waters? They have carried drowning men on their backs to the shore. So, does that restore your image of dolphins a little?' he asked, pulling her towards him.
'Nice save, Fraser. Yes, that's a much better story.'
They decided to unclip Darcy's lead. Like a bullet from a gun, he took off down the hill, running too fast for his short legs. Head over heels he tumbled, before getting up only to

tumbled over again, it was incredibly endearing. They shared his relief when he finally reached level ground.
They walked along the pebbled coastline, scanning the water for seals or dolphin. Darcy sniffed around the rockpools, rolling in anything that appealed to his senses. A large flat rock lay on the ground ahead of them. Kira to it and clambered on, Fraser joined her. It made the perfect lookout spot.
'Tell me about when you were young?' she asked him.
'When I was a boy, I liked to come down to this beach in my red swimming trunks to splash around in the sea, no matter what the weather was like. My favourite thing was standing on the shore trying to skim flat stones across the top of the water. I counted how many times it hit the surface; trying to beat my score from the previous time.'
'Can you still skim stones?' she asked.
'Can I still skim stones?' he repeated. 'Skimming stones is a skill that once learned, is never lost. It's like reading a book or riding a bike.'
Jumping from the rock, he began scanning the ground for flat pebbles. By the time he was finished, his pockets bulged with ammunition. Down at the water's edge, he stood with a flat stone between his fingers and thumb. Tilting sideways, he made a few mental adjustments then threw the skimmer horizontally. The stone splashed down into the water without skimming the surface.
'You'll find it easy enough to beat that score,' Kira heckled.
Completely ignoring her, he took another stone, blew on it for luck, then tried it again. It skimmed once, before sinking. From behind him, he could hear Kira laughing hysterically at his feeble attempts.

'Hold on, it just takes a minute to get warmed up,' he said, making excuses.

By the fourth stone, three or four skims across the surface could be counted. His determination was to be admired; he did not stop until the stones were skimming off as far as the eye could see. He took a bow when Kira stood up on the rock and gave him a round of applause. Darcy had waited at the water's edge, debating whether to chase the stones.

They walked back along the beach, then up the tree lined path. Halfway up the slope, Kira said, 'I need to stop for a rest for a moment. I feel so out of puff. It must be the change from city air to clean fresh highland air. My lungs don't know what the hell is going on.'

She rested on the wall for a few minutes until she felt ready to make the journey back to the car.

'Thanks for bringing us here, Fraser,' she said. 'I've had a lovely time, so has Darcy.'

'It was my pleasure. I've still got lots more places to take you,' he said, reaching for her hand.

'I can't wait.'

Chapter 32

Jeremy got dressed up in black jeans and a black polo neck jumper. Hurling everything out of his tidy drawers, he searched frantically for a black hat to complete his ensemble. The search proved fruitful, when he found a 'Thinsulate' fleece fabric hat, under one of the many shoe boxes. He admired himself in the long mirror which was on the wall at the top of the stairs. With the hat pulled down over his eyebrows, he posed like James Bond with an imaginary gun. Liking what he saw, he commented to himself, 'I'm a menacing, unseen shadow. I can go where I like, I can do what I like.'

To his surprise, the sensation of an erection began pushing hard against the tightness of his jeans. Oh yes, he was back in control, just the way he liked it.

Pacing the floor impatiently, he waited for the hour of midnight. All he wanted was to get in his car and head in the direction of the Jacksons' house, but timing was key. The whisky decanter caught his eye. *No harm in a small snifter just to take the edge off,* he decided. He splashed the whisky into the crystal tumbler, held it up to the light to check his measure, then topped it up to the brim. There was still at least half an hour to wait before he could leave, so the whisky would pass the time nicely. He made himself comfortable on the chesterfield and began to feel his taut nerve endings uncoil. It was a good idea to have a drink before the mission for medicinal purposes. The effects of the alcohol washed over him, making him feel deliciously invincible. Reaching over for the decanter, he debated

whether another stiff one would be in order. No, he decided against it, the witching hour was nigh.
On the opposite side of the street from the Jacksons' house, Jeremy took up his position. Shrouded by the darkness in his car, he watched the activity of the lights. The living room light, downstairs, had now gone out. The light at the top of the landing went on, as did the bedroom light at the front of the house. The landing light went off. The big light in the bedroom went off but a small light went on. Presumably, one of them liked to sleep whilst the other read with a bedside lamp on. *I will lie in wait, watching.*
It took longer than expected for the house to go into complete darkness. *They're late bedders for a couple of old cronies. I won't make a move yet, best to wait until ma and pa Jackson have safely arrived in the land of nod,* he decided.
When he sensed the time was right, he stepped out of the car, looking up and down the street for potential witnesses. The coast was clear and he made a run for it, moving stealthily across the road. Reaching the target property, he edged his way to the rear of the house, with his back to the wall .
'Phase one, complete!' he whispered, making a small ticking gesture with his finger.
Removing his fleece fabric hat, he scanned the ground for a rock of a substantial size. *Well, looky here,* he rejoiced. A neatly tended rockery with a varying range of stones was waiting to serve his purpose. It wasn't easy to make his selection in the darkness. In fact, the first two rocks he lifted were of an acceptable size but when he held them in his hand, he realised they carried no weight. Then hidden away under a flowering shrub, he spotted a beauty; big and heavy,

fit for purpose. His hat would act as a perfect silencer for the task. The large stone was fitted snugly into the hat before he closed his hand tightly around it. In his head, he counted one, two, three before swinging the stone-filled hat with full force at the window pane. Cracks appeared. *One more whack should see it right.*

Drawing the rock back once again, he thrust it with all his might at the already weakened glass. 'There she blows!' he whispered to himself, as the window caved into the kitchen sink.

The back door was located beside the window, he reached in with his gloved hand to find the bolts. As far as he could tell, there were two bolts which he was able to reach and draw back. He then retrieved his arm slowly back out of the jagged space in the broken window. *If my calculations are correct, I should now be able to enter the property.*

'Hell's fire and damnation,' he muttered under his breath. The door was still locked. He could only assume that there was a bolt somewhere on the door, which he could not reach. The only thing left for him to do was to pull out the large pieces of glass that remained in the window frame. It wasn't the outcome that he had hoped for, but it couldn't be all plain sailing. He was prepared for every obstacle that may be presented in his way. The minute you let a minor hiccup faze you, game over.

His leather gloves offered him valuable protection as he gently slid out the shards of glass. It was a slow, delicate process, but he took his time using a rewarding method which entailed wriggling the glass loose from the frame. Once extracted, the pieces of glass were laid out on the grass. This phase was carried out silently and methodically.

Before long, the frame was completely devoid of anything sharp that could hinder him. It was now time for him to climb nimbly through the space that he had created. The sink was directly behind the window, so reaching his hands inside, he held onto the side of the ceramic basin. Slowly, he pulled himself through the opening, sliding forward until his outstretched arms reached the floor. His feet and legs were through, he now had to simply slither forward until his whole body had passed over the sink.

He landed with an ungainly thump on the linoleum floor; he instantly sprung to his feet, brushing the splinters of glass from his clothes. Taking a moment to listen for sounds of the occupants, he concluded that they were still asleep. The property had now been entered. Phase two complete. Tick.

He glanced at the back door, noticing that there was a large bolt at the top. *It would have been impossible to reach that one,* he thought, sliding it back in preparation for his escape.

Now, he was going to prowl, cat-like around the house in search of family photos. Sounds of a bed creaking could be heard above him. Stopping in his tracks, he froze, waiting for silence. Silence came, allowing him to prowl again. What he was doing was dangerous, yet oh so thrilling. He could feel the familiar stirring in his trousers again; it felt good.

Leaving the kitchen, he entered the hall. There was a dining room to the right; he decided it was a good place to start. Photos in frames were set out on the sideboard; he took a closer look. The orange glow from the streetlamp gave just enough light for him to see. Studying the photo at close range, he saw the face of a dark-haired boy in his early twenties smiling up at him. The young man was laden with a backpack, the backdrop was exotic. His t-shirt replicated the

Rolling Stones' Sticky Fingers album. Jeremy knew exactly who this was; he despised the very sight of him. The large obnoxious tongue poking out from the t-shirt, made Jeremy feel enraged; it was personal. The cheesy smile and the cocky t-shirt were signs that he was being laughed at. 'You won't be smiling for much longer, halfwit,' he said, in a faint whisper.

He continued his silent search for photographs from the past. What he needed was an album of photos. Dropping down onto his knees, he quietly opened the cupboard doors on the sideboard. There were table mats, tablecloths and a pile of CDs, but no photo albums.

'Damn it to hell! Stupid fucking family,' he murmured.

I can't give up hope, he thought, *there is still a lounge to be searched.*

He left the dining room sharply as he couldn't stand to look at the face of the smug bastard in the photo for a minute longer. The sight of his arch enemy had stifled the arousal that he had been experiencing down below. Anger, coupled with revenge, broiled within him.

He'll get what's coming to him, he vowed to himself.

As he walked through the hall, he suddenly heard movement from upstairs. Someone was getting out of bed. There was the sound of footsteps walking across the room above. The footsteps entered another room. A door shut, a toilet seat clicked up or down, he couldn't say for sure. There followed a long flow of relief hitting the water in the toilet bowl. Flush.

'That's it, toddle back off to bed,' he whispered. 'Be a good Jackson and go to sleep.'

Standing statue still in the alcove under the stairs, he waited for the wonderful sound of silence.
When he was certain that the occupants of the house were asleep, he got back on the job. He tiptoed into the lounge, looking, searching for what he had come for. Unfortunately, no framed photos were on show. A tall cabinet displaying a few cheap bird ornaments, stood against the wall. There were four drawers under the shelf. Sliding the first one out slowly, he removed his glove in order to feel around the contents. It appeared to contain phone chargers, European and American adapters and cables of some kind. Gently pushing the drawer shut, he opened the second drawer, peeking in. The light was dim in the room, but from what he could make out, he had stumbled upon a most welcome sight. Stacked neatly in the drawer were four photo albums. It was more than he could have hoped for. He pulled them out, opening them, one by one. They were full to capacity with little square snapshots of the past that were going to lead him straight to Kira. He retrieved all four albums, then shut the drawer ever so quietly. Tiptoeing out of the room, he walked furtively along the hall to the kitchen where he had conveniently left the back door unlocked for a smooth exit. Phase three completed beyond expectations. Tick, tick, tick.
Once out the back door, he hastened round to the front of the house. Still remaining vigilant, he ran across the street and into his car. In no time, he was heading back in the direction of Palmerston Place. He gripped the steering wheel as he pressed his foot down hard on the accelerator. *Jeremy, my boy, you are one smooth operator*, he told himself, unable to keep the smile from his face and the swelling from his jeans.

He simply couldn't believe his good fortune. Not one but four, information packed photo albums were now in his possession. What was he going to uncover within the pages of the books; it was beyond exciting.
In the investigation headquarters, previously known as the dining room, he laid the four albums side by side. The temptation was to start the trawl immediately, but the hour was late, almost morning, and he knew that tiredness could lead to sloppiness. No, he would start afresh tomorrow, it would be something to look forward to. Now, he needed to rest. The evening had been a high octane rollercoaster and he had loved every minute of it. He could hardly wait for the next mission.

Chapter 33

Mrs Jackson felt a draught on her bare legs as she walked downstairs in the morning. Wrapping her dressing gown around herself, she tied the belt tightly at the waist. The house was colder than normal, and the sound of the traffic outside more audible. Something wasn't right. Nervously, she walked along the hallway, into the kitchen. The first thing she noticed was the broken glass in the sink. The window pane was gone, only the empty frame remained. Her heart thudded as she ran to the foot of the stairs, shouting for her husband to come quickly.

She ran from room to room looking for anything that was missing or out of place. Everything appeared to be as it should be.

Bill stumbled sleepily downstairs. 'Right, what's this all about?' he asked, rubbing sleep from his eyes.

'Come and see the kitchen window,' she told him, leading him by the hand.

'Oh, that is not good,' he said, heading to the cupboard which held the heavy duty refuse bags. Tearing one from the strip, he began carefully lifting the sharp splinters from the sink to the bag. 'I don't think we should jump to any conclusions here. It could have been a bird that flew into the glass. I mean, have you seen the size of some of these bloody crows?'

'Yes, I think you're right. Nothing has been disturbed or stolen. It's just unfortunate timing with that shady customer coming to the house yesterday.'

Mr Jackson thought for a moment, 'Maybe we should phone the police to come out and take a look around. It might put our minds at rest. What do you think?'
'No, I don't want the police, Bill. Not until we know for sure that Fraser is not in any kind of trouble.'
Ann Jackson left her husband clearing up in the kitchen whilst she went to the hall cupboard to fetch the hoover. Under the alcove, she saw what looked like two footprints. She switched on the overhead light then knelt down to inspect the prints more closely. Yes, unfortunately she was right, they were undoubtedly footprints, impregnated with splinters of glass. A cold chill enveloped her as she visualised the intruder that she had the misfortune to meet, standing, hiding in the alcove as they slept.
Bill stared at the kitchen window with the missing glass. *It may well have been a large bird that did this but since when did a bird ever clear out every piece of glass from the frame?* He peered through the empty space where the window had been, and sure enough, by way of confirmation, he saw the long fragments of glass laid neatly in a row on the ground. This information would be kept to himself but something drastic had to be done.
The electrical socket in the hall held the plug of the hoover. Bill flicked the switch.
'Hey Bill, can you push the plug of the hoover in. It must have come loose,' Ann shouted from the lounge.
'No, Ann, it hasn't come loose, I switched it off. We need to talk.' He joined his wife in the lounge, guiding her to the sofa to sit down.
'I've made a decision; I'm going to lift some of my pension pot to secure the house. It's time we got double glazing in all

the windows. Apparently, it helps to keep the heat in as well as the intruders out. I am also going to contact a security company to install cameras and an alarm. I think this is something we should have done years ago. We'll certainly sleep easier in our beds at night.'
Mrs. Jackson nodded in agreement. 'I think that's a great idea, Bill. There's no point in hanging on to money when we are feeling afraid in our own home.'
'That is so true, Ann. I'll get on to it today. First, I need to call a glazier.'

Chapter 34

Fraser started work early on the Monday morning. Much as he had enjoyed the time off, his business badly needed him back at the helm. The office space upstairs that he had created for himself was uncluttered, with no distractions. The desk and chair were intentionally positioned at the veranda doors, with the view across the fields behind him. Darcy was asleep in his basket in the kitchen, which meant that Fraser was unable to make coffee. If he wakened the dog, it would waken Kira, and he did not want to do that. She had been sleeping until lunch time most mornings and Fraser believed that it must be doing her good.

By mid-morning, he was still working his way through the pages of emails that had been left unanswered for the past few weeks. They were taking him longer than usual to get through as he had to start each one with a lengthy, heartfelt apology. He stopped typing for a moment, on hearing a noise coming from the hallway. In the quiet of the room, he heard scratch, scratch, whine, whine. The sound of a little paw scraping on the woodwork of the door made him smile. *The poor pup is looking for his breakfast and some company. I'll need to wake Kira,* he decided, reluctantly.

Darcy nearly fell over himself with excitement when the office door was opened. Fraser laughed at the speed of his wagging tail. As he scooped him up into his arms, the pup licked all over his face with his tiny rough tongue. They walked along the hall to the bedroom where Kira was sleeping soundly. Fraser took Darcy's paw, stroking Kira's cheek with it. She did not stir. Fraser put the dog on the floor

and sat on the bed beside the love of his life. He swept her damp hair from her forehead; her cheeks were flushed.
'Sorry to wake you Kira, but I can't get any work done because this little pest won't give me peace.' Darcy licked his hand.
'I'm so sorry,' she said, feeling embarrassed. 'What time is it?'
'It's after ten. He's just looking for food and a companion.'
'You must think I'm so lazy. I am normally an early riser. Leave Darcy here with me, you get back to your work.'
He kissed her, leaving the pup scrambling to climb up the duvet.
Kira got dressed into her grey tracksuit before heading downstairs with Darcy. The dog ate his breakfast while she took a cup of sweet tea through to the lounge to admire the view. The village of Portmahomack looked so pretty and yet the harbour area looked completely deserted. This made Kira think that it was a perfect time to venture out to explore her new surroundings. It would be best not to say anything to Fraser as she knew he would probably talk her out of the idea.
'Darcy!' she shouted, waving the red lead for him to see. 'Come and sit nice, we're going out,' The little dog did not need to be told twice, he was at her feet within moments.
They strolled past the five houses in the row which were similar to the one that she and Fraser owned. Taking a close look at them all, she decided that their house was the nicest by far. Darcy walked beautifully in step beside her as they headed down the brae that led to the harbour.
None of the harbour front seats were taken, they had their pick. Kira chose the one that she and Fraser had sat on that

first day when they arrived. Darcy was content to sit on her knee whilst she enjoyed the experience of being outdoors. The gulls circled and swooped overhead. What noise do gulls make? She listened, hearing squawks, cries, squeals. A story she had once read came to her mind. *The seagulls circle the shoreline when a storm is coming, they are driven away from the open water. What is the word that fishermen use to describe the sound they make? I can't remember. I think it begins with an 'm'. No, I can't get it.*

A storm was coming, a dark fateful storm and there was nothing that she could do about it.

I don't know how much longer I can hold onto this, she thought with a heavy sigh. *he needs to know. Oh, wait a minute! 'Mewing', that's what fishermen call the sound of the gulls.*

Kira suddenly became aware of someone standing to the left of her. It was an older woman and she was staring. Feeling unnerved, she got up from the bench to walk in the direction of home. The woman followed her on the other side of the street. Kira could see the woman pointing her mobile phone at her. *Is she taking a photo of me,* she wondered, pulling up the hood of her sweatshirt. Quickening her pace, she noticed that the lady was keeping up with her. Kira began panting for air. An overwhelming need to stop and rest came over her. Her legs were fatigued, her lungs burned. *Maybe I'm imagining things,* she thought, fighting to keep the panic at bay. *I'll catch my breath here. Hopefully she'll walk on.* As she stood panting at the wall, she glanced in the direction of her follower. To her distress, she saw that the woman had also stopped. *Who is she? Why is she following me? I wonder if she thinks I'm someone else.* With the little strength she had left in her, she forced herself to the top of the hill. To Kira's relief, the woman turned, walking back down towards the harbour. Kira sat down at the kitchen table, crying; the experience had really shaken her up. Darcy laid his head on her lap. She wondered if the little dog was comforting her.

It wasn't until Kira and Fraser sat down for the evening, that she mentioned the incident at the harbour.

'Kira!' Fraser said, trying to mask his exasperation. 'You can't go out to places where there are people. Your face will probably be on the news and on the front of newspapers. The public have possibly been asked to come forward with any sightings or information about you. You could jeopardise everything that we have here.'

'I'm sorry. I wanted to give Darcy a walk and give you some peace and quiet,' she explained. The idea of displeasing Fraser upset her terribly. Tears rolled down her cheeks as she sat silently scolding herself for her stupidity.

'Kira, Kira, your nose is bleeding. Put your head forward slightly. Look, pinch it here,' he told her, demonstrating on the bridge of her nose. The incident at the harbour had upset her more than Fraser had realised; he was worried that she was ready to crack under the pressure of being alone and housebound during the day. Soon there would come a time when they would be able to walk freely around the town, but these early days were crucial, as Kira's disappearance would still be fresh in the minds of the public. They needed to wait until the police had come to a dead end in their search for her.

'I'm so sorry,' she sobbed, holding the bridge of her nose. 'I know how hard you've worked to make our new life run smoothly. I could have ruined it all.'

'Don't upset yourself, there was no harm done this time. All I ask is that you be as vigilant as you can. If you really have to go out, then wear some kind of disguise. I promise it won't be like this for ever.'
'I give you my word that I won't take any more chances. That incident was enough to give me a fright.' Kira leaned her head on Fraser's shoulder. She couldn't allow herself to think about what would happen if Jeremy ever found out where she was.
Alma Glass-Waters had followed the girl up the hill. The hair was different, her frame was slighter, but she was certain it was the missing girl, Kira Carmichael from Edinburgh. Perhaps she would contact the police to report the sighting; after all, she did have photographic evidence.

Chapter 35

A resounding bang on the front door awakened Jeremy from his sleep. He decided to ignore it. It was probably just those goons from the bank. His spirits were sky high as the sun shone through the window onto his bed; he wasn't going to let anything spoil that feeling. Today, he had a very important job to do. Chuckling heartily, he imagined himself sitting at the table looking through the photo albums with an enormous magnifying glass. 'I am Sherlock the Terminator, nothing can stop me once I get the scent of the crime in my nostrils,' he announced, in a deep and dramatic voice. He laughed hysterically, secure in the knowledge that he was close, damned close. The net was closing in.

Instead of going straight to the dining room to start his photo album investigation, he decided to make himself a light breakfast. It had been a long time since he could be bothered to cook anything for himself; in fact, most of the time he had completely forgotten to eat at all. But today was different, this was the start of something new in his life. The long months of suffering in purgatory's waiting room were over, he was moving on to higher places.

The kitchen was bright, with sunlight shining across the breakfast bar. He whistled, 'Don't Stop Me Now,' whilst he prepared poached eggs on toast. A pot of strong Earl Grey tea would accompany it nicely. The sun streamed through the window, warming his face. *The sun shines on the righteous,* he thought, basking in the glory. Those albums were sitting waiting to be investigated, but he was going to take his time and simply enjoy the feeling of anticipation of what he may uncover.

When he could wait no longer, he headed upstairs to his bedroom to search through his walk-in wardrobe for the smoking jacket that he had inherited many years ago. The jacket had been given to Jeremy after the passing of his grandfather. He never really knew his grandfather, but he was told that he wore the jacket almost every day when he became housebound. Made from rich blue velvet, it had ornate silver buttons, its collar, cuffs and lapels were satin. It was highly suitable for the day's investigation.
Before sitting down at the dining table, Jeremy flicked up the hemline of his jacket, like a pianist would do before playing a masterpiece. He cleared his throat, then cracked his knuckles in preparation for his inspection. Every single photograph, which lay beneath the layer of protective cellophane, would be scrutinized closely.
Any photograph featuring a small dark-haired boy, was removed from the page. The first album was full of rich holiday pickings, giving him a healthy pile of potential evidence.
The second album was Mr and Mrs Jackson's wedding album; he discarded that immediately. The third album looked exceedingly hopeful as it contained many childhood photos of Fraser with his parents. The last album was a dead loss. Each photo was more sickening than the previous one. They were all photos of Fraser as a baby. The day he was born, the day he came home from the hospital, granny holding him, grandad smiling at him and so it went on and on and on. Jeremy slammed the album shut. 'That's quite enough of that rubbish,' he said aloud, feeling sick to his stomach. *This guy really knows how to push my buttons,* he thought.

In all, he had managed to salvage twelve photos from the books, and these would at least allow him to make a start. If he didn't find the information he needed from them, he would have no option but to go back to Mrs Jackson. This time he would show her just how serious he was about finding her son. No more Mr Nice Guy.
Jeremy scrutinised the pictures for any tiny detail that would point him in the right direction. The first photo was Fraser with his parents in a small boat out at sea. There was no name on the boat, there was nothing in the background but sea and sky. The next photo showed Fraser standing next to a boat in a harbour. *Clue number one,* he decided with glee.
The following two photos were discarded, but the one after that was very interesting. Fraser and his mother were standing smiling for the camera. In the background was a very distinct red and white striped lighthouse perched on the peak of a long peninsula. *Ah ha, a lighthouse,* Jeremy thought, rubbing his hands together in an exaggerated gesture. *I believe I have just found clue number two.* Zoning in on the detail of the picture, Jeremy noticed that Fraser had a little dog zipped into his jacket. *This family are beginning to make me sick. Do people like this really exist?*
There were beach photos with large nameless vessels in the background; useless. Then in one of the photos, a pod of dolphins could be seen in the water, and Fraser was standing on the shore pointing at them, laughing. There couldn't be many places in Scotland where dolphins could be seen. *Clue number three,* he nodded. The last photo was of Fraser and his father standing in front of a building. The name of the establishment was on a sign to the left hand side of the picture. Some of the lettering had been cut out of the photo

as the focal point was father and son, not the setting. The writing that could be seen in the photo read, 'Glen Mor'. This was his final clue to research.
Taking a pen and paper from the drawer in the dining room unit, he wrote:

Small harbours in Scotland.
Lighthouses in Scotland with bold red and white stripes.
Common places for dolphins to be seen in Scotland
Buildings named 'Glen Mor..' in Scotland.

Removing his laptop from the leather briefcase, he plugged it in to the socket to charge. He wandered through to the kitchen to make himself a cup of coffee, while he waited. It had been a successful morning; he was feeling positive about the results he had uncovered. A thought occurred to him that he may go down to the Sir Arthur Conan Doyle Centre later in the evening to find out if Claire Voyant was available to give him a reading. *Sometimes it's helpful to know what is ahead of you,'* he thought. *Forewarned is forearmed. After all, I do like to cover all bases.*

Chapter 36

Celia Carmichael never missed a meeting in the church hall. She had formed solid friendships for the first time in her life. Not the kind of friendships that she and Ramsay had with the couples in their circle. These were proper 'bare your soul' type friendships she had never experienced before. Each week when she arrived at the meeting, a man called Andy Wallace caught her eye with a wave to let her know that he had kept her a seat. The chairs were laid out in a circle so that everyone could see whoever was sharing their story. Celia didn't share her feelings often to the group, although she was very open as to whether it had been a good or bad week for her. On occasion, she would talk about Kira; how clever and successful she was, what a wonderful daughter she had been. Celia made a point of never talking about Kira in the past tense, that would infer that she was gone for good. As far as Celia was concerned, life would return to normal as soon as Kira was found.

Andy Wallace's son had gone missing in Thailand. He had gone on holiday with two of his friends where they had met a group of English girls. Apparently, he had arranged to meet with one of the girls on an isolated beach at night. That was the last time anyone saw him. In the girl's statement, she told police that she had headed back to her apartment around 11pm. The police suspected that he had gone for a swim whilst under the influence of alcohol and subsequently drowned. His father, Andy, knew that there was more to the story than the authorities were letting on. He shared his concerns often with the group, highlighting at one of the meetings that the same fate befell another young boy just like his son. He brought the newspaper along with him to read the story to the circle of fellow mourners.

Celia liked Andy Wallace. She looked forward to sitting with him each week at the meetings. He was a working-class man, slightly rough around the edges, with a broad Edinburgh accent. Andy was not the sort of character that she would ever associate with under different circumstances, but grief was grief, and it didn't matter who you were, the pain was identical. It was very flattering that out of all the attendees at the meeting, he chose to sit beside her, every week without fail.

Often, he pulled his chair an inch closer to Celia's; she liked when he did that. Sometimes she could smell him, the odour really appealed to her nose. It was an aroma of the leather from his jacket, aftershave from the cheaper end of the market and a slight whiff of alcohol. She would never have admitted it publicly, but Celia thought that Andy smelled sexy. His cheeky comments towards her made her laugh heartily. One week, when she arrived wearing a skirt a little shorter than usual, he shouted across the hall, 'Celia! You've got a great pair of pins on you.'

This comment had made her blush; her response was to giggle like a teenager. She thought about it long after he said it.

One evening after the meeting, Celia gave Andy a lift home in her Maserati. Whilst raving about her beautiful car, he told her that she was very fortunate to have such nice things. She had never felt fortunate before. Getting into her expensive car every day and driving it had not been worthy of a second thought. Having no money was not something that she had ever experienced, nor had she ever had to live in a small

house. All of these privileges in her life, were completely taken for granted. Not once did she ever spare a thought for anyone who had nothing.
Andy gave Celia precise directions to his home. Although they lived in the same city, she had never been along the streets that he led her down. Andy lived in a local authority house which he had bought from the council. He had painted it, double glazed it and landscaped the garden. It was obvious that not all of his neighbours took the same pride in their property as Andy did.
Pulling the car up to the front of his house, she waited for him to get out. It appeared that he wanted to sit in the car to talk for a while, which pleased her. Celia found him interesting to listen to and he took her seriously when she talked. Andy made her feel like a different person, which suited her fine because she hadn't liked Celia Carmichael for a long time. When he finally made a move to get out of the car, he had leaned over, kissing her cheek. He told her that the meetings had been so much better since she started coming to them. Celia blushed again, saying nothing. Taking the precious compliment to her heart, she locked it away to dwell upon later.
When Celia arrived home that evening, Ramsay was still shut away in his office. She shouted up the stairs to let him know that she was home. The reply that came back was more of a grunt than words of welcome. Climbing the stairs, she approached his study and knocked on the door.
'What? I'm busy,' he spat.
As she entered the room, Ramsay immediately switched the screen off.

'Ramsay, you've locked yourself away for months now. Surely there can't be that much evidence to dig up,' she questioned, appealing to him to come out and get on with his life.
'You don't know anything, woman,' he snapped. 'Do you want Kira back or do you not? I can't let you hinder the case for me. Now, go to your bed.'
Celia left the room, shutting the study door behind her. She went into her bedroom to change into her nightdress. A feeling of sadness consumed her as she sat on the edge of the bed with her head in her hands. Ramsay's study door suddenly opened, and she heard him coming out, but it was only to go into the bathroom. There was the sound of a flush, then the shower was switched on. It was an opportunity for her to creep through to his study for a snoop around.
There were stacks of papers, piled high behind the door. They were written in small, neat handwriting. Glancing at the top page, she could see that he had written information about missing people. There was documented information about every person he could find on the internet who had ever gone missing. There were teenagers, men, women, children and even old people who had gone missing from care homes. The people were from all over the world, dating back to 1960. The pages he had compiled came up to Celia's thigh. A tall stack of irrelevant nonsense that had been more efficiently stored on a computer. Seeing all of this, she realised that he hadn't researched anything, he had just written and written a lot of unnecessary information for absolutely no reason.
Clicking the space bar on the computer, she directed the mouse to the word 'history'. The images that appeared on

the screen before her made her feel physically sick, 'Big Latino Jugs', 'Hot Cheap Girls', 'Big Girls Are Hotter'. Disgust was all she could feel for the man she had shared the best part of her life with. *So, this had been his idea of finding Kira,* she thought, running through to the bedroom. Retrieving her discarded clothes from the chaise longue, she pulled off her nightdress and redressed herself. Taking her brown leather Louis Vuitton holdall from the wardrobe, she packed a few items of clothing into it. A Val Scott painting hung on the bedroom wall. Celia pulled the right hand side of the gilt frame towards her, revealing a safe behind it. When she entered Ramsay's father's date of birth into the keypad, the door mechanically opened. There were neat piles of cash sitting in rows; she helped herself to more than half of the money. The sound of running water from the shower stopped. Ramsay would be out soon. Dashing downstairs with her bag, she headed out the front door to her car, which was parked in the driveway.

Ramsay would think that she had disappeared the same way that Kira had, until, that is, he checked his computer. As soon as he entered his study, he would be faced with a tawny skinned young girl pouting at him, holding onto her enormous Latino jugs, on the screen before him.

Chapter 37

Kira loved highland life and everything good thing that came with it. She took Darcy on a short walk every day whilst Fraser was working. Carefully avoiding the village, she would go instead in the direction of the fields behind the house. While Darcy ran around chasing his tail and snapping at butterflies, she would sit on the fence, laughing as she watched him.

It was obvious that Fraser was becoming a bit stressed with the workload that had built up over the previous few months. Kira wanted to help him. She offered to do the books for the business although she had no experience in this type of work. Finally, he agreed, teaching her the basics over the course of three evenings. Kira was sharp, and she picked it up in no time. This new working relationship meant that Fraser's hours in the office were shorter, giving them more time to be together.

The skies were grey when Kira awoke on the Sunday morning. It was the kind of dull, drab sky that was fixed for the day; no breaks in the cloud. Although she was sleeping later in the morning, she did like to be dressed before she went downstairs. Seeing herself in the mirror, wearing only her underwear, she noticed that she could now see bones around her hips and ribs that were never visible before. Having always been curvaceous with a tendency to put weight on easily, she liked her new slender shape. The dark hair had really changed her look, but she now saw from her reflection that she was totally unrecognisable. She had to admit that she liked the new Kira the best, maybe because it represented the happiest phase of her life. When she pulled on her tracksuit trousers, they hung loosely on her frame. They would not stay up even when she tied the drawstring waist tightly. Something had to be done about this. Her image was more casual than it used to be, but she still wanted to look attractive to Fraser.

She peered her head in the door of the office. 'Excuse me love, do you mind if I order some new clothes on the internet? None of my stuff seems to fit me anymore. It must be all the walking I'm doing every day with Darcy.'

'Kira, you don't need to ask my permission for anything. Buy what you like, get whatever you need. Nothing here is mine, it's all ours,' he told her.

This was a stark contrast to her life with Jeremy where she was constantly reminded that he was the substantial earner in the household. He insisted on her seeking his permission for everything that she had ever bought.

In the late afternoon, Kira stood at the window as she always did, admiring the view. Taking her eyes off the sea for a moment, she looked down at the untended plot at the front of the house. Their home was newly built which meant that there had been no previous tenants to establish a garden. The summer would be arriving soon, so she decided to make it her project.

With a piece of paper and a pencil, she sat down at the kitchen table to sketch a plan of the garden. Trees, shrubs, bedding plants were all needed to spruce up the plot. The back didn't matter as it was used mainly for parking, but in the future, she would come up with ideas for that too.

Once she had researched all varieties of garden plants that would thrive at this time of year, she placed an order with a garden centre. Fast growing trees for privacy, flowering shrubs and pretty bedding plants were all on her list, as well as garden tools. Amongst her order was one small extravagance that she felt sure Fraser would allow her, had she asked him. It was a sundial which sat on a concrete column. It would be erected as a centrepiece on the lawn.

Darcy came into the kitchen looking for her, sniffing and whining to get her attention.

'Oh Darcy, we are going to have so much fun doing the garden.'

The little dog looked up at her.

'No digging up plants and no burying bones. Okay.'

I don't think I'll tell Fraser about the garden project. I'll keep it for a surprise, she decided. *On the other hand, that would be two secrets that I would be keeping from him. Is that fair?*

Chapter 38

It took Jeremy just under two hours of research to find out that the lighthouse in the photos was Tarbat Ness Lighthouse. With the help of the internet, he worked out that the Moray Firth, which is in the same area as the Lighthouse, was a popular location for dolphins. By matching the photo of the harbour with images of harbours in the area, he found a perfect match to the village of Portmahomack.

The last piece of the jigsaw to confirm the location was the discovery of the Glen Morangie whisky distillery. As soon as he had searched the words 'Glen Mor', the homepage for the whisky appeared on his screen. The webpage explained that it was known as the distillers of Tain who had been honing their craft for more than 175 years. It also told him that it was situated near the harbour village of Portmahomack. Jeremy smiled because accompanying the useless information about the whisky, was a photo of the distillery. If the father and son Jackson idiots were removed from the picture, it would be identical to the one on the screen.

The name Portmahomack had resonated with Jeremy, he had a feeling that he had heard it before. That evening, he had lain in his bed, staring at the bowls of fruit in the cornicing, when a sudden realisation struck him. Amongst all the witnesses that came forward with claims of Kira sightings, there had been a woman from Portmahomack who had taken a side-on photo of a girl. The memory of the photo had come back to him. He recalled the dark haired, skinny girl in the picture. She had been wearing a baggy grey tracksuit, and a little dog on a red leash had been walking by her side. He remembered that the facial features were a good match to

Kira, but the rest of her did not fit the profile. *Good disguise,* he thought. *That bitch has thought of everything. What she doesn't realise is that you have to get up a little earlier in the morning to outsmart Sherlock the Terminator.*
The next plan of action would be to go to the police to ask them about the witness statement. Hopefully, he would be able to ascertain the address of the house in Portmahomack where Kira had been seen entering. When he had that information, the next stop would be a visit to his parents' house, as there was something there that he badly needed. He would call round on the pretence of enquiring about their well-being, then he would sneak through to 'borrow' the essential item without anyone noticing.
The evening air was mild, almost warm, Jeremy had noted, as he strolled down to the Sir Arthur Conan Doyle Spiritualist Centre. He had no idea what events were on, but he thought he would go in to see what was happening. There was something mystical about the atmosphere that he relished. Perhaps it was the mystery of the unknown that he liked, or the idea of being armed with inside information. A warm welcome always awaited him as he walked through the door. He would even go as far as to say that the people on the door made a bit of a fuss of him. Something in his demeanour must have led them to believe that he was successful and highly thought of. *I wonder if they would be so kindly to me if they knew what I was planning,* he sniggered to himself.
The doormen approached Jeremy, asking him if he needed any help finding what he was looking for.
'Well, actually, I was hoping that I could meet Claire Voyant for a private reading. I don't have an appointment, but it is

rather urgent,' he said, trying to appeal to the softer side of the gentleman's nature.
'I'm afraid Claire is not here this week. We have a male psychic on tonight who is new to us, but he comes highly regarded. His name is Walter Bailey-Hardwick. He's here for one night only this month. Would you like me to ask if he has any openings in his schedule for you this evening?' the man asked helpfully.
'I had hoped for Claire, but I may be open to the new psychic if he's available. I'll wait here you whilst you ask him,' Jeremy said, feeling disappointed.
Two of the regular ladies approached him in the foyer, to offer a little conversation whilst he waited. He was charming towards them until he saw his messenger. 'You really must excuse me,' he told them, leaving them in mid-sentence.
'Mr Bailey-Higgins will see you now Mr…eh?'
'Ward, Jeremy Ward.'
'Mr Ward. May I inform you that he is due to start his booked appointments in half an hour. I told him that you needed to see him urgently, so he has fitted you in.'
'That was terribly good of you. I'm very grateful. I shall be putting in a good word about you to your superiors,' Jeremy lied.
The helpful gentleman reddened with embarrassed. His manner became over helpful to the point of being annoying as he showed Jeremy upstairs to the medium.
'Here, let me get the door for you,' the man offered. 'I'll show you in myself. There you are. Let me introduce you to…'
'I'll take it from here,' Jeremy snapped.

Walter Bailey-Hardwick was a morbidly obese man with features that Jeremy thought resembled those of the character, Jabba the Hutt. Seeing him sitting there wearing a ridiculous mauve kaftan, it struck Jeremy that this garment was probably the only option that would fit him. Looking closely at his hair, Jeremy could see the netting through Walter's threadbare wig. Jeremy's respect level for this individual was depleting by the second.
'Come in, sit down, young man,' Walter said, raising a beckoning hand above his head.
Jeremy caught sight of the psychic's white, dimple fleshed arm inside his wide kaftan sleeves. He developed an urge to say, 'Maybe some other time', but he reluctantly did as he was told.
Walter held Jeremy's hand in his own, staring at the lines on his palm. 'I see here that you like to travel.' He glanced up at Jeremy for confirmation.
'No, I don't.'
'Oh, I must be wrong. I have seen that you plan to take a trip in the next few days…up, up! It could be up in the air or up north. Does this mean anything to you?'
'Maybe,' Jeremy said reluctantly, thinking, *This big guy is good.*
'I see someone who I think is your father, he is ill or hurt?' Again, he glanced at Jeremy for a sign that he was on the right tracks.
'My father is alive and well, living not far from here.'
'I'm sorry, it's just that I see him injured.' At this point, he changed the subject completely. 'Have you have had any dealings lately with men dressed in suits, Jeremy?'

Jeremy made no response. *Now, that is none of his fucking business,* he thought. *I didn't take time out of my day to hear about those pests.*

'You must speak to these men. It will make things worse if you don't. Jeremy, you need to make peace with yourself. You are a troubled young man. This is not a good state of mind to be in. I think you need to shut the door on something that is not good for you.'

'What makes *you* think *you* know what is good for me? Eating too much food isn't good for you but you're not going to listen to my advice, are you? I've heard enough. I'm leaving.' Jeremy stood to leave.

Walter rose above the insult that had been hurled at him, saying, 'Sometimes lost things don't want to be found.' Jeremy glared at him in such a way that it left Walter feeling seriously alarmed.

The over-helpful gentleman in the hallway escorted Jeremy down the stairs, informing him that he could pay by cash or card at the reception. Jeremy had no desire to pay at all for the useless advice he had just been offered, but he did not want to make a fuss.

Taking out his bank card, he told the receptionist that he wished to pay for a reading from Walter Bailey-Hardwick.

'That will be £45, please,' she said, turning the card machine around to face him.

Inserting his card in the slot, Jeremy entered his pin number. Rejected. He tried again. Rejected. Again. Rejected.

'I'm sorry sir, but your card has been declined. Do you have another method of payment?'

'No, there is plenty of money in my account. Do I look like a man with no money?' People were turning to stare. He needed to calm this scene down a bit.
'I'm terribly sorry. I live on this street, so would you mind if I walked along to my home to get the cash for you?' Jeremy said, in the politest manner possible. 'Believe me, I am a very regular customer in here.'
'That would be no problem. We'll see you shortly,' she told him with full trust.
Strolling arrogantly out the front door, his thoughts were typical. *They can go whistle for that money.*
The declined card affair had really irked him. It was the focus of his thoughts when walking along to his house. As soon as he was inside the front door, he raced through to the investigation room to log onto his laptop. He entered the relevant details of his bank account.
'Funds on hold', were the words that came up on his screen. Fortunately, he had another account. 'Funds on hold.' Next up was his savings account. 'Funds on hold.' Calmly, he reached forward, lifting the glass fruit bowl from the middle of the table. Raising it high above his head, he screamed obscenities as he threw it at the wall. The bowl smashed and the splinters of glass flew across the room. *These fucking goons have frozen my fucking bank accounts. They will regret that decision,'* he assured himself, as he walked through to the hallway to get his phone from his jacket pocket.
After pressing the 'Father' button from his contacts, he waited for the dialling tone.
'Hello, father, it's Jeremy.'
'Hello Jeremy. How are you?' his father inquired formally.
'I'm good thanks. How are you?'

'Your mother and I are well, thank you.'
'I was thinking of coming over to see you tonight,' he said, sounding his father out on the idea.
'It's rather late for that, Jeremy, is it not?'
'Yes, perhaps it is. When would be a good time to call?' he asked.
'Hmm, let me think. Hold the line please.' Holding the phone away from his mouth, he shouted, 'Iris, that's Jeremy wondering when he can come over. What should I tell him?'
Jeremy narrowed his eyes, hearing his mother shout back, 'Tell him to come on Tuesday around half past four.'
'Jeremy, your mother thinks that Tuesday at four thirty would be a good time to visit. How would that suit?'
'That would suit fine,' Jeremy told him. *Fuck that,* he decided there and then. *I have a much better idea.*
'Did they ever get any leads on what happened to Kira?' he asked.
'No, father. There have been no leads, no sightings,' Jeremy lied. 'See you Tuesday at four thirty. Goodbye.'
'Goodbye, Jeremy,' his father said, hanging up the phone.
Jeremy threw his phone on the floor, he then donned his black jeans, black polo neck jumper and black fleece fabric hat. His gloves were already waiting on the hall table for him. *It looks like Sherlock the Terminator is coming out again,* he thought, feeling that wonderful tingling sensation in his trousers.

Chapter 39

Tears rolled down Celia's cheeks as she drove across the city. There was only one place that she could go discreetly without feeling judged. How long had Ramsay had been visiting those dreadful pornography sites? The whole occurrence had made her feel cheated on and lied to. The lonely days and nights she had experienced, waiting for him to solve the mystery of their daughter's disappearance. It had been loneliness that had driven her to the meetings at the church hall. Getting together each week with like-minded people had given her a brand new perspective on life.

Driving through the unfamiliar rundown area, she searched for Andy's neatly tended house among the streets. Gangs of hooded teenagers stared at her car as she passed them. Afraid and alone, she circled slowly around the blocks of identical houses. Suddenly, there it was, an oasis in a desert of deprivation. Andy's property, so out of place in the middle of a neglected neighbourhood.

In utter despair, she ran to the front door. Andy answered the door wearing his pyjama trousers and a football top, the tattoos on his arms were visible to her for the first time.

'Celia! What are you doing back here?' he said, looking at his watch. 'It's after 11 o'clock. Come in,' he quickly added, putting his arm around her waist to usher her through the door. 'Give me your car keys. I'll drive your car up the side of the house. This is not the kind of area you can leave a car like yours unattended.'

Celia walked into Andy's house whilst he moved her car. The lounge was surprisingly homely. It was glaringly obvious to see where Andy had been sitting before she had arrived. His armchair had a stool in front of it for his feet, and beside the chair sat a small table within reach. Rested on the table was a can of Guinness and a packet of dry roasted peanuts. An American football game was in full swing on the television screen in the corner. Celia found the sight quite alien, albeit rather endearing. At this moment in time, there was nowhere on this earth she would rather be. It occurred to her that Andy Wallace was the only true friend that she possessed.

'What's this about?' Andy asked her when he came back into the house.

Celia sat down on the tired brown sofa. 'I couldn't take anymore, Andy. I needed to get away.'

'What happened?' he asked, putting the television off.

Celia told Andy about Ramsay shutting himself away for weeks on end, working on solving Kira's disappearance case. She explained how she had trusted him, believing that he was following leads, becoming closer every day to finding their daughter. She then disclosed to Andy the reality of the situation with a stack of handwritten, irrelevant nonsense and the large breasted, porno girls.

'Celia, I'm going to be honest with you as a friend. I, of all people, know that when your child goes missing with no explanation, you drop into freefall. Basically, you do whatever it takes to keep you sane. You feel helpless, so you do something that you think is going to help. Ramsay has created this 'investigation' to give himself a purpose, to make him feel useful. Can you understand that?' he asked her, gently.

'Yes, I do see that, but how do you explain all the bare bosomed, Latino ladies that he has been looking at?' she sobbed.
'Again, Celia, I am going to be very blunt with you here, but we are friends and I think you want honesty. I believe that Ramsay has probably always looked at the large breasted, Latino ladies. The porno girls are nothing to do with Kira's disappearance or his grief. I think it is probably just something that he likes, as do many other men. I know that's harsh, but we all have secrets,' Andy disclosed.
'I want to stay here with you for a while, Andy. Would you mind?'
'Look Celia, I have lived here on my own for a long time. I am unsociable, I go to my bed in a drunken fug every night so that I won't dream about my son, Lewis. I am not a fun person to be around because I'm broken and depressed. My wife left me for those very reasons. You wouldn't be happy around me because I'd pull you down. You're a positive up-beat person that would be better off without me.'
'I understand what you're saying Andy, but I'm happy when I'm with you. You make me feel special and important. Please, could I just stay for a couple of days?' she begged.
It was difficult to believe that this rich, elegant lady was beseeching him to let her stay in his privately owned council house in a dodgy part of town. *Life doesn't half take some surprising twists and turn,'* he marvelled.
To Celia, Andy was like a diamond in the rough. As she looked across the room at him, a stomach punching thought flitted into her mind. *Ramsay and I went to incredible lengths to stop Kira from being with the boy she loved because he was not in her social class.* How could she ever forgive herself?

'I need to show you something,' he told her, walking over to the drawer in the display cabinet. He pulled out a letter which was on Police letterheaded paper. 'I got this yesterday.' He handed it to Celia. 'Here, read it.'
The police were informing him that a British man living in Thailand had contacted them with information about the missing Scottish boy, Lewis Wallace.
The man had been watching the BBC news in his apartment in Thailand, when he saw a special feature about missing people. Photos had appeared on the screen of Lewis, who had disappeared several years before. The man had recognised him instantly as being a boy he had seen begging on the streets. He had reported to the police that the boy had severe injuries and was in a very poorly state.
'Oh, Andy! What are the police going to do?' Celia asked.
Andy broke down. 'Nothing, absolutely nothing. Celia, I think it's my son.'
'Why don't you go out to Thailand and look for yourself,' she suggested.
Andy laid his head into his hands, 'Do you not think I would if I could?' he asked in despair. 'I have borrowed so much money in the past few years to chase every lead. Celia, the well is dry. The first believable sighting I've had, and I can't go to save him.'
Suddenly taking charge of the situation, Celia announced, 'Tomorrow, I am booking two flights to Thailand. When can you get away? I'm going with you.'
Andy knew that he mustn't get his hopes up. 'Celia, I can't borrow the money because I can't pay you back.'
'Who said anything about paying money back. This is my treat; I can afford it. Andy, you are the first real friend I've

ever had. You're about the only person right now that I actually care about, apart from Kira. If I can book it tomorrow, can you get away?' she asked him.
'Yes, yes! I could leave right now,' he said, feeling overwhelmed by this woman's generosity.
'In that case, I'll book the first available flight.' For the first time in her privileged life, she actually felt useful.
'I need you to promise me one thing, Celia.'
'Anything.'
'Please tell Ramsay where you're going. He's lost his daughter so it wouldn't be fair to torture him any further. Just tell him the truth, you're helping out a friend.'
'You're right and you're a very good man, Andy Wallace. I'll send him a text.'

Chapter 40

Jeremy's parents lived in Arboretum Road. The high wall and mature, leafy garden hindered the stake-out phase of the mission. Driving slowly along the road, he gauged what would be the optimum vantage point to observe the light activity. It wasn't long before he found the perfect spot. From the darkness of his car, he watched the living room light go off, the upstairs lights go on. All he could do now was wait patiently for darkness.

An old orangery was situated at the rear of his parents' Victorian house. The glass structure was an original feature, but it had seen better days. The plan was for him to gain entry to the property via the orangery. Once inside, he would enter the main house through the connecting door.

This is going to be so easy to pull off, he thought. *I know what I'm looking for, I know exactly where to find it.* The house was so extensive that he could have a party downstairs and his parents would sleep like babies through it.

The house had been in complete darkness for over twenty minutes when Jeremy decided that it was time to go forth in action. Getting out onto the pavement, he quietly clicked his car door shut. Staying vigilant, he ran across the street to the high wall that surrounded his parents' property. Following his previously prepared plan, he walked in the shadows of the trees until he reached the front gate. If his memory served him correctly, the gate made a loud squeak when opened. With this in mind, he decided instead that he would leave it shut and simply hold on whilst he swung his legs over sideways. When he was in the garden, he darted across the sprawling lawn, past the orchard, round the corner to the

orangery. *Phase one, complete,* he commended himself, making a ticking gesture with his finger.
The timber around the glass in the orangery had perished, he kicked at it until it crumbled, then disintegrated. Using his shoulder, he gave it a nudge; a section of the glass caved in. The space that he had created was large enough for him to crawl through. It was so incredibly easy.
Inside the dilapidated orangery, he moved to the second phase of his plan. This part involved gaining entry to the actual house. He remembered that his parents didn't always lock the adjoining door, so he tried turning the round, wooden handle. Locked. *Damn it! Fear not my good man,* he told himself. *As always, I've come prepared.*
Rolling up the leg of his jeans, he took from his sock an old Christmas card, tweezers and a thin, wooden doweling rod. *The tools of my trade,* he smiled. He slid the card under the door, being careful to position it under the lock. The doweling rod was then poked through the keyhole until it hit the key, causing it to fall out of the lock, onto the floor. With great precision, he tweezed the card through from under the door. 'Come to papa,' he whispered to the little metal object resting on the Christmas card. This trick featured in a film he had watched when he was young. In truth, he never dreamt that it would actually work but he had always wanted to give it a try.
'And for my next trick,' he announced in a lowered voice. 'I shall open the door of this impenetrable establishment.' He stifled great laughter as he turned the key of the adjoining door. Entry gained. Phase two completed to an exceptionally high standard. Tick.

There were two things that he had come for and he knew exactly where to put his hands on them both. The first was money. He crept quietly into the kitchen where he reached for the tea caddy tin at the back of the cupboard. How many times had he seen his mother taking money from it when he was a boy? *The 'tea caddy' idea is such a cliché,* he thought. *How dumb can you get*? Prising off the lid, he dipped his hand in for the contents. Sure enough, there it was, a big wad of cash. *Too easy,*' he scoffed, stuffing it into his pocket. *You are going to have to be a little more cunning that, mother dear. I could teach you a thing or two.* Phase three completed with ease. Tick.

Jeremy's father's study was situated at the back of the house, to which Jeremy now headed. There was no need to tiptoe, but he did. The musty odour reached his nostrils bringing with it most unpleasant childhood memories. There was no time for him to feel sorry for himself, he was there to do a job of work. *Focus on the mission,* he affirmed to himself. *There is no point in boohooing about the past. I have turned out the man I am in spite of my parents.*

It was quite a walk to the back of the house, but the door lay ahead of him like a pot of gold at the end of rainbow. The door was slightly ajar; an invitation to walk in and make himself at home. Theoretically, it was his home, a home filled with miserable memories. A queasiness stirred his stomach contents. He made a conscious decision that once he had gotten what he came for, he would never step foot near this antiquated dump ever again.

For a few moments, he stood there, just looking, feeling once again like the unhappy boy he used to be. He choked down a lump that unexpectedly appeared in his throat. *Come on you soft fool,* he warned himself. *You have work to do. The past is the past. How does that saying go? … What doesn't kill you, makes you stronger. Yeah, I'm stronger because of these apologies for parents.*

Ah ha! he thought, seeing the tall wooden cabinet in the corner of the room. *Now, that really has cheered me up.* Sauntering purposefully over to it, he turned the key in the lock. The door creaked open when he pulled it. Like an apparition before him, he saw the wonderous object, resplendent and erect. A thrill passed through his body at the sight of the shotgun. When he was young, he had sneaked into the study many times just to stare at the magnificent specimen. Prising it out from the stand that held it, he nursed it in his arms. He immediately felt powerful just holding it. The shotgun's long, hard barrel coupled with the smooth polished wood of the butt, instantly aroused him. He had wanted to get his hands on this shotgun since he was a child. His fantasies often featured him stealing it and blowing his parents' heads off. But not today, he had far better plans for it. The shotgun cartridges were stacked up in the drawer under the cabinet, he remembered seeing them there many years ago. Fortunately for him, nothing had changed, and he lifted two boxes before he left. Without a backward look, he left his father's study never to return again. With a pocket full of cash and a shotgun in his hands, he made his way back to the orangery. *I am unstoppable,* he thought. *I always manage to get what I want, that's why I know that I'll get Kira back.*

As he reached the adjoining door, he heard someone behind him.

'Where do you think you're going, you bloody thief!' his father's voice boomed.

Urine ran down the insides of Jeremy's legs. His father had always had that effect on him.
'Who the hell are you? What are you doing in my property?' Mr Ward demanded.
Jeremy relaxed in the knowledge that his father didn't appear to know it was him, nor had he spotted the rifle. The familiar sound of his father's heavy footsteps were close behind, drawing nearer and nearer. Frozen to the spot, he stood stock still until he knew his father was directly behind him.
The formidable Mr Ward reached out to grab him. Jeremy swung around, whacking the butt of the rifle across his father's head. Mr Ward dropped like a stone onto the ground. A pool of dark red blood oozed out like a halo around his crown. Seeing his father lying there unconscious, sent a flashback to his mind. It was of Walter Bailey-Hardwick at the Sir Arthur Conan Doyle Centre, saying 'I see your father injured.' Jeremy stood reflecting for a moment, *That psychic may have been fat and annoying but credit where it's due, he is bloody good.*
Leaving his father to bleed out on the floor, he ran through the adjoining door, then out of the gap in the orangery. *Oh dear,* he thought, *I didn't intend for that to happen, but collateral damage occurs in all high pressured situations. It was simply not my fault.*
Overall, he rated the home invasion a roaring success. Now, he was back in funds and armed with a loaded weapon. The incident with his father had been unfortunate but he could safely say, mission complete. Tick, tick, tick.

Chapter 41

Kira sat on the carpet playing with her little dog. Taking part in a tug of war, for a floppy toy rabbit, she rolled around the floor with the pup. Fraser appeared downstairs for lunch. Heading straight to Kira, he kissed her on the lips. He patted Darcy's soft coat before taking over Kira's role in the fight to retrieve the rabbit. Kira sat back watching the two of them wrestling so earnestly.

'What would you like for lunch?' she asked, getting up from the carpet.

'Toasted cheese with tomato please, if you're offering.'

'I'm offering,' she said, walking towards the kitchen area.

'Hey, Kira, wait.' She stopped, walking back towards him. 'What's that on your arms?'

Kira studied both arms, seeing patches of bruising on them.

'That little dog is rougher than he looks!' she told him. 'So be warned. He plays dirty.'

It poured with rain all afternoon so when Fraser went back into his office, Kira had a look through the books that had been sold off from the library. 'The Count of Monte-Christo,' by Alexandre Dumas, was her choice from the selection on offer. The name of the novel was familiar, but she knew nothing of the story. She settled down on the sofa facing the view of the sea and began reading the story. Eventually the rain had passed over, allowing the sun to stream through the window onto her face. Darcy jumped up beside her, laying his head onto her knee. He fell fast asleep in the warming sunlight.

Kira read the first few chapters of the novel; she was hooked. She could relate to the main character who was wrongfully

imprisoned, then forgotten about, but able to escape and reinvent himself as someone completely different.
Had she not also been wrongfully imprisoned in a life with Jeremy? The ball and chain she was shackled with had been so heavy, it had become impossible to drag around in her day-to-day life. Now, she had escaped and reinvented herself as a casually dressed woman in love, a bookkeeper, a dog owner and a country girl. Simple goals, but huge changes for her. No one from her past would recognise the person she was today. It was not only her looks that had been transformed.
In the background, there was a dark force threatening to ruin everything for her. But it wasn't here yet, so in the meantime, she would enjoy living and loving with all her heart. Laying her book to one side, she rested her head on the back of the cushioned sofa. With the warmth of the sun's ray on her face, she shut her eyes, falling into a deep sleep.
Fraser finished the email that he was working on before switching off his computer. The backlog of work that had been mounting had almost all been dealt with. Having Kira working on the accounts for him had been a game changer. *She is not only beautiful,* he decided, *but she is one of the smartest people I know. I am the luckiest man alive.* Closing the office door to keep Darcy out, he then came downstairs to see his napping family.
'Right, you two, get up. Let's go for a walk before dinner. That pup needs to run off a bit of steam.' Darcy bounded over to Fraser, instinctively understanding that he was getting a walk. This threw out the theory of the lead being the trigger for a dog's excitement. 'Let's find a ball for this little guy,' Fraser said, rummaging through the box of toys

that he had picked up for him in a charity shop down in the village.

Kira rose unsteadily to her feet, heading to the hall to find her wellingtons. *Fresh air will be good for me,* she thought, feeling a little disorientated. She reached up to the hook where Darcy's lead hung, shouting for him to come. The little dog immediately ran over to her, sitting obediently at her feet. Patting his head, she told him that he was the best boy ever.

They climbed the gate near the back of their house, into the clover filled field, which appeared to stretch for miles. Kira told Darcy to sit as she unclipped the lead. He bolted for freedom.

Fraser took Kira in his arms to tell her once again how much he loved her.

'Kira, you're the only thing that I've ever truly needed in my life. I was never happy without you. I didn't care about anything else, just you. You are my purpose, my life and my future. Waking up beside you every morning is like a dream come true.'

He then shouted at the top of his voice, 'I'm crazy about you!'

Darcy heard Fraser shouting and obediently came running over. 'I wasn't talking to you, daft mutt!' Fraser said, picking up the tennis ball and throwing it across the field. Darcy ran at full speed, tripping over his own feet as he went.

Kira stood laughing at him. 'How on earth do dogs learn to fetch a ball when no one ever shows them?' Darcy ran back towards them, dropping the saliva covered ball at their feet. He stood panting for it to be thrown again and again and again.

When Darcy finally lay down on the grass, no longer interested in fetching the ball, Kira turned to Fraser saying, 'I think we can go home now. This little pup is done for the day.'
Fraser carried Darcy in his jacket back across the field. He listened intently as Kira related the events that she had read so far of The Count of Monte Cristo.
When they reached the house, Fraser guided Kira to the sofa. 'I want to have a serious talk with you,' he told her.
'Oh, I don't like the sound of that,' she shuddered.
'No, it's not a bad thing, it's just about the future. I want to talk about marriage and having a family.'
Kira hugged him, tears stung her eyes, 'I want all of the above.'
'Good, well that's all sorted then. What's for dinner?'

Chapter 42

The William Tell Overture suddenly accompanied Jeremy's vivid dream. It awakened him with a start. The ringtone of his phone was blasting harsh notes at him from the bedside table. His hand reached out from under the duvet, feeling around for the irritant. 'Yes?' he said, through gritted teeth.

It was his mother was on the other end. 'Jeremy, I'm at the hospital. Your father was attacked by an intruder. It happened through the night. He is in a critical condition. You need to get here quickly. We're at the Royal Infirmary, in the high dependency unit.'

'Oh mother, that's shocking news. Poor father. Did he get a look at the intruder?' Jeremy asked.

'I don't know because he hasn't regained consciousness. He may be able to tell us more when he comes round. Just come quickly, Jeremy. I don't want to go through this alone,' she begged him.

'I'm on my way,' he promised with conviction before he hung up the phone. Plumping his pillow up with two hands, he snuggled back under the duvet.

A police siren from outside woke Jeremy from his deep sleep. He expanded a satisfying stretch as he yawned. *Damn it,* he thought, sitting up in bed. *I have such a busy day ahead and now I will have to trail across town to the fucking hospital. This is extremely inconvenient.*

It didn't take long for Jeremy to get showered and dressed. The bathroom mirror showed him that a shave was not necessary today. *Looking good, Jer,* he told himself. *The rugged, stubbly look really suits me.* In a section of his wardrobe, there hung almost every colour of crew neck jumper. *I think I am in the mood for pink today. Ha, ha, I'm in the pink, so to speak.* The jumper was not for wearing, it was to tie around his neck. After all, it's how all the toffs wore their sweaters.

On the way to the hospital to visit his poor father, Jeremy made the executive decision to make a detour to the police station. It was imperative that he get the address of the house in Portmahomack where the eyewitness had spotted Kira entering. That was far more important than visiting an unconscious man in hospital who would be oblivious to the fact that he was there.

The duty officer was standing at the main desk when Jeremy entered the police station. Playing the part of broken-hearted fiancé, he explained who he was. With a sniff and wipe of the eye, he asked for a list of all the witness statements, even the ones from outside the United Kingdom.

'You see, I've decided that I'm going to follow every lead by investigating every single one of the sightings, even if it costs me all the money that I have in the world. I am going to devote my life to finding my Kira.' He broke down crying. He felt he was being highly convincing.

By the look on the duty officer's face, it was clear that he was deeply affected by Jeremy's plight, to say nothing of the determination and grit he was displaying. 'Mr Ward, I commend you on your commitment.' Within a matter of minutes, he had handed over the full list of witness sightings to Jeremy, wishing him the best of luck in his quest.

Jeremy nodded humbly, his bottom lip quivering. He left the police station with exactly what he had come for. *In a different time, in a different world, I should really have worked for the Secret Service.*

It was downright bothersome having to drive over to the hospital, but Jeremy knew that it was necessary to play the dutiful son for a couple of hours; it was the least he could do. Scrutinizing the eye witness accounts would have to be put on hold for now. Driving across town to the Royal Infirmary, he turned the radio on to sooth his jangled nerves. Rocky Raccoon by The Beatles came through the airwaves. Jeremy banged on the steering wheel several times. *This song is especially for me!* he delighted, laughing at the irony of it. The song told the story of Rocky's girl being stolen and him seeking revenge with a shotgun. *Uncanny or what?*
Jeremy sang along, emphasising the relevant parts to his situation by pointing into the air as he drove. *This has been a direct sign that the mission I'm on is the only thing that matters,* he confirmed to himself.
Through the hospital gates, he took a left to the carpark for the high dependency unit. Just for fun, he drove at high speed then pulled firmly on his handbrake, skidding neatly into a parking place. It was so nicely done that he glanced around to see if anyone had noticed him.
A nurse, who had been standing at the window, shook her head at the disrespectful stunt.
He sauntered casually along the corridor in the hospital, whistling the confirmation song that he had just heard on the radio. In the distance, he saw the sign for the high dependency ward. Several metres before the entrance to the unit, he began sprinting all the way in the door, panting for breath. His mother would see that he had really made an effort to be with her.
'Mother, how is he? I can't believe this has happened,' he said woefully.

'I know, I know, Jeremy. It's just awful. They've said that he may not fully recover. It's a possibility that he may need round the clock care when I get him home. The doctor suggested that I think about looking for a suitable care home for him, but Jeremy, I could never stick your father in some institution,' she sobbed.

Jeremy stared at her for a moment thinking, *Hmm, well you had no problem sticking me in one for the best part of my life.*

However, he continued play acting the concerned son. 'Oh, that's horrendous. No, mother, you simply couldn't 'stick' him in an institution. *You* could give him round the clock care, bathing him, changing him and feeding him. Couldn't you?' he suggested.

Mrs Ward did not answer but Jeremy could see the cogs of reality working overtime in her mind. 'Jeremy, could you move in and stay with me for a while? I don't like living by myself in that big house. Please? I'm frightened to be alone.'

Jeremy stared at her again in disbelief. *You didn't want me in the house when I was a boy, you didn't want me coming over the other day, but now you are begging me to stay.*

Taking her wrinkled hands in his, he spoke softly, 'You know that I would love to help you, but I have some very important business to attend to out of town. I'm so sorry, mother.'

'Will you come and stay after that? Please, Jeremy, I'm beseeching you. I don't want to be alone.' She clung to him in a manner that resembled a hug. Jeremy realised that it was the first 'hug' he had ever received from his mother.

'I'll do what I can,' he said, throwing her a few rationed crumbs of mercy.

'Oh, thank you Jeremy. Thank you so much. You're a good boy. You've always been a good boy,' she grovelled.
How would you know? You don't even fucking know me.

Chapter 43

In the shop at Edinburgh Airport, Celia picked up items necessary for her trip to Thailand. She was unsure how long she and Andy would be away, so it was better to be fully prepared. Although she wasn't a woman with a faith, she had prayed the previous night that the boy that had been spotted begging was indeed Lewis Wallace. At this moment in time, nothing else mattered to her than Andy's happiness. Of course, her greatest wish would be to find Kira, but right now this was Andy's search. He was going to need her support throughout this time whether the outcome was good or bad.

Andy was overwhelmed with gratitude towards Celia for footing the bill for the trip, but he was not his usual cheeky chappie self as they sat together at the airport. His mind was preoccupied with what lay ahead of him, he had to stay strong and focused. His precious son had disappeared so long ago, now he was going to find someone who could quite possibly be him. Deep down, Andy had always known that his son wasn't dead. It was that inner knowledge that had kept him sane over the years.

His mind drifted to the worst-case scenario. They find the boy that the eyewitness reported, and it is not Lewis. It would be another devastating blow for him. Would he be strong enough to get back up? What was the alternative, to stop searching? No, never, the one thing he was certain of was that he wouldn't give up until the very end, whatever that end looked like.

When they had taken seats on the shuttle flight to London, Andy turned to Celia to explain, 'Celia, I don't want you to think that I'm not grateful to you just because I've been sitting here quietly. It's just that I've got to get my mind set right for the task ahead. I've had so many disappointments with dead ends. I can honestly say that every time my hopes have been dashed, it kills a small piece of me inside. I'm only a shell of the man that I was before Lewis disappeared.'

Celia reached for his hand. 'You don't need to explain anything to me. Sit there beside me as quietly as you like. I am simply here for support. Just try to keep your spirits high but your expectations low. We'll get through this together. If it's Lewis, then we'll find him.'

Reclining his seat, Andy closed his eyes and against his better judgement, he imagined the moment when he became reunited with his dear son.

Celia glanced down at Andy's strong arms which were tattooed with logos of his favourite football team, his hardworking hands calloused. A heavy sense of guilt fell over her like a weighted overcoat. *Why did I ever make social class an issue when it came to love and happiness? Please forgive me, Kira.*

Chapter 44

Ramsay walked around the house wearing only his underpants. The sense of loss he was experiencing was agony. Celia had told him that she was off to Thailand to follow a lead with a friend. *What friend?* he wondered. *Celia doesn't have any friends, not real ones. What lead is she following? It can't be anything to do with Kira because she didn't have her passport when she disappeared.* It was all so confusing for him.

It's understandable that she's upset by the naked girls on my computer, but she should have stayed to talk about it. What kind of woman just ups and leaves to go heaven-knows-where, with heaven know who? It didn't make any sense to him. *Where could she have met this friend?* There was talk of her attending meetings once a week, but he didn't remember her mentioning anyone that she was friendly with, certainly not friendly enough to accompany on holiday. Perhaps he should have paid a little more attention when she had spoken to him.

Time weighed heavily on Ramsay, filling his day was impossible. Going out wasn't an option, and he had no desire to see anyone. The house had lost its soul and the emptiness of loss echoed throughout the rooms. The only food he had eaten since his wife left, was toast, dry. Normally, he would have been excited about Celia going out of the house because that was when he liked to enjoy the girls on his computer. Now, he had all the time in the world to look at the girls, but he had no desire within him. If he never saw those ridiculous, pouting females again, he certainly wouldn't be broken-hearted. All he wanted was for his wife to be home, safe and sound. *Thailand? She would never dream of going to a place like Thailand, especially without me.*

As he sat at the kitchen table, going over everything in his head, he suddenly spotted the postcard with the painting of Mull on it. Snatching it from the shelf, he turned it over to read the message from Lynette Cochrane, inviting Celia to the join the support group at St Mary's church hall.

I may have to go along to this meeting tomorrow night, he thought. *I need to find out what the hell is going on.*

Chapter 45

Kira's new clothes arrived by courier. They were two sizes smaller than she had been wearing and there was not a short flowery dress in sight. The package also contained a hat that covered her forehead, flaps to cover her ears and straps for under her chin. It wasn't attractive looking, and she felt like Uncle Buck, but it did hide most of her face. Now, she could walk down to the village without fear of anyone recognising her. Leaving her previous life behind had meant that she had no savings, bank account or credit cards. The shame of asking Fraser for money had now gone, they were a partnership for life. When she showed him her disguise, he had to agree that it was pretty good.

'Don't forget to stay vigilant. Don't hang around in the one place for too long and if you see anything that makes you uncomfortable just make your way home immediately,' he warned her.

'I promise to follow all of your instructions to the letter, sir,' she said, saluting.

Darcy walked smartly beside her on the way down the steep brae to the harbour. This time her visit did not include looking out to sea or admiring the boats, it was the shops that interested her. An art gallery was the first stop on her travels. The colourful paintings in the window caught her eye, tempting her through the door. Before she stepped inside, she motioned across the room to the gallerist for permission to enter with Darcy. The woman responded with a nod, so Kira carried Darcy in her arms. The shop was tastefully lit with overhead spotlights illuminating the artwork that hung on the walls. Kira wandered around looking closely at the detail in every picture. The painting that caught her eye was a very large canvas with a dramatic scene of the islands surrounding Mull. The signature of the artist was written in the corner of the painting. Taking a close look, Kira saw that the picture had been painted by an artist called Coral Mac.

'Do you like that piece by Coral Mac?' the gallery owner asked.

'I absolutely love it. You could stand here staring at it all day. It's not like anything I have ever seen before. Is it very expensive?' Kira asked, unable to take her eyes off the painting.

'Well, it depends on what you would call expensive. It is a rare piece from an artist who lives in Mull, but her work sells worldwide. It's an investment,' the woman explained.

'How much of an investment?' Kira probed, perfectly aware that the woman was avoiding the question.

'This particular piece is £37 000, but we occasionally get smaller works which sell for less than half of that. Her work is sold abroad at a far greater cost.'

Kira smiled, saying, 'It's worth every penny and more, but I'm on a budget at the moment and it is sadly out of my reach. Would you have anything around the £200 mark?'

The gallery owner showed her all the prints that she stocked in her price range, but Kira felt that after seeing the Coral Mac painting, nothing else quite hit the mark. Thanking the woman for her help, she left the shop empty handed.

A shop selling handmade crafts was the next place of interest for Kira. The owner seemed agreeable to having a dog in the shop. Again, out of respect, Kira carried Darcy in her arms. The shelves were filled with pottery, dried grasses, scented

candles. The white handcrafted mugs were irresistible to Kira, with their bright red poppy design, back and front.
'There is a matching teapot that comes with this set,' the shop owner told her, bubble wrapping the mugs. 'Would you be interested in seeing it?'
'Yes,' she laughed, 'I would be very interested.'
'I'll take it,' she said when the owner returned. Lifting a scented candle from the shelf, she said, 'Here, I'll take this too.'
The shop's name, Harbour Cove, was written across the carrier bag that Kira left with. It was way heavier than she thought it would be.
There were so many little independent shops along the main street that, in a way, it reminded her of Bruntsfield where Ivan's estate agency was situated. Without allowing herself to dwell on matters, she fleetingly wondered how Connie, Derek and Ivan were doing. Had they forgotten about her; moved on as though nothing had happened. What was her replacement like? Was she any good at selling houses? There was nothing in her past life that would tempt her back, everything she could ever want was right here in Portmahomack. No thoughts of her parents ever entered her head; she would have shooed them out if they had.
Fresh fruits were arranged on racks outside the small grocer's, further along the street. Kira pointed to the pears, cherries and bananas. The grocer filled brown paper bags with the fruits she had chosen. The bags felt heavy in her arms by the time she left. Dizziness came over her on the walk back towards the harbour.

'Darcy, you're going to have to walk by yourself. I have too much to carry.' Laying him down on the pavement, she took hold of his red lead. 'Walk nicely, please.'

Darcy walked in step beside her until he spotted a seagull with a crust in its beak. He decided to chase it, pulling Kira along the pavement with him. 'Stop Darcy!' she shouted, running along with him, clinging to her shopping bags. The seagull finally flew out of sight and Darcy lost interest. It dawned on Kira that they had been out for several hours and that the little dog must be hungry.

They reached the foot of the hill, Kira stared up towards the top. *I can't do it, I'll never make it. It's too steep and my bags are too heavy.* Darcy began to tug frantically at the leash. 'No, Darcy. Behave!' she shouted. Two steps towards the summit of the hill and Kira's legs buckled. She dropped to the ground. The bags fell from her hands, the sound of broken china followed, then out rolled the cherries in the direction of the harbour. Darcy sat by Kira's side as she started to cry.

'Hey Miss, are you alright,' shouted a teenager from behind.

'Not really,' Kira told him.

'Give me your bags and the dog. I'll help you to your feet.'

There was no option but to trust him. He pulled her up, supporting her under her arm. 'Hold on to me. We'll walk slowly together. Is there someone I can phone?' he asked.

'No, I don't have a phone. Thank you for helping me.'

'No problem. One step at a time. We'll take it slowly. Put your weight onto me.'

Kira could hardly remember getting to the top of the hill, but the next thing she knew she was in Fraser's arms. The boy handed over her bags along with the dog. Before he left, he said, 'I hope you'll be alright, Miss.'

Fraser thanked the boy for his help. Kira stood at the door shaking, feeling overheated. She removed her fur lined hat. The boy glanced at her for a moment then said, 'Do I know you? You look familiar.'
Fraser thanked him again, shutting the door abruptly.
'What on earth happened to you?' Fraser asked.
'I don't know. My bags were heavy, Darcy was pulling, and the hill was steep. I was also burning up in my disguise hat, so that didn't help. I just felt overwhelmed. I'm going to go and lie down for a while,' she told him, reaching for his arm to support her in the walk upstairs.
Fraser sat on the sofa, looking out to sea as Kira slept. Darcy finished his food in the kitchen then walked through to climb up on Fraser's lap. Fraser thought about his parents for the first time since he had left Edinburgh. Shifting the sleeping Darcy onto the seat beside him, he headed to the kitchen to fetch the 'pay as you go' phone that he had bought for emergencies.
'Hello, mum.'
'Fraser, son, I've been out of my mind with worry.'
'I just wanted to tell you that I'm oaky. I'll see you both as soon as it's safe to do so.'
'Are you in trouble, son?' she asked.
'No, mum. I'm not in any trouble. I love you and dad. I miss you both.'
'Son, we love you too. There is something I need to tell you, Fraser. There's a very bad man looking for you, I think you're in danger.'
'Mum, mum…are you there, mum?' he asked. The signal was breaking down.

Mrs Jackson was so happy to hear from Fraser, but she was unsure whether he heard her warning. All attempts she made to call the number back, failed.
It was for the best that the poor phone signal had cut Fraser off from his mum. In fact, he knew that he shouldn't have been calling her at all. At this early stage, he couldn't afford to have any slip ups. The less his parents knew, the better. In years to come, his mum and dad would be able to come up and stay with them. He reflected on their short conversation and the final thing she said to him. *There's something I need to tell you. What could my mum need to tell me,* he wondered. It crossed his mind that perhaps his father was sick, but there was something in the way she said *we love you too, son,* that told him that everything was fine with them both. *Maybe she just wanted to tell me that Kira Carmichael, my ex-girlfriend is missing. Yes, it's probably just that.* Pushing the conversation to the back of his mind, he made a conscious decision not to phone again until it was safe. Kira's disappearance would become old news eventually.

Chapter 46

There had been no business class seats available on the plane, which meant that Celia had no option but to travel economy class. The flight had been arduous for her but not a word of complaint passed her lips. When they arrived at Suvarnabhumi Airport in Bangkok, they collected their luggage and sped off in a taxi, which was conveniently waiting outside.

The driver pulled up in front of the Bangkok Marriot. He lifted Andy's holdall and Celia's battered-looking suitcase out from the boot, placing both items on the marbled hotel steps. Celia desperately tried not to be embarrassed by her luggage, it was the only case Andy had to lend.

The air conditioned foyer of the hotel was a welcome relief from the oppressive heat outside. The uniformed receptionist smiled, handing them their room key and wishing them a wonderful stay in Bangkok. For Andy's sake, Celia hoped that it would indeed be wonderful but expectations had to remain low.

The room was luxuriously comfortable with views across the city. Celia had purposefully booked a room with two single beds to avoid any awkwardness. In her heart of hearts, she wished that they were sleeping together in a king size bed, but she suspected that Andy did not need any further complications in his life at that moment. Just having him as her friend was enough for now. It dawned upon her that for the first time in her purposeless, selfish life, she was needed and it felt joyous. There was nothing that she wouldn't do for this diamond of a man. Her life, until now, had evolved around possessions and outward appearances but losing

Kira and meeting Andy had turned everything on its head. It was almost like seeing life through brand new eyes; eyes that showed a very different perspective.
'We won't even bother unpacking,' Celia told Andy in the bedroom. 'I don't think we should waste another second. Let's see if this boy is your son.'
'Thank you, Celia. That was exactly what I was thinking. We'll go down to the bar and I'll make the call.'
It would have been so easy for the man who recognised Lewis, to simply walk on, to just forget all about it. Andy felt so much gratitude towards him for taking the trouble to contact the police. Whether this boy was his son or not, someone cared enough to report it.
The phone number for the eye witness was on a piece of paper that Andy had tucked safely in his wallet. Before he made the call, he asked Celia what she would like to drink.
'No, don't be silly,' she told him. 'You phone the man, I'll get the drinks.'
'Celia, you have made this trip possible for me, please let me at least buy you a drink.'
This mattered to Andy, she could see that. 'In that case, I will have a double gin and tonic, please.'
'Whoa, steady on woman, I didn't say that I could stretch to a double,' he joked.
He really is the funniest man, she thought, laughing heartily. His little jokes tickled her.
After ordering, Andy sat back down. Soon, the barman was bringing the drinks over to the table.
'Well, here goes, Celia,' he said, taking his reading glasses from his inside pocket. 'Look at me. I'm shaking.'
'Hello,' said the voice on the other end of the line.

'Hello, Mr Hardy. My name is Andy Wallace. I was given your number by the police. I believe you think you may have seen my son.'
'Andy, call me Chris. Where are you?'
'I'm in the Marriot Hotel in Bangkok,' Andy told him, feeling an instant warmth towards the man he was speaking to.
'Give me about an hour. I'll come over and meet with you. Are you alone?'
'No, I have my good friend Celia with me,' he replied, reaching for her hand.
Tears burned in Celia's eyes.
'Sit tight until I get there,' Chris Hardy told him.
When the conversation was over, Andy began to sob. Over the years, his strength had depleted, leaving him emotionally fragile. In an instant, Celia was out of her seat, standing behind him with her arms around his neck. She whispered strengthening words of comfort in his ear.
The pain Celia felt in her heart was intolerable. She ached not only for Andy but for her own precious daughter.

Chapter 47

Ramsay parked his car around the corner from St. Mary's Cathedral. Entering the grounds by the gate at the front, he suddenly felt extremely anxious as he didn't know what to expect. The postcard had informed Celia that the meetings were held in the hall at the back of the church, so that was where he headed. The hall soon became visible to him, with its door open and the lights ablaze. A few people were milling around when he approached, offering him a warm welcome and introducing themselves to him. 'Ramsay' was all he told them.

No one had sat down within the circle of seats; Ramsay was the first. It intrigued him to see the obvious friendship bonds between the people there. Before he arrived, he had formed a preconceived notion that the hall would be full of depressed people sitting around crying for their lost loved ones. The jovial laughter that he could hear around him came as quite a surprise. It almost felt like he was intruding on a private party. He wondered if Celia was one of the gang or if she sat quietly each week waiting for the others to sit down.

An elderly gentleman, wearing a tweed cap, pulled the heavy front door shut, which seemed to be a signal for everyone to take their seats. When the room fell silent, the woman in charge opened by saying, 'Bob, would you like to start with the announcements?'

Bob nodded. 'A couple of announcements, folks. The meeting next week will be moved to the Monday night. The minister of the church has asked if they can use the hall for their yearly treasury meeting. So that's Monday next week, at the usual time. The next thing I wanted to bring up was the outing for this year. It has been suggested that North Berwick might be a pleasant location for the trip. Obviously, it's a joint decision, so if you put your ideas forward, then we can look at the options as a group. I've set up a suggestions box at the door. There are slips of paper and a pen there, so go on, share your ideas. That's about it, folks. Over to you, Lynette.'

'Thanks Bob. We have a new member with us tonight. So, can we give a warm welcome to Ramsay.'

Everyone looked at Ramsay, then applauded. This embarrassed him terribly causing his cheeks to redden. It was this first time he had experienced the sensation of blushing in many, many years.

'The reason we clap for our new members is because we know that it takes courage to come along and meet with complete strangers. I hope that you will share your story when you feel ready. Thank you for joining us.' Everyone clapped again. Ramsay gave an awkward half smile in conjunction with a nod.

Lynette carried on chairing the meeting. 'I have some developments for you all tonight.' Lynette waited for everyone's attention. 'Andy got some news from the police through the week. There has been a possible sighting of his son.'

Everyone looked pleased, but with obvious reservations. Most of the people in the room had received word at some point of a possible sighting of their loved one. Had it turned out to be their missing family member, they wouldn't still be attending the meetings.

Lynette carried on. 'So, let's keep Andy in our prayers as he travels to Thailand with our good friend Celia for support.'

The shock hit Ramsay like a freight train. This statement was painful to listen to and no one seemed in the least surprised that Celia had gone off with this Andy character. When Celia told him she was away with a friend, he had automatically presumed that it was another female. He had heard enough. As he rose abruptly to his feet, his chair fell on its side. Unable to conceal his emotions, he strode towards the door. His heart pounded; his face burned.

'Ramsay, are you alright?' Lynette shouted after him.

'No, I'm not bloody alright. I've just found out that my wife, Celia, has gone galivanting across the world with another man!' He marched out of the door, slamming it shut.

'Well,' Lynette said, 'That wasn't a great start to the meeting tonight. I had no idea that was Celia Carmichael's husband. That was very unfortunate, but let's move on. Does anyone want to share anything with us this week?'

Chapter 48

Jeremy's mother sat by her husband's bedside comforting him. Although he was in a coma, she had been told by the nurses that there was a good chance that he could hear her. She described how alone she felt; how frightened she was in the house. Against the advice of the nurses, she talked about the intruder and the fact that nothing appeared to be missing from the property. 'Why would he come into our house?' she sobbed. 'I've been telling you for years now that the old orangery needed pulling down. It's not safe because the wood around the windows is all rotten.'

Laying her head on her husband's motionless arm, she sobbed hysterically. 'Why did this have to happen to us? We are good people. Why us, why us?'

The nurse on duty entered the room with a cup of tea for Mrs Ward, who had now made an effort to pull herself together. Some idle chat about the clemency of the weather was exchanged between the two women. The nurse then sat down on one of the visitor's seats. 'Do the police have any idea who did this to your husband?' she asked.

'No, the burglar had been wearing gloves. Apparently, they have no leads as to who he was.'

Mrs Ward glanced at her husband's fingers, noticing that they were twitching. Sitting forward, she took his hand in hers. His eyes flickered open. The nurse immediately stood up, moving in closer.

'Mr Ward, are you with us?' she asked, turning to Mrs Ward. 'Quick, your husband is trying to say something.'

Mrs Ward moved her ear down next to her husband's mouth in order to hear anything that he wanted to say.

'Yes, darling. What is it? What do you want to tell me?' she asked.
A barely audible rasping came from the patient's mouth as he said, 'Jeremy, Jeremy.'
'Yes, darling. I'll get Jeremy,' his wife told him.
The ECG readings on the heart monitor spiked frantically. The nurse ran off to get the doctor.
Again, the patient whispered, 'Jeremy, Jeremy,' as he clawed at the blanket on the hospital bed.
'I know, I know, you want your son by your side. Now listen, darling, you are going to be okay. You will get well again and be back home with me in no time. Jeremy will come and stay for a while to make sure I'm safe, then I can send him home when you return. It will be back to normal soon, just you and me, together.'
Visibly distressed and frustrated, Mr. Ward fell back into the relief of the coma.

Chapter 49

Jeremy threw open the suitcase. Packing for a trip was one of the many things that he did well. Neatness and order were his rules of thumb. Unsure of how long he would be away, he decided to pack too much, rather than too little. The mission that he was embarking on was going to take as long as it took. Underpants, pyjamas and socks were ironed, before being folded expertly into one half of the case. Cotton shirts, unworn, still in their cellophane wrappers, were placed at the other side, along with his folded slacks. Toiletries and three pairs of polished shoes were fitted into the mesh compartment on the lid of the suitcase. A separate bag was placed on top of the packed items, it contained his black Thinsulate hat, gloves and polo necked jumper; an outfit that he was becoming extremely comfortable with.
He made a booking at 'The Oyster Catcher' to stay for a few days. The hotel had a choice of two rooms, so he paid a little extra for the one with the view of the harbour.
Might as well make a holiday out of it, he thought. *After all, it is my parents' money that I'm using.*
Ever so carefully, he swaddled the highly polished shotgun in a padded jacket that belonged to Kira. It was most unlike him, but apart from the hotel reservation, he had no definite plan for when he arrived in Portmahomack. The idea of watching the happy couple from afar, certainly appealed to him. *I will be the fox spying on the chicken coop, with similarly dark intentions.* The image of this made him laugh out loud. Yes, for once, he would be flying by the seat of his neatly ironed pants but the fine tuning could be tweaked when he arrived. Despite everything he had been through, he found

himself feeling excited to see Kira again. His ideal scenario was that Fraser had her tied up against her will in the basement. In this perfect scenario, Kira would be overcome with happiness when he arrived to save her. The thought of her running into his arms, telling him how much she loved him, filled him with joy. The joy soon dissipated when he thought of her walking along the road with a stupid dog, heading home to her boyfriend. All the lies and the cheating had broken his heart. Why had she done it? Didn't they have a good life together? After all, he had let her do nearly everything she wanted. She had a beautiful house in one of the best streets in Edinburgh. Their sex life had been regular and spontaneous. A tingling grew within his trousers when he thought of Kira coming home from work, wearing her short dress. Oh, the anticipation when he waited behind the door to hear the key being turned. The swelling grew. How could she give all that up? It was impossible to fathom the workings of her mind.

Was it possible that Fraser Jackson could have been wearing a disguise each time he booked an appointment? Was it possible that she didn't recognise him? Did he perfect a plan to abduct her? Don't be so fucking stupid! That bitch probably planned the whole thing.

He gave himself a serious talking to about being soft on Kira. There was no benefit of the doubt in Kira's case. They both knew exactly what they were doing, and they both needed to be punished for what they had done. He made a mental note to himself to save a bullet for that mangy dog of theirs.

The car was all packed up for the trip and he was now ready for the off, but after setting off he suddenly remembered something. Pulling on the handbrake, he left the engine running whilst he ran into the house to collect that little something that he had salvaged from the police station after the re-enactment. *Can't possibly forget that,* he thought. *It's an integral part of the whole mind game operation.*

Before long, he was driving at top speed, destination Portmahomack. The sweet, sweet smell of revenge was in his nostrils, thrilling him with every sniff. It was going to feel wonderful when he inflicted on them a portion of the pain that he had been subjected to all this time. From the moment Kira disappeared, bad fortune had plagued him. He had run his company into the ground and his house was going to be repossessed. The money in his bank account had completely dried up and worst of all, he was going to end up living with his mother. It had been a slippery slope that had propelled him downward, fast, ending in a painful thud at rock bottom. *When this mission is completed,* he told himself. *I will be back on the up and up. Jeremy Ward is never down for long.*

At the top of his voice, he began singing 'Rocky Raccoon'. It had become the theme tune for this particular mission. Smiling smugly to himself, he marvelled at his own investigative skills. In fact, it could truthfully be said that he had unravelled the entire mystery single-handedly. Basically, he did what the police could never have done. Perseverance had been the key to his success; he had quite simply stopped at nothing to get the answers he needed. His mind drifted back to the meeting with Claire Voyant. How expertly he had disentangled her little pieces of information about the 'classics'. It had been a good job, well done, and he was perfectly entitled to accept the full credit.

This last phase of the mission was going to be the most triumphant. It was going to make him feel much happier, certainly more carefree. Once the assassinations had been carried out, he would be able to rebuild his life. A new business plan would be first on his agenda, then perhaps he would find love again. Children weren't out of the question. *I will make a wonderful father,* he told himself. These thoughts of his new life gave him strength. *Not long now,* he thought. *The end is in sight.*

Chapter 50

The lounge bar of the Marriot Hotel in Bangkok was fairly busy when Chris Hardy excused himself past the people standing around the doorway. By the way he scanned the room on arrival, Andy could tell that he was his man. He looked just as Andy had pictured him, a balding businessman wearing a white open neck shirt.

Andy caught his eye by waving his hand above his head. Chris smiled, walking over to join them. Andy and Celia stood up as Chris approached the table. They shook hands, introducing themselves.

'Thanks for meeting with us, Chris. Can I get you something to drink?'

'I'll take a cup of coffee,' he said. 'It's very difficult to get a decent cup of coffee around these parts, but I know that it's good in here.'

Andy rose from his seat to head to the bar, but Celia placed a hand on his shoulder, gently guiding him to sit down. She knew when to take a step back, she was only there for support. Leaving the men to talk, she made herself scarce.

'I'm sorry to be meeting with you under these circumstances,' Chris said.

'I'm just grateful that you took the time to phone the police in Scotland to report it. I don't hold out a lot of hope, but I would never forgive myself if I didn't follow every lead that comes in, just in case.'

'I get that,' Chris sympathised. 'I can't imagine what you must be going through.'

Anxious to get started, Andy asked, 'Tell me what you saw.'

'I have an office not far from here,' he explained. 'Every lunchtime, I go out to get food from a little café on the corner of the street. For a couple of years now, I have given money to a boy who sits in a doorway near the café. He looks British. We have exchanged a few words in the past. I think he has had a head injury because he appears to be quite slow in his responses. I didn't think anything about it until I was watching the BBC news channel. They were running a programme on missing young people in the U.K. It had been on the back of that young girl Kira Carmichael who went missing after showing someone a property for the estate agency she worked for. I don't know why they let young girls go alone to these properties. It's just asking for trouble.'
Celia arrived back at the table with Chris's coffee. Knowing that Celia had heard this comment about Kira, Andy then explained that the missing girl was her daughter.
Chris looked embarrassed as he turned to Celia. 'I'm so sorry, Celia, I didn't realise.'
Celia waved his apology away, reassuring him that he wasn't to know it was her daughter. Chris had not been tactless but hearing her daughter's name being mentioned by a man in Bangkok seemed to stop her heart for a moment. *The whole world must know that she is missing,* she thought. It was the most unexpected things that brought her to tears when it came to Kira. Speaking openly at her meetings was never an issue but seeing a poster on a lamppost with Kira's smiling face on it was like a punch to the gut.
Andy brought the conversation back to the subject of Lewis. 'So, you saw the BBC news programme about missing young people.'

'Yes, all the faces of the missing youths appeared on the screen. That's when I saw Lewis. I noticed his resemblance to the boy living on the streets here. Of course, I could be way off the mark and if I am then I'm truly sorry, but I had to make the call just in case.'
'I appreciate that Chris,' Andy told him. 'So, what do we do now?'
'I'll take you to where the boy sits every day. You can make your mind up if it's your son. Are you ready to go now?'
Andy gripped Celia's hand. 'Ready as I'm ever going to be.'
They left the Marriot Hotel together, Chris drove them to where the boy resembling Lewis would be begging. Tightening his grip on Celia's hand, Andy could feel his entire body tremble uncontrollably and his skin felt cold. The erratic beating of his heart began to alarm him. A sudden need to throw up overwhelmed him. 'Chris, I'm really sorry but could you stop the car for a moment.'
Andy stumbled out of the car at the roadside, apologising for himself. Focusing on the pavement below him, he bent over double, his hands resting on his knees. A few seconds passed, then his stomach contents heaved up over the roadside. He remained in the same position, standing motionless before he retched again. After drying his mouth with his sleeve, he got back into the car.
'Sorry about that folks. I'm just nervous.'
Chris turned into the underground car park beneath his office block. All three walked together in silence to street level. Andy's legs lost power, making him unsteady on his feet. Celia moved in close to him, saying, 'Lean on me, we'll walk together.'

Andy put his arm around her, she, in turn held tightly on to him. Their steps were in unison; a walking version of the three-legged race. This simple act made Andy feel stronger, giving him confidence to go on.
'This is the café I visit,' he pointed, 'and it's in that doorway over there, where the boys begs.'
'I can't thank you enough, Chris. You are a good man. There are not enough people like you.' Andy struggled to keep his emotions in order.
Chris turned to him, 'I'll have to head back to work now but please let me know how this turns out. I suggest that you sit on the wall across the road and wait. He should be here within the hour.'
The next hour would be a pivotal moment in Andy Wallace's life. He took up a position on the wall across the street to watch for a poor beggar boy who could potentially be his only son.
Celia sat next to him, rubbing his back gently in a circular motion.

Chapter 51

Mrs Ward had not left her husband's bedside since the incident happened. How could she? Staying alone in that antiquated house was not an option. In hindsight, perhaps over the years, they should have given up a few of their holidays and used the money to renovate the place. It wasn't that she didn't care about her husband's poorly state, it's just that she now worried for herself. What would happen if all she had left in the world was Jeremy.

'Stay calm, my love. Don't be worried. We will get you home when the time is right. Jeremy will move in and help me to look after you.' Her husband became distressed. 'You must try not to upset yourself, darling. We are lucky to have a son who will take care of us in our old age. He'll soon realise that it's time to give back for all that we have done for him. Deep down, he is a good boy,' she added, trying to pacify the restless invalid. Mr Ward tugged at his wife's hand, attempting to draw her close to him.

'What is it dear? What's wrong?' she asked, leaning in towards him.

'Jeremy, Jeremy,' he mumbled.

'I know, love, Jeremy will get here when he can. He has some very important work to take care of, but he will come to you as soon as possible.'

At this point, Mr Ward became so distressed that his wife called hysterically for the nurse.

The young nurse entered the room with a silver tray in her hand. When she neared the patient, she removed a hypodermic needle from the tray and shot him skilfully in the arm. As his body turned limp, she gave his wife a reassuring nod.

Mrs Ward stroked his hair back from his forehead, saying, 'There now, that's better. No point in getting yourself all worked up. I know you want home, but you have to get well first.' *I think I'll call Jeremy, he needs to know that his father is calling for him. It is his duty to be here.*

The music was blaring in Jeremy's car, as he drove on the scenic roads leading to the north of Scotland. His happy mood was soon spoiled when he saw the screen on the dashboard lighting up with, Incoming Call - Mother.

What the fuck does she want now? he wondered.

'Hello Mother. How are things?' he asked, feigning concern.

'Oh Jeremy, it's awful. Your father has regained consciousness, but he's just saying your name over and over again. Please get here as soon as you can.'

'I'm very tied up for the next few days, mother, but when I return, I will be right there to give you both the care you deserve. Why do you think father is saying my name over and over?' he asked, gauging the situation.

'I can only presume that it's because you are his son, and he loves you. Sometimes when you have had a brush with death, it can make you re-evaluate everything in your life. He's been getting very distressed when he says your name.'

Yeah, I'll bet he does, he thought.

'Stay strong mother; when I return, I'll take control of everything.'

Jeremy drove through the main street in the town of Pitlochry. The tartan and tweed shops made him smirk, they were purely for the tourists. *Who is actually dumb enough to buy that nonsense,* he thought. *The idiotic tourist think that*

Scotsmen wear kilts, ha! I haven't seen anyone in a kilt for at least twenty years. Grudgingly, he had to admit that the flower baskets swinging from the Victorian lamp posts were a nice touch, as was the mountainous backdrop that surrounded the town.

This had been his first trip up to the top of Scotland. The further he drove, the more it felt like the pressures of the city were melting away. *Perhaps when this mission is all over, I'll settle into a new life in the highlands where no one knows me.*

Jeremy had an important job to do before he reached his destination, but the town of Pitlochry was a little too bustling with tourists for his liking. He drove on through without stopping. *The next town I come to, I'll stop,* he decided.

It wasn't long before he was met with a sign for the village of Blair Atholl. *That will do nicely.*

This quaint little village had exactly what he was looking for, a general store with a red post box outside on the pavement. 'Perfecto' he announced aloud to himself. Reaching into the back seat, he grabbed the item that he had acquired from the day of the reconstruction. Taking it hadn't been easy, but he had a way of making things disappear without anyone noticing. At the time, he had only taken it as a sentimental keepsake, but he had a much better use for it now. Memories of the day that Kira's last known movements were re-enacted, flooded back to him. The actress they had chosen to play Kira looked nothing like her. This had angered him immensely. When she returned to the police station to change her clothes, he heard her speaking. She was not refined like Kira; in fact, he thought that she was as common as muck. He despised her for thinking that she was anything like his Kira.

The lunch options were limited in the general store, but he spied an egg sandwich which looked almost edible. A bounty bar would be his reward for eating it. There was a hatch within the shop, which crudely presented itself as a post office. After buying a padded envelope and stamp, he left to sit in his car. This next section of his rather sketchy plan was a last minute idea that had bounced into his head. The purpose of it was purely to fill his intended victims with fear, catch them off guard and instil paranoia in them. It was genius really. He took the list of eye witness statements from the glove compartment and began scanning through them for the address in Portmahomack where Kira was reported to reside. In bold capital letters, he copied the postal information onto the padded envelope. A conspiratorial smile sat lightly on his lips. A delicious tingle appeared from nowhere. *Let the game of cat and mouse begin,* he laughed.
It had always fascinated him as a boy, watching his parents' cat playing with a mouse before he killed it. It would seem that the cat wanted to prolong the pleasure for as long as it possibly could. He could relate to that; some things were worth dragging out to the bitter end. Bearing that thought in mind, he got out of the car and dropped the package into the post box. The bin was positioned outside the shop, he purposefully dropped his sandwich wrapper into it, checking to see who was watching. *Look what a good, law abiding citizen I am,* he thought, chuckling all the way back to his car.

Chapter 52

The day that Kira struggled on the hill with her shopping had been the first of many similar episodes. Fraser eventually insisted that she could no longer leave the house on her own. Providing she rested and didn't overexert herself, Kira felt well. Fraser made sure that he bought foods that she especially liked, encouraging her to eat little but often. They both took Darcy for his walk at lunchtime. Fraser went alone with the little dog to the back field at night.

Kira read a lot through the day, enjoying the view of the everchanging landscape across the Moray Firth. They didn't go for long walks at the weekends anymore, but on the pleasant days, they sat in the garden while Fraser cooked them lunch on the barbeque. Life had changed considerably but it was not for the worse. For Kira, there were good days and bad days. She embraced the good and lay down to the bad. Fraser had wanted to take Kira to a doctor, but she insisted that she did not want that. The more people she interacted with in the outside world, the greater the chance of her being discovered. She could handle the situation on her own; a doctor could not tell her anything that she didn't know already. Kira had made her mind up that nothing was going to spoil her life in Portmahomack with Fraser and Darcy.

There was never a need for her to push thoughts of Jeremy or her parents from her mind; they did not enter her head in any form. The day she disappeared had seen the rebirth of the new Kira; the Kira that she was always destined to be. For now, her energy levels had depleted a little, but the magic between her and Fraser had only intensified.

Chapter 53

Andy and Celia sat nervously across the street from the doorway where the boy in question usually sat begging. The waiting was almost unbearable for Andy. Having Celia there to talk to him kept his mind off the enormity of what was going on. He couldn't possibly have made the trip without her, not just financially, but emotionally too. Celia could see that Andy's nerves were taut as he looked both ways, up and down the street.

'I'm going to sing a well-known theme tune to a television programme. You have to guess what it is,' she said as a distraction.

'Go for it,' Andy agreed, still glancing both ways along the road.

Humming the first few notes of a theme tune, Andy guessed, 'The Antiques Roadshow' straight away.

She laughed, telling him to have a go. Clearing his throat, he began humming a theme tune. Celia did not recognise it. 'Is it one of these sports programmes? Because if it is, then that's not fair.'

'It's 'Match of the Day'; everyone knows that tune,' he told her.

'Andy, look, here comes a boy,' Celia interrupted, taking hold of his hand.

A young boy limped along, dragging his left leg. His left arm lay motionless at his side. There was a noticeable scar on his forehead and his mouth drooped a little on the left side. Shuffling along to the doorway, he used his only working arm to aid his descent into a sitting position. The sandals he wore were little more than a sole, his clothes were ill fitting.

'Come across the road so that we can get a closer look,' Celia suggested.
'I don't need a closer look,' Andy replied. 'That's my boy. That's my Lewis.'
Running at speed towards the boy, he stood before him. The boy shook his tin at Andy in a hope of some spare change.
Crouching down on the ground, Andy sat level with the boy.
'Look at my face, son. What do you see?'
The boy stared at Andy. Tears filled his lifeless eyes. He sobbed. Andy had never seen a more pitiful sight. His heart felt physically wounded by what he saw. A human being, a precious boy, his wonderful son.
'Dad?' the boy managed to say.
'I've come to take you home, son. It's all over. You're safe now.' He scooped the boy up from the ground into his arms.
'Celia, take my phone. Can you call Chris Hardy for me.'
In a state of shock, Celia fumbled with Andy's mobile phone until she found the contact for Chris. With trembling hands, she pressed the call button, then handed the phone back to Andy. Celia was overcome with emotion at what she was witnessing: the pain, the joy, even the envy of a father and son being reunited.
'Hello Chris,' Andy said, holding onto his son, 'I'm going to ask for another favour. It is my son; I've found my boy. Could you take us back to the hotel please?'
Chris Hardy broke down in tears on the other end of the line.
'I'd be delighted,' he cried. 'Sit tight, I'll be there in five minutes.'
Celia cried uncontrollably with happiness for Andy and his son. The tears were also with sorrow for Kira.

Back at the hotel, Celia ran a hot bubble bath for Lewis. She knew that he was going to need urgent medical attention, he was so obviously broken, body and soul. Whatever experience he had been through in the past years, it had left him a husk of a young man. He bore only a flicker of resemblance to the boy in the photos that Andy had once shown her.

Andy picked up his phone and proceeded to dial the police station in Edinburgh.

'Hello, could you put me through to the duty officer. My name is Andy Wallace. My son, Lewis, went missing several years ago in Thailand. I've got to tell him the news. I have found my boy! My son is coming home!'

The response from the police was heart-warming. The case had been high profile for many years, and there was not a father among the officers who had not dared to imagine how awful it would be if it had happened to their son.

Getting Lewis out of the country with no passport, no identification, was not going to be easy. The police in Scotland were going to do what they could, but in the meantime, Andy made an appointment with the British Embassy. One thing was certain, Andy Wallace was not leaving Thailand without his son by his side.

Chapter 54

Jeremy reached Portmahomack around 7pm. The sun was setting behind a distant mountain, shedding a fiery lambency over the boats in the harbour. Parking the car at the rear of the hotel, he collected his holdall from the boot. Rather than checking in straight away, he decided to take a seat on a bench across the street at the harbour. The last rays of the sun were disappearing for the day and he wanted to take a moment to watch them. Boats had been a passion of his ever since he was a boy. Memories of a school trip flooded his mind. It had been a three-day trip around the remote islands of Scotland. He could honestly say, hand on heart, that it had been a highly enjoyable experience, apart from one small annoyance. Rupert Maynard was an obnoxious boy who had been assigned to the lower bunk in the same cabin as him. Rupert had mocked his pyjamas for their pattern of jungle animals. He, himself, had joined in the laughter along with everyone in the cabin. He pretended that he didn't care, but he knew that he would get his revenge. That night whilst everyone slept, he climbed down the bunk bed ladder. Without making a sound, he sneaked Rupert's trainers out from under the bed whilst he slept. A smile broke out on his lips as he thought of himself, age 10, walking upstairs onto the top deck, raising the trainers high into the air, then hurling them overboard. 'Let's see who's laughing now!' he had said, watching the shoes bobbing on the waves, getting smaller and smaller as the boat sailed away.

When only the red afterglow of the sunset remained in the sky, he decided to check into the Oyster Catcher. Tomorrow the game of cat and mouse would begin with stalking the

happy couple. This would of course build up to the inevitable crescendo.
Jeremy was shown to his room which boasted a view over the harbour. It came as a great relief to him that the room was clean, a little fussy for his liking, but nonetheless, immaculate. He showered and changed before going down to the bar to order something for his dinner.
The best he could say about the meal was that it was adequate. Dessert was not his forte, but a couple of brandies helped to make him feel replete. There was a lot on his mind but nothing that a little alcohol wouldn't wash away. Although, he was there in the highlands out of necessity, he realised that this had been his first holiday in almost two years. With that thought in his mind and the fact that he was spending the biscuit tin money from his mother, he made his mind up to have another brandy; a double. *Go on Jer, spoil yourself, you're worth it.*
The third brandy began to kick in, giving Jeremy a warm, relaxed glow. The bar was filled with what he presumed were local people as they all appeared to know one another, and they were a little unsophisticated. The fourth brandy that he ordered made his head spin. This was a feeling that he did not like. It forced him into the decision that it was time for bed. The long drive had tired him out, so a comparatively early night, he decided, would not be the worst thing in the world.
When he had scrambled under the offensive chintzy bed covers, he lay back to straighten things out in his mind. His head was spinning but his thinking was clear. Tomorrow, the happy couple would receive his package. This would give them a jolt right back into the past. This would be

enough to tarnish the shine of their happily ever after future. Another fundamental part of his objective to unsettle them was to enter their home without their knowledge. Whilst inside, he would leave enough evidence for them to suspect his visit. *Ha,* he thought, *this is more fun than I could ever have imagined.* The thought of the dog suddenly came into his mind. The fly in the ointment for him was the dog, there was a good chance that it may bark, alerting his targets. *Why would Kira get a dog?* he scorned, as he imagined them fussing over it, laughing at its antics. Fuming, he pushed the thoughts out of his head. He was, however, reasonable enough to know that it wasn't the dog's fault. The dog just happened to be in the wrong place, at the wrong time. He made the decision that if there was a way that he could let the dog live, then he would; after all, he wasn't a monster.

The brandies worked their magic, bringing sleep to Jeremy before he could think through his plan to its final conclusion. When he awoke, he looked around the room to remind himself of where he was. 'Ahh, Kira,' he thought.

Admittedly, he was excited about seeing her again, although he wished that the circumstances had been different. Throwing off the chintzy quilt, he yawned out a stretch. *Better get an early start,* he decided. *So much to do, so little time to do it in.*

He donned his black outfit simply because it made him feel menacingly powerful. Leaving his room, he headed downstairs to see what would be dished up for breakfast. Being a creature of habit, he sat down at the same table, in the same seat, as the previous night. The table had been set up nicely for breakfast with teacups, toast rack and a selection of little pots of jam. Lifting the napkin from under his cutlery, he gave it an exaggerated flick in the air before resting it on his lap. When the waitress came over to ask him what he wanted, he replied, 'The works!' A full Scottish fry up breakfast was what he required. 'Oh, and I will have a pot of Earl Grey tea,' he shouted after her.

The waitress returned to the table later with Jeremy's breakfast. 'Thank you my dear,' he said, smiling. 'I wonder if you could give me clear and concise directions to Harbour View Road.' *Why bother with satnav when I have a perfectly good source of information right here.*

'Yes,' she replied. 'It's a row of delightful new-build houses at the top of the hill. There are six of them altogether. Each one has been designed uniquely. They were built by a local building company last year. What a view they get from up there!' she gushed.

Jeremy smiled, nodding at her. *I ask a simple question and I get bombarded with all that shit!* he thought angrily. *All she had to say was it's up the fucking hill.* That kind of thing made him extremely cross. *I guess I was wrong about asking her. Satnav never spouted that kind of garbage at me.*

With anger stewing away within him, he got up from the table, leaving his breakfast uneaten. 'People just don't think before they speak,' he muttered under his breath.

On the short walk to his car, he decided to drive to the house first in order to case the joint. There was a mental tick list that needed to be completed. Were there bushes around for him to hide in? What was the most intruder-friendly entry point? Did the house have curtains or blinds on the windows? These questions needed to be answered in order for him to move forward with the mission.

In second gear, he crawled along the single-track road to the house at the end. It was the finest one in the row, he had to admit. He could see that the back door was the entrance closest to the road, the front door faced the sea. He very quickly ruled out the door at the front, it was way too risky. The back door looked like it could be infiltrated with ease. There was plenty of dense shrubbery growing all around the house, giving complete privacy from the neighbours.

In the lane behind the house, he sat in his car watching for signs of life, and he saw none. There was a car in the drive, and from this single fact he presumed that the occupants were home. *I think I'm going to have a long wait,* he thought, sliding down on his reclined seat. *Good things come to those who can last the pace. I ain't goin' nowhere, buckaroo.*

Chapter 55

Permission was eventually granted for Andy to fly Lewis out of Thailand, back home to Scotland. Ultimately, he had one person to thank for that and that person was Celia. She made calls to every politician listed in her phone. They were all friends of Ramsay's and delighted to help. The red tape was sliced through, speeding up the process considerably. Lewis was checked over and although he was in a very bad condition, he was deemed fit to travel. They were booked on the next flight out of Bangkok, due to land at Heathrow. Lewis spoke very little. Andy feared for his son's mental state, but he was committed to supporting him in every way possible.

The last lap of the journey home ended when they flew from Heathrow to Edinburgh. They collected their suitcases then made their way to the 'arrivals' door. Suddenly, they were overwhelmed by the flashing cameras of the press. The reporters were crowded four thick around the barriers. Questions were being simultaneously shouted at Andy and his son, from all directions.

'How does it feel to be home, Lewis?'

'What happened to you out there in Bangkok?'

'What are you going to do now, Mr Wallace?'

'How did you manage to find him?'

Lewis put his hands over his ears, shutting his eyes tightly. Neither of them were prepared for this onslaught; all they wanted to do was go home. Microphones were thrust forth into their faces while the flashing continued. The questions were fired non-stop, round after round. Eventually, Andy gave them a short statement.

'I am thrilled to have my son home with me. A British citizen working in Bangkok recognised him from photos that were shown on a BBC news programme. I flew out to Thailand with my friend to check out the sighting. I didn't hold out much hope because I have been disappointed many times in the past, but it was him, my boy. I don't know what has happened to him whilst he has been in Bangkok. I'm not even sure that he knows himself what happened. He will need a lot of love and care, so I beg for you to give us privacy at this time. It is a dream come true for me, a miracle, but it will be a long road ahead. Thank you.'

It was a welcome relief for Andy to see the journalists backing up and slowly dispersing. Meanwhile, he led his distressed son and Celia through the crowds, to the front door. Andy approached the first taxi in the long line waiting outside the airport. The driver lifted the cases into the boot while Andy helped his son into the back seat.

Every news channels aired the story of a man who never gave up believing that his son was going to be found alive. It was the happy ending that everyone yearned for. Renewed hope was given out to all families in a similar situation. The story revealed that Lewis Wallace had received a head injury that appeared to have paralysed him down one side of his body, giving him partial memory loss. It was unknown whether he had suffered a swimming accident, possibly colliding with the rocks or if he was attacked and robbed. He retained no memory of that fateful day on the beach when he completely dropped off the radar. It was also reported that Lewis would get all the medical and psychological help that he required. His loving father had every intention of caring for his son in his own home.

Many viewers contacted the news channels pledging financial gifts for Andy and Lewis. Cards and presents arrived by post from people who had been deeply affected by the story. Andy was given the privacy that he had asked for; he was grateful for that. Lewis was unrecognisable as the carefree boy who had left to go on holiday that earth-shattering summer. The boy had changed but the love his father held for him had remained the same.

Ramsay watched the news channel in disbelief. Seeing his wife on the screen, standing by a man she hardly knew, made for difficult viewing. He witnessed her resting her hand on the man's back, walking through the airport. He had no idea what her plans were now that she was back from Thailand, but he wanted her home. She was his wife; he loved her dearly. The thought of living the rest of his life without Kira and Celia tortured him. Perhaps he hadn't given her the attention she had needed. There was no doubt that losing Kira had driven an even wider wedge between them. It had been easier to shut himself away than to face Celia's look of disappointment when she realised that he couldn't bring their beautiful daughter back. Celia had turned to strangers for comfort because he wasn't there for her. If she could find it in her heart to give him a second chance, he would make it up to her. All he could do now was wait to see if she still wanted him in her life.

Andy took Lewis home, asking Celia if she would come along for moral support. She agreed to stay until Andy felt confident to care for Lewis on his own. There was absolutely no doubt that Celia was in love with Andy Wallace, but she realised that she would be no more than a hindrance to him. There was no place for her in his life. Andy's focus was now all on his son; Celia totally understood that. If she could have one more chance with Kira, she would do things so differently. It was painful to admit, but deep down she had always suspected that Jeremy hadn't been kind to her. There had been signs of his controlling behaviour towards her, but she chose to turn a blind eye and say nothing. The idea of the wedding with the influential guest list had clouded her vision. *I only ever saw what I wanted to see,* she reflected.

Now she had no place to truly call home. The feelings she had for Ramsay fell short of the mark and could never rival the love she felt, albeit briefly, for Andy. Andy had made her a better person. He had enabled her to see what the truly important things in life were. He also made her feel attractive, sexy even. Ramsay had never brought any of these good, good things out in her. On the other hand, Kira had tied them together in happiness as well as sorrow. No one could ever share or break that bond. Now she had to decide where her future lay. Would there ever be a place for her in Andy's future? Was it worth hanging on to find out? Was she strong enough to get a place of her own to go it alone? Were the foundations of her marriage solid enough to build on?

There were no answers to any of these questions right now, but she hoped that time would reveal the right path to take.

Chapter 56

Jeremy's father passed away at 6.35am on the Sunday morning. The reading on the heart monitor flat lined. Mrs Ward was in shock, unable to digest the information. There was a daughter in Canada, but she no longer had any contact details for her. Jeremy was all she had in the world and now she needed him desperately.

The police investigation had developed into a full-blown murder inquiry. The detective in charge began to suspect that whoever broke in and attacked Mr Ward that night was familiar with the layout of the house. A forensics team moved quickly to uncover any possible DNA left behind by the perpetrator. However, so far, the only DNA found was that of the three family members, Mr. and Mrs. Ward and their son, Jeremy. There was urine found on the floor of the crime scene, but the lab results had not, as yet, been returned. When asked about the urine on the floor, Mrs. Ward suggested that it may have belonged to their cat. It was also concluded that the absence of fingers prints would imply that the perpetrator was wearing gloves.

Mrs. Ward left the hospital that day with a plastic bag filled with her husband's dirty washing. As she had never felt the need to learn to drive, she phoned for a taxi to pick her up from the main entrance. Although she was broken hearted for the untimely death of her husband, there was a burden weighing more heavily on her mind. *What about me, what the hell will happen to me?*

The driver dropped her at the front of the house. Walking down the path to the front door, she noticed that the garden looked a little unruly. *That's a job for Jeremy,* she thought.

Inside the house, she heard the echo of the front door shutting behind her. The air felt cold with musty tones. Only the other day she had suggested to her husband that the house was too large for them, as were the sprawling lawns that surrounded the property. Now she was alone; well, alone until she got Jeremy home.
At the back of the house where the dreadful crime took place, Mrs Ward could see the dark red, almost black stain on the floor, marking the spot where her husband had lain. It was terribly upsetting. A thought occurred to her as she stared at the dried in blood. *If I sell the house, I hope the fact that there was a murder here won't affect the sale price.* Complete renovation of the property was needed, from top to bottom. A sudden regret entered her head. *Why did we spend all that money travelling the world?* She knew full well that the pot was now dry. *Never mind, Jeremy will look after me.*

Chapter 57

Jeremy staked out Kira's house for several hours. Very little activity took place during this time, which frustrated him enormously. The back door had opened at one point when the dog was sent out to do its business. No one accompanied the animal, it wandered back into the premises alone when it was finished. The lights in the house remained on for the duration of the day and into the night. A closer inspection was required, so he exited the car and moved skilfully towards the back of the house. Dusk had fallen on the town, not pitch darkness, so he had to take great care not to be seen. Hiding in the bushes, he surveyed the illuminated windows for movement. There was none.

He crept over to the kitchen window, stretching up to look in. The package that he had posted was sitting unopened on the kitchen table. *Damn it to Hell*! he thought. *Why do people not open their fucking mail?*

The package contained the replica of the Pretty Woman dress. Kira had worn an almost identical dress the day she disappeared. Jeremy had felt certain that it would unnerve her when she saw it again. Phase one had not gone according to plan, he could feel himself getting angry. When he looked up at the windows, his anger turned to rage. *These windows do not have single-paned glass. I can bet my ass that there is not a rotten frame among them,* he seethed. Things had been so easy in the previous breaking and entering jobs. Old, neglected properties were much more suited to his needs. Now he was looking at brand new double glazed windows with solid hardwood frames. 'No, no, no, no!' he said aloud to himself, his face burning in sheer temper.

Gaining entry to this property was not going to be easy. *This is a fucking fortress,* he thought. 'Okay, have it your way,' he said, as he began climbing the drainpipe in order to reach the little balcony jutting out from the upstairs window. 'It takes a lot more than this mere hiccup to stop me,' he whispered.
It was a tough climb with nothing substantial to grip on to, but he managed to reach the balcony. One hand at a time, he reached up to grip the concrete floor above him. For a short period, he hung there, not knowing whether he had the strength to pull himself up. Shutting his eyes tightly, he thought of Kira and Fraser humiliating him, taking everything from him, forcing him to hurt people. With an almighty burst of energy, he hauled himself up onto his feet. 'Did it!' he said, feeling proud of his achievement. *Nothing can stop me because I am Sherlock the Terminator.* He stifled a snigger.
Now that he was on the balcony, he could peer safely through the window. He identified the room as a type of workplace, an office. There was a desk with a lamp shining on some paperwork, next to this he could see a computer with printer. Through the door of the office, he could see clearly into the well-lit hallway. A sudden jolt of agony ran through the entire length of his body, causing him to freeze rigid to the spot. What he saw hanging in the hallway over a door, made him turn around to throw up over the side of the balcony. The sound of his vomit could be heard splashing as it hit the concrete slab below. It was something that he could not help. The sight of the white lace wedding dress, just hanging there, taunting him, was more than he could stand. He needed to get away, quick. The wedding dress had knocked him off his game. Unable to think straight, he knew

this could cause him to make multiple mistakes. Tomorrow he would return when he was calmer. 'Abort mission,' he whispered. 'Abort mission.'

Climbing back over the balcony railing, he held on, preparing to drop to the ground. The plan was to relax, drop, roll. Hanging downward, gripping on with his fingers, he prepared himself for the fall. The strong stench of vomit wafted up to his nostril. He counted to ten. One, two, three… When he reached number seven in his countdown, the back door opened and Fraser came out. Jeremy dangled above him, barely able to cling on a moment longer. From his unfortunate position, he watched closely as Fraser walked along the road alone, no dog, no Kira. Straining to see where he was heading, Jeremy lost his focus, which, in turn, made him lose his grip and fall to the ground. He was not relaxed, he did not roll; in fact, he jarred nearly every bone in his body. Straightening his buckled frame, he painfully hobbled along, hurrying as fast as he could to catch up with Fraser. *Where is he going,* he wondered, *and where the hell is Kira?*

Fraser walked down the hill, but instead of walking in the direction of the harbour, he took a left. Jeremy followed closely behind. The single-track road was lined with dense shrubbery; Jeremy used this to his advantage. At the end of the road a resplendent, red sandstone church stood. The church was set amidst a graveyard filled with headstones in various states of disrepair. Jeremy hid behind a column shaped memorial, which was topped with a stone urn. He furtively peered his head around to see the church entrance. Fraser had gone in, leaving the heavy arched door slightly ajar. Jeremy crept up to the opening to hear what was going on. The clergyman and Fraser were seated in a pew, discussing matters. Jeremy listened closely, but he was unable to decipher what was being said. *I may need to invest in some equipment for my future missions. A listening device will be top of my list, followed by spy cameras.* The minister was pointing to the front row of pews, he then pointed to the back of the church. Jeremy's stomach somersaulted when Fraser turned around to look back at the aisle. *So that's what you really look like, you ugly sod. Age has dealt you a few nasty blows since that carefree photo of you wearing the Rolling Stones t-shirt.* In his heart of hearts, he recognised that the young man was handsome, if you liked those type of looks. However, he would never have admitted that to anyone, especially himself.

What the fuck are they discussing? Jeremy mused. *What are they planning*? It didn't take long for the penny to drop. After seeing that white, lacy dress, he knew exactly what they were planning. Taking another look through the partially open door, he saw that the two men were walking towards the exit. It was time to take cover. A tall headstone near the door was the perfect spot. With his back against the engraved epitaph, he sat silently, listening, watching, waiting.

'It will be a lovely service,' the minister assured Fraser.

'I know. I just want to get everything right. It has to be a perfect day for Kira.'

The minister nodded. 'Don't worry. It will be, just leave everything to me.'

Fraser shook hands with the minister, thanking him for everything. 'I'll see you tomorrow at two, then.'

'Yes, tomorrow at two.'

Fraser left the churchyard, heading in the direction of his home.
The minister switched the lights off before exiting the church building. Using both hands, he locked the heavy door with the large, antiquated key. For a moment, he stopped to listen. Was that the sound of crying he could hear? Yes, there was definitely a sobbing sound resonating from the headstones. It wasn't the first time that he had heard strange noises coming from the graves of the dead. 'Rest in peace,' he announced. 'Rest in peace.'
The engine of the minister's car could be heard driving off, leaving Jeremy alone in the churchyard. The vague plan he had sketched out would need to be abandoned, things had changed; Kira was getting married. There would be no game of cat and mouse, no menacing, no more watchful waiting. *It ends tomorrow*, he told himself. *Now I have an exact time and location, 2pm at the Portmahomack Church.* The evening's revelations, although distressing, had unwittingly put him right back in the driving seat. Just the way he liked it.
The injuries from the fall had left him limping his way back along the deserted road towards his car. This mission had not exactly gone to plan, but as usual, he had used the skill of improvisation. It was good to be back in control, but he couldn't deny that he felt deeply hurt, physically and emotionally. *How could Kira betray him like this? How could she have left him?* He could make no sense of Kira's choices; she had been his betrothed and now she was planning to marry that clown.
Back at the Oyster Catcher, he tended to his bleeding wounds. They were somewhat worse than he had originally thought. Using the complimentary bubble bath provided, he

ran a deep, foamy bath. This would be perfect for soaking his aching limbs in. His body was sore, his feelings were hurt, but he was pretty sure that Sherlock Holmes and the Terminator had suffered a few knocks in their time.

Chapter 58

Whilst Fraser stood in front of the mirror knotting his tie, he thought over a conversation that had taken place a few months previous. Kira had surprised him by preparing a special dinner. The table had been set so beautifully with flowers from the garden which she had displayed in the poppy teapot because they didn't own a vase. When they sat down to eat, she confessed that she had been harbouring a secret from him. Having gained his full attention, she continued by explaining that she had been faced with a momentous decision before she disappeared. The choice that she had decided upon had been borne out of love for him.

The knot in his tie was not quite right, he redid it several times until it was. It had been a long time since he had dressed up in a fine suit and silk tie, he was completely out of practice. He wanted to look his very best for Kira. It was her special day and everything had to be perfect, she deserved it. There were no words to describe how much he loved her.

Earlier that morning, the minister had opened up the church to allow the florist to arrange the flowers for the special day. The congregation was small, so only the first pew was decorated with a garland of colourful flowers. Roses and lilies were displayed in large ornate vases throughout the church, filling the air with their sweet scent. Tall ivory candles were inserted into the ancient candle holders, which were fixed to the stone walls around the church. The first hymn chosen to be sung was Morning Has Broken. This would be followed thereafter with The Lord's My Shepherd.

Everything had been meticulously planned to make the day perfect. The sun was shining with barely a breeze blowing.
Fraser arrived at the church; he nervously took up his seat on the front pew. The minister gave him a smile of encouragement. Fraser nodded back. There was an elderly lady in a simple, green dress sitting on the pew opposite. She had been the church cleaner for many years. Three of the church elders were in the same pew as the woman, but they had spaced themselves out in order to fill the row. An organist played a loop of hymns as background music before the start of the service.
Fraser felt his stomach churn over as the minister indicated to him that it was time to begin. The music changed to a recording of Kirsty McColl singing 'Thank You for The Days'. Fraser rose to his feet when he saw the Church Treasurer bringing Kira down the aisle. The minister stood at the front, waiting for the music to finish.
He began.
'We are gathered here together to celebrate the life of Kira Jackson. Kira had been suffering from a rare form of leukaemia and was sadly taken from her newly wedded husband, Fraser, last Tuesday. Kira made the brave decision of refusing all medical treatment for reasons which were important to her. She was a wonderful human being who was loved by all who knew her.'
Kira lay in a rosewood coffin which rested on a stand with wheels. The coffin was covered with small bouquets of flowers tied together with yellow ribbons. Fraser stared at the coffin where the love of his life lay. She had told him that she had been attending hospital appointments when they had first met. The specialist had informed her that she

needed to start her chemotherapy programme immediately. She chose to have a short life with Fraser, rather than a longer life without him.

Fraser was so grateful to the minister for agreeing to marry them at Kira's bedside. He wanted to see her in a beautiful dress one more time. It was her great desire to end her life as Mrs Jackson.

The minister told the congregation to rise for the first hymn, 'Morning Has Broken'. As the first few notes played, the small gathering rose in unison. The organ music drowned out the singing, but the sentiment of the song was not missed.

Everyone retook their seats as the minister announced that Kira's husband Fraser was going to share some thoughts and memories of his wife with everyone.

Fraser stood composing himself for a moment, at the front of the church. He then took his handwritten notes from his inside suit jacket pocket. Clearing his throat in a nervous gesture, he began.

'My darling Kira, I lost you once a long time ago,
And the parting of that moment filled me with saddest of woes.
But destiny smiled upon me and led you back into my life,
I was even blessed to have you as my wife,
Now I've lost you again,
How can I go on…' Fraser broke down as he glanced at the coffin which held his sweet Kira. The people scattered around the pews, bowed their heads. Tears were shed for a girl they never knew.

He dried his eyes and swallowed hard to remove the lump from his throat.

He continued. 'Kira, I want you to know that I will think of you every moment of every day. Shakespeare once said, '...parting 'tis such sweet sorrow,' but there is no sweetness to be found within my sorrow. I live for the day that we will be united once more, but this time it will be for all eternity. Rest in peace my dear wife, for I...

Outside the door, Jeremy stood with the loaded shotgun in his hands. Fuelled to the brim with revenge, he felt completely in control. Softly, he sang the words of Rocky Raccoon, to himself.

He turned the handle of the heavy arched door, then booted it open with his foot. He cocked the gun, shouting, 'The party is over!'

Everyone turned around, staring in disbelief. Jeremy fixed his eyes on Fraser, who was standing at the front of the church. As he aimed the shotgun at him, Fraser took a step to the side, revealing the coffin on the stand behind him. The treasurer slipped out his mobile phone from his pocket, pressing 999.

Jeremy looked at the scene before him. What he saw with his own eyes would not register in his brain. A coffin stood in the place of a bride dressed in white.

'Where is she? Where's Kira?' he shouted, firing the gun randomly, hitting the pulpit. 'What's going on here?' he screamed, his face burning with rage.

Fraser began to walk down the aisle towards him.

'Don't come any closer,' Jeremy threatened.

'I want to explain to you about Kira,' Fraser said softly. 'Are you Jeremy?' His tone was calm. 'Kira has passed away, Jeremy.'

'You fuckin' liar!' Jeremy shouted, aiming the gun, shooting him on the left ankle. Fraser fell to the ground. Jeremy kicked viciously at him.
'Where is she? Where's my Kira?' he shouted towards the minister.
The minster ran down the aisle to where Jeremy was still kicking the injured man.
'Let's talk about this rationally,' the minister offered, leading Jeremy away from Fraser.
Using the full force of his adrenaline pumped strength, he rammed the butt of the rifle at the ageing minister's head.
The minster fell to the ground.
'Who's next?' Jeremy shouted, with the two seriously wounded men lying at his feet.
The treasurer now had the police on the loudspeaker of his mobile phone. They could hear that there was a dangerous situation playing out. The treasurer pretended to talk to Jeremy but for the benefit of the police.
'Come on, now. Let's calm down. This is the house of God you are in. The Portmahomack House of God,' he said.
'Shut the fuck up, moron. I'll leave when I find out where Kira is.'
The treasurer tried again. 'Look, we have two men here who are seriously injured and will need an ambulance. Please can we get help for them?'
'Listen, Ghandi, you clearly don't understand what is going on here,' Jeremy spat. 'This conman has made Kira disappear before. This is all a lie, a sham. You fools have bought into the whole thing.'
Storming down to the front of the church, he took hold of the heavy, walnut lid of Kira's coffin, tossing it to the side. It

landed with a thud on the stone floor. In sheer bewilderment, he stared down at the beautiful, pale face of Kira, in the open casket. His fingers reached down to touch her face; it felt cold, waxen. He began shouting at the corpse. 'Kira, Kira. Get up! It's over, I know what you've done. I know about the classic characters and the meetings. I know everything. Get up!'
The faint sound of sirens could be heard in the distance. Jeremy snapped back to reality. Holding tightly on to his rifle, he ran down the aisle and out of the church. A police car and ambulances were tearing down the narrow road. Jeremy leapt into the bushes. Continuously looking over his shoulder, he ran at full speed, across the field, down towards the harbour. One of the police cars had driven straight down the hill to find him. He stood at the water's edge, hearing the siren becoming louder and louder. *What will I do now? he* asked himself. *See what you made me do, Kira, it's all your fault. You should never have left me.* Panic rose within him, the police siren was deafening.
From the corner of his eye, he noticed that one of the small boats in the harbour was called, *The Scarlet Pimpernel*. 'Ah, ha!' he laughed. 'Classic!'
Taking a mighty leap from the harbour, he jumped aboard. The boat's rope which was knotted around a metal ring on the stone wall, loosened with ease. Then, using the last of his strength, he yanked the wire of the motor. It fired into action, first time. *Ha! I am invincible. No one is ever a match for me. I am Sherlock the Terminator.* He steered the boat out of the harbour, towards the open water. The small vessel sped off across the choppy waves. The uniformed policemen, who

were standing at the harbour wall became like toy figures as the distance between them widened.

A call was made to the local coastguard who arrived swiftly in a lifeboat. The police jumped on board. The boat sped out to sea in pursuit of Jeremy.

The engine in *'The Scarlet Pimpernel'* began to splutter, puffing out black smoke. The boat slowed down until it reached an abrupt halt. Jeremy felt defeated. The reality of the situation was that he had reached the end of the road. The lifeboat was now visible in the distance, moving at full speed towards him.

Lifting his father's rifle, he put it in his mouth.

It was no good, he couldn't do it. Instead, he aimed the rifle down, blowing a substantial hole in the bottom of the boat.

By the time the lifeboat arrived, the Scarlett Pimpernel was fully submerged.

A dive team were brought in to search the waters. It wasn't long before one of the divers brought to the surface the limp, lifeless body of Jeremy Ward.

Chapter 59

After a short stay in hospital, Fraser was discharged with a bottle of painkillers and a pair of crutches. It was good to be back in the house that was full of the essence of Kira. The elderly lady who had been at the funeral had taken good care of Darcy whilst Fraser was away. On hearing of his release from hospital, she arrived at the door holding the dog in one hand, a pot of stew in the other. Hugging him tightly she told him, 'Things will get easier, son. I promise.'

*

Mrs Jackson switched off the hoover when she felt the vibration of her phone ringing in her apron pocket.

'Hello,' she said to the unknown caller.

'Hi Mum. Could you and dad come up to Portmahomack to stay for a few days. I really need you,' Fraser asked, fighting back the tears.

Chapter 60

Ramsay had grown a thick, grey beard because he had lost all desire to shave. Showering and dressing were burdensome chores that he indulged in only when necessary. He dined on beans on toast every night, which he ate in front of the television set. Most days, he wandered aimlessly around the house in his dressing gown with the rope belt hanging loose. The curtains in his home were rarely opened, making it difficult to differentiate day from night, he didn't think it mattered.

All alone, he sat in the kitchen feeling wretched. The ring of the doorbell made him jump, it had been quite some time since he had heard it. Closing over his dressing gown, he tied the belt tightly, he wouldn't want to offend the caller with the sight that lay beneath. He made his way through from the back of the house to see who could possibly be visiting him. To his joyous delight, he saw his wife, Celia, through the glass door. He quickened his step to greet her.

'Celia, hello,' he said. His knees weak, his emotions a blend of laughter and tears.

'Hello, Ramsay. You look terrible,' she told him. 'If we are going to make a go of this marriage, then you're going to have to make more of an effort with your appearance!' She ended the sentence with a smile.

Ramsay wound his arms around her neck, clinging to her for dear life. A loud childish cry came from deep within him as he rested his head on her shoulder. The wool of her cardigan, the smell of her hairspray, her familiar bony frame; it was all too much for him. It was the most wonderful day of his life.

'Celia, my precious Celia, I was nothing more than a shell when you weren't here. I can't live without you. I realise now that I haven't treated you the way you deserve to be treated and I am so sorry for that. I will spend the rest of my life making it up to you.'
An idea suddenly came to him, 'Hey! Let's book a holiday in that beautiful hotel in Mull where we went one summer with Kira.' The mention of her name brought unstoppable tears flooding down his ruddy cheeks. 'Celia, I am so sorry I couldn't bring our lovely daughter back. I feel like such a failure.'

Chapter 61

The warm summer sun shone down on the town of Portmahomack. Fraser walked with the aid of his crutches to where Kira had been laid to rest. Mrs Jackson was by his side with Darcy on the lead, her husband following close behind. They strolled together along the narrow road which led to the Portmahomack church. The shrubs were in full bloom, the birds sang the sweetest songs. At the back of the churchyard, next to the wall, was the grave where Kira lay. Fraser took a bouquet of white roses which were tied with a yellow ribbon and he laid it beside the black marble headstone, which read:

Kira Jackson, beloved wife of Fraser.
'Don't feel sad because it's over. Be happy because it happened'.

Printed in Great Britain
by Amazon